STANLEY THOMSON

356

*Recall the Truth,
Fear the Perception*

Copyright © 2021 by Stanley Thomson

All rights reserved. No part of this publication may be reproduced, distributed, or transmitted in any form or by any means, including photocopying, recording, or other electronic or mechanical methods, without the prior written permission of the publisher, except in the following way.

Thomson, Stanley (author)
356
Recall the truth, fear the perception

978-1-922722-15-7
Historical Fiction

Minion Pro 10/12

Manuscript and editorial assistance by Stella Thomson.

Cover and book design by Green Hill Publishing

DEDICATION

*"I unhesitatingly dedicate this to my wife Carole.
Patience is a flower that groweth not in every
garden, I'm grateful that yours blooms in mine."*

And to my sons Christopher and Paul
with love, pride and admiration.

ABOUT THE AUTHOR

Stanley McGill Thomson was born at 356 Easter Road Leith in Scotland where he lived for the first two years of life with parents Bill and Janet and beloved brother David. His father was a Congregational minister and among Stan's earliest memories was sitting on a windy hill outside the Scalloway Church, on the Shetland Islands. The family moved to Cumnock then to Dunfermline from where they emigrated to South Australia in 1958.

Education was at Salisbury North and King's College in South Australia. He left school at Wentworth in NSW to commence a career within the PMG (now Australia Post)

For several years he and his first wife Pamela ran the General Store in Hepburn Springs Victoria where they had moved from Melbourne with their sons Christopher and Paul. It was from there that he made his foray into Radio at stations such as 3CV, 5PI (Port Pirie) 5SE (Mt.Gambier) and then to a 30 year career with the ABC proudly based in the South East of South Australia but broadcasting regularly interstate and nationally. Carole and Stan joined their lives in 1988 and they lovingly share 6 children, enjoy many grandchildren and are proud of being great grandparents. Stan is an ardent supporter of the Arts and was a long serving Trustee of Country Arts SA and board member of the Riddoch Art Gallery in Mt. Gambier.

VI

1947 and the world was still trying to come to terms with peace. There was a sense of optimism tinged with suspicion. Could we really trust each other? Since 1939 we had been literally killing each other on battlefields and tearing our families apart at home.

The last three years of the 1940s were uneasy as people started to trust, started to understand (maybe), started to make plans. Plans which for the first time in four or so years did not include using weapons of destruction, or stockpiling food.

The Erskines of 356 Easter Road, Leith experienced post-war Scotland in a way that tore at their family's core. Truth and trust were the casualties in a schism that never healed.

PART ONE

ONE

"You're kidding me it's not possible is it?" Craig Erskine looked around him to see if his orgasmic type of outburst had been heard then he quickly turned his eyes back to the building realising that it didn't matter if people had heard him.

Here he was looking at a blood stain and a bullet hole in the grim looking grey wall of the tenement building to which his Mother had brought him, as a newborn 72 years ago. He admitted to himself that he was looking at the marks through perceptive eyes. The perception grew from the fact that decades ago it was he who was principally responsible for their existence.

Craig had often pondered on the concepts of perception and truth and had argued that while truth may be absolute, perception is a form of that absolute truth. His truth. It was based on an incident that occurred outside the front door of 356 Easter Road Leith, where he had lived with his parents, Bill and Janet Erskine. This was during a time when Europe was shaking down her skirts as it began to move forward after the conflict of 1939-45. Obviously the previous war of 1914-18 had had a profound effect on Britain when it turned out that the 'war to end all wars' was a misnomer.

It happened again, and now Scotland was re-establishing her role on a world stage that hadn't known peace for six years.

This was Erskine's first trip back to his homeland. He had promised himself such a trip if he survived seven decades. Although he had never forgotten the event that took place on the pavement outside, so many years ago, he had managed to place it in his cerebral 'filing cabinet'. Now that he was here, he felt a shudder throughout his body as he stared at the pattern that he chose to see as his blood stain and a nick in the wall that could well have been a bullet hole.

Three hours earlier he had arrived at Edinburgh airport from Adelaide via Dubai.

Due to the fact that he still had a European passport, passage through customs and security was thankfully swift. He was travelling light in terms of luggage so he was able to sprint in time to catch the departing Air Bus into the city. As the bus made its way past Murrayfield he remembered being taken there by his uncle to see the New Zealand All Blacks play Scotland. He was amazed at how much he had remembered of that time and hoped that the same would happen when he got to number 356.

As he walked along Edinburgh's Princes Street nostalgia poured out of almost every doorway. He recalled badgering his parents for a strawberry milkshake, from a shop simply called The Milk Bar. It was now a Tattooist and souvenir shop with a swarthy looking human object of his own design standing at the door wearing a plaid shirt opened to reveal a tattooed crest and the words "you'll nae tak oor freedom!" The exclamation mark actually resembled an arrow and it pointed up and over the curve of the stomach and disappeared below a shabby looking tartan skirt, not to be confused with a kilt. Craig wondered just what sort of freedom the message alluded to, feeling quite sure that neither William Wallace or his alter ego, Mel Gibson had a man's nether regions in mind when they gave out that famous exclamation.

When the man caught Craig's enquiring look, he stepped aside and gestured for him to enter. He brandished, rather than presented a tray of pencil sharpeners bearing a stick-on picture of the Forth Railway Bridge.

Craig was close enough to notice that the pictures seemed to have been hastily affixed, probably so as to be removed later and replaced with London's Tower Bridge when the unsold sharpeners would be sent to a similar shop in England. Craig quickly averted his gaze not daring to engage any more eye to eye contact with this unhappy looking inked individual.

Then Jenners Store loomed into sight, just opposite Waverley Station. Memories of afternoon teas with adults came to mind with silver service and warnings never to use a steak knife to butter your raisin bread. He well remembered the scowling look coming from his Father but even to this day he never fully understood what was so wrong with the practice.

Surely a knife is a knife? And who would die or be injured if I went ahead and did it?

Craig had spent his young adult years within cooee of Sydney's Bondi Beach yet it was Portobello sands he remembered most. Also it was cockles from Limekilns that sparked his tastebuds more than Moreton Bay Bugs.

His reverie was disturbed by a woman with a thick European accent.

"Do you know where a chemist shop is?" Just a straight out almost abrupt question, leaving no room for ambiguity. His past experience with Europeans had taught him that they are not wasteful with time or energy or excessive talk when all they need is an answer to their questions.

"I do" said Craig and cheekily left it at that. "Well where?" came the quick response.

Then something remarkable crossed Craig's mind and he was quietly grateful to the woman for the intrusion. He had not been here for over 60 years yet he could recall exactly where the chemist shop was.

Turning to the impatient woman he said.

"If you cross over to where that piper is playing, you will find a ramp to take you down to Waverley Station." The woman was obviously puzzled and a little angry or was that just the European style of response heard by a sensitive Anglo Saxon ear?

"I don't want a train I want a chemist."

Craig took a deep breath as he managed himself into a more helpful mode.

The clarity of the memory was alarming. He and his family had just alighted from the Dunfermline–Edinburgh train, and he was marched straight into Boots the chemist at Waverley. Craig had had just one strawberry milkshake too many and his Mum took him to buy some tummy easers. A whole lifetime had passed by, since he had vomited on the Waverley Station steps, earning the scorn of passersby and humiliated parents.

A hint of a smile remained as he walked up the remainder of Edinburgh's famous thoroughfare and turned left towards Easter Road.

TWO

He was soon standing outside number 356. While his body was perfectly still, his eyes feverishly searched the portico, and the join where the tenement wall and the pavement met. His attention was focused on the spot close to the step, as if the harder he stared, the more apparent the bloodstain would become.

Eventually, his eyes raised their gaze up to the second floor and a window at which he remembered looking down at the street, watching adults live out their lives, and his childhood mind trying to make sense of it. Craig Erskine always thought that, even then he was more of a looker than a player, a spectator rather than a participant.

The sight he looked down upon, that he remembered most, was his Father coming home from the war which he did on a daily basis. His Mother used that expression when he asked her where Dad worked.

"Your Father is off to the war, son," she would say, "he works at the war." His young mind didn't really comprehend what war was.

The war which was actually officially over, still remained a point of discussion, debate and fear. There was so much talk of countries that Erskine didn't know then, such as Germany and France, and people with the names of Churchill, Eisenhower and Hitler.

He remembers his mind being in a whirl when he heard that people in Germany and France were actually fighting with guns. That a man named Hitler was hell-bent on bringing his guns and bombs over the channel and the sea to cities such as London to kill.

Erskine also learnt that many men from Scotland and England had actually armed themselves and went out in ships and on aeroplanes to meet such threats in nearby Europe and also the far flung Orient to kill people. To go to the war.

So when he pondered on his Mother's expression about his Dad 'going to the war' his child's mind couldn't make much sense of it. For one thing, the war was over and anyway he had never seen him carry a gun. His friends had shown him photos of theirs who had 'gone to the war' and they had carried weapons. Craig's hadn't, he wasn't like the Fathers of his friends. His came home each night, while his friends' Fathers didn't. They had slept in mud and blood and many didn't come home at all.

"Although Mum told me he was 'off to the war' each day, he didn't go to war like they did," he told his friends. One of those friends was Jim Baxter whose Mother received a telegram, the contents of which she knew before opening it. Baxter senior had gone missing in action. It was his son, Jim who verbalised the thoughts that many in Leith had. "Tamson, yir faither wis and still is a coward. He comes hame every nicht, bit mine doesna."

Erskine understood the sentiment in Baxter's outburst. The day following the discussion he had had with his friend, Craig found a white bird's feather in his school desk. In contrast to the abuse that his fellow students hurled at him in the playground about his Father, no one talked about or explained the significance of white feathers. The taunting was always confronting him, it was there at playtime, it was in the school lunchroom and in the barbs thrown at him on the way home.

Craig carried it home. It manifested in ways that challenged normal behaviour. Like an aching tooth, he wanted the pain gone. He wanted to shut out the world...the taunting, the fear and the bullying that seemed unique to post war Britain as it sorted out its attitudes.

Craig resolved within himself to bring it to an end. There was only one way, and that was to root out the cause, and that meant confronting his Father that night.

He dare not think what he would do if his Father admitted to being the 'coward of Easter Road' as his friends called him.

So, it was a nervous lad that sat by that second-floor window at 356 Easter Road, Leith so long ago. It had been raining, and the cobbled roadway and granite-lined pavement glistened in the decreasing light of early evening. He stared downwards as closely as one would peer at an artist's canvas, eager to understand the painting that was before him.

Then as the last of the sunlight faded, he saw him. Normally there would be an expected feeling of happiness in the young boy's heart, seeing his Father returning home. Especially if there was a surprise gift such as some Edinburgh Rock that would take him ages to consume. Instead there was a degree of loathing. This man was causing him unhappiness, this man was the reason that his friends taunted him, this was the man who was a coward.

Each day it seemed that young Erskine was learning more about 'the war' and he was about to find the significance of white feathers.

THREE

The elderly man, known to everyone as Mac, lived in the bottom flat of the tenement, and had three budgerigars in his back room. Young Craig had become fascinated by the birds' ability to repeat words that old Mac had taught them. Mac allowed Craig in sometimes but didn't like the birds to be too active as the noise might alert the landlord, who frowned on their existence.

Mac Penfold was born in Australia and left the family farm to join up to fight in World War 1. His readiness to volunteer for any assignment earned him respect and recognition from his superiors and soon became a commissioned officer in the 9th Lighthorse Regiment.

The 9th was raised in the state of South Australia and had a unique history, in that it was the first defence force to have a mix of regulars and reservists training together. Mac suffered most of his injuries on the Gallipoli Peninsula of Turkey. Colonel Albert Miell was killed there and was replaced by Lieutenant Reynell who met his death while attacking the infamous Hill 60 held by the Turks. Mac had been alongside both men when they died, and the same blast had shattered his leg and blistered his face with bomb fragments. Following his medical evacuation in 1915 he was demobbed in Edinburgh and for the most part hid himself away from people's gaze. He avoided mirrors like he used to avoid the enemy at Gallipoli.

He made his home in Leith and became a keen bird fancier. The birds didn't notice the painful limp or the gaping wound left by a shell attack. The birds didn't care that he dribbled when he talked, his face misshapen after numerous surgeries.

They didn't realise it then, but Penfold and his men were to be part of one of the most significant Australian wartime events on the Gallipoli Peninsula, in an allied fighting unit known as the Australian and New Zealand Army Corps.

Craig never understood fully what Mac was trying to tell him when he talked about the original Anzac Day, but he was enthralled with what he heard, as he helped clean the makeshift aviary in the ground floor back room of 356 Easter Road.

"We were part of a big push to capture the Gallipoli Peninsula which would clear the Black Sea for the Navy ships," said Mac. His original Aussie accent was still discernible beneath the Scottish brogue that had begun to influence his speech.

"If we could have taken Constantinople, it would have been curtains for the Ottomans, and a hell of a shock for their commander, Ataturk."

Ataturk was later to be heard actually commending the bravery of the Anzac force, and the two warring sides shared a mutual respect. A commendable attitude in some quarters, maybe, but some questioned the ability to 'respectfully' place a bayonet in another human being's stomach.

Craig asked a question that had bothered him since first noticing the old man's limp. "What about your leg?" pointing to Mac's left limb that was forever disfigured.

"When did that happen?"

Mac stopped tending the budgies for a while and looked out of the back room window, as if reliving the blast that altered his life.

Craig, however, noticed a smile appearing on Mac's lips and wondered why such a memory would be happy.

"Ye ken son," Mac falling into the Scottish vernacular, "From day one, I think I knew that I wasn't going to have an easy time of it. I was originally put on board the HMAS Sydney but a day or so after leaving Albany, a few of us were whisked off and transferred to the battleship Prince of Wales, because Sydney went up to the Cocos Islands to tackle the German raider, Emden."

Craig could not have been a more eager listener – he was only just starting to realise what war was about, and thinking that maybe in another 20 years' time, he could be involved in a similar conflict.

Mac took some time in describing the transfer from one ship to the other. "It was a choppy sea that night and a few of us fell overboard, and although we were pulled back into the lighter, we were dripping wet and bloody cauld!"

Mac stopped talking for a second, to stifle a sneeze, the result of too vivid a memory perhaps.

"Anyway, we got on board the Prince of Wales which landed us at Gallipolli. The next couple of days in the trenches soon made me forget having a cold. Sometimes I can still hear the bullets pounding into the mound."

Craig, was still a little puzzled at why Mac was half laughing as he told his story, but he was soon to find out the reason.

"Three days in," continued Mac, "I was feeling absolutely lousy so they sent me to the hospital ship to see the quack."

Craig had no idea what a quack was other than the noise Mum made when telling stories about farmyards. But it didn't faze him as he leant in closer to Mac, all thoughts of budgies gone from his mind.

"So the doc examined me and gave me three days off, and complete rest. He gave me a strong sedative and I swear I was asleep by the time they stretchered me out to another room to get over it all."

"How long were you in that room?" asked Craig.

"Almost three days, and I reckon I slept for most of that time, I had no idea where I was, and I cared less. However, when I came round I started to think of what was going on, and realised that I had been asleep while everyone else was being blown to pieces on the peninsula. I was no coward laddie, I can tell you that, so I was keen to get out of that stretcher."

The word 'coward' hit home with Craig, as he knew he still had that confrontation with his Father ahead of him. He quickly put it at the back of his mind as he pushed Old Mac for more of the story of him recovering from the flu in Turkey.

"I was so bloody thirsty," said Mac "I sat up and looked around and saw a bloke, probably a medic of some sort, sitting with his back to me, writing at a desk. Excuse me, mate could I have a drink?

"Well I have never seen a fella jump so high and look so scared."

"Why?" asked Craig.

Mac's smile started to broaden now as he explained that the room that he had been put in was actually a small mortuary and the guy at the desk was doing the paperwork for the despatch of three bodies that were alongside where Mac was lying.

So, when Mac woke up with no doubt a sheet falling off his face, and asked for a drink, the attendant thought it was one of the dead soldiers!

Mac was soon sent back to the lines, but not for long. Four days later he was back in the hospital ship, with a shattered left leg.

There was a strip of land on the ridge surrounding the Gallipoli Peninsula which was called the Nek, a derivation from the Afrikaan word for a mountain pass. It was a type of bottleneck which was so easy for the Ottomans to defend. The allies commander Lieutenant Colonel Albert Miell was killed there and was replaced by Lieutenant Reynell who met his death while attacking the infamous Hill 60. Mac had been alongside both men when they died, and the same blast shattered his leg.

Reluctantly Major Michael (Mac) Penfold was repatriated to Dorset Military Hospital. Having no family left in Australia, he decided to stay in the UK as his injury barred him from further service.

As well as bringing home a physical injury, Mac brought the psychological scars so well known to other returned service personnel. Among them was guilt that he was not alongside his comrades, and he also felt a strong fear of being labelled a coward by others, because he looked reasonably healthy.

Mac's injuries put paid to any possibility of him returning to the war. He eventually moved to Scotland and took up residence at number 356 Easter Road in Leith and found solace in cage birds and went on to become a leader in the Loanhead and District Cage Bird Society which managed to keep its regular meetings going throughout both World Wars.

His pleasure now came from tending to hens, cockerels and budgies, but he had an abhorrence of white feathered birds. His friends believed it was because of the connection with white feathers and cowardice.

Young Erskine's mind was alerted when he heard this because he thought there may have been a connection between this and the reason that white feathers were put on his school desk. Craig asked Mac to explain the connection.

His query received a stony silence from Mac.

"Can you hear me, Mr Penfold?" he asked when he saw that Mac was just standing staring out of the window, with millet seed in one hand, the other holding apart the wires of the cage. The task of feeding the birds had come to a complete halt through the mention of white feathers. He turned to face Craig, and he looked at him for what seemed ages.

"Wait here, lad," he said and slowly moved away and out of the basement door. Craig heard his measured steps on the stair, then silence as he reached the upstairs room.

It wasn't very long before Mac began the return journey, his steps still measured and his stare seeking out the young lad whose question had caused a sudden change in the mood of the room and the dynamics of the relationship of the elder and the younger. Craig had no idea what was to follow but he felt the gravity of the moment.

FOUR

Mac held a tattered-looking book under his arm. It had a military emblem on its front page. "Come here lad, sit by me," said Mac in a heavy, almost sad, tone.

"You're about to hear something that I have not shared with anyone before."

Craig did as he was asked, his mind racing with trying to make a connection between the white feathers and the serious nature that had begun to dominate his time with Mac and his birds.

"The war was only about a month old, when I arrived from Australia, and straight away I was sent to serve with a Pommy outfit on a special mission."

Craig didn't dare stop the flow of conversation, but was eager to ask what a Pommy was. It could wait.

Mac continued, "There were five of us and all they would tell us was that we were off to somewhere in France. I was a bit excited about that because I had heard of France and it sure sounded an interesting place. I just wished I wasn't going there to fight."

Craig had no idea where this was heading, but he sensed a timely need for silence and attention.

If there was such a thing as solemn brightness, it came to Mac's eyes. Brightness because he hadn't visited this episode of his life in such a long time and was eager to test his emotions, and solemnity due to the tale that he was about to share, for the first time, with someone outside of his compatriots and brothers in arms.

"Maybe you have heard of Julius Caesar," Mac looked at his young friend, not really expecting a positive answer. So he was a little surprised when Craig said, "The old Roman who was stabbed in the back by his friends? Yes we saw that film at the Scotia cinema on Haymarket, with that woman who was in Gone With The Wind. Apparently it was made while London was being bombed and Mum said that Vivien Leigh had an accident and lost her baby." Craig was feeling excited about being able to add to this conversation.

Mac gave a half smile, thinking that there was something to thank the ever-growing film industry for in helping to perpetuate Shakespeare's work, even though a whole generation would now think of Cleopatra with a Vivien Leigh-like visage.

"What's Julius Caesar got to do with why you went to France?" queried Craig. "Nothing really, it was just a way of explaining the area of France I was sent to,"

responded Mac. "Caesar went there because of the valuable flint tools that the tribes there dug up and formed into tools and weapons."

"Funny if the dagger that Caesar was stabbed with was made with that flint!" mused Craig.

"Ironic," said Mac, overlooking the fact that Craig probably didn't understand what that meant.

Mac went on to explain that the area where the World War I Battle of Mons took place was originally called Castrilocus, after the mini fort of Castrum that the Romans built there. It eventually became known as Mons, after the mountains around Castrilocus.

"A fine place for a battle," was one thought that Julius Caesar voiced, according to the scribes of the time.

A prophetic thought, given the number of skirmishes that took place there, the latest of which was the Battle of Mons, the first significant action of World War I. It was a victory of sorts for the British allied forces, because they inflicted huge casualties on the Germans, and managed to hold the line. However, it did end in a retreat by the Brits, partly because of the French army removing their support and exposing the allies to the German onslaught.

The Brits weren't particularly proud of a retreat from the German forces, and it did nothing to bond their French allies to them. Franco-Anglais political relationships have never been easy as far back as the Battle of Agincourt.

Craig noticed that Mac had drifted off as he was talking, seemingly letting his mind prepare for what he was about to relate.

The young boy pulled at Mac's sleeve which had the effect of turning the old soldier's eyes back to Craig, who asked him, yet again, what this had to do with Mac heading to France. There was also the overhanging question about white feathers.

"I had just finished my training in Aldershot, when the Battle of Mons was starting and if I may say so myself, I was a pretty good soldier."

"What were you best at?" asked Craig.

"Rifle shooting," was the response. "And, as I found out later, it was my marksmanship that landed me in this special mission to France."

"You see I wasn't sent as part of a bunch of soldiers to fight in the actual battle. I was selected to carry out a single job with four others, then be sent right back to England."

Mac's voice was starting to sound stronger and his eyes had lost that stare of deep thought that had haunted him from when he first started to tell his story to Craig. It seemed as though his reluctance to tell the lad much had passed, and he welcomed the eager audience that Craig had become.

Young Erskine was becoming a little restless, as he noticed the clock on Mac's kitchen wall. It was getting close to teatime and he would hate it if his Mother came to fetch him. He actually doubted if his Mother knew where he was right now. So, he wanted Mac to hurry with his story.

Mac went on to explain that by the beginning of September 1914, the British Expeditionary Force had considered its losses and decided to move back. Cognisant of the thoughts that must be running through the minds of the soldiers, top brass reiterated the rule that anyone who appeared to be arranging their own retreat would be severely dealt with, and it would be far worse than a stint in prison.

This was wartime and the defence forces were free to adopt certain emergency wartime procedures. The harshest applied to deserters.

FIVE

It was this policy that brought 19-year-old Private Highgate a notoriety that no one would wish for. He had joined the forces in his hometown of Shoreham on the English south coast, and soon found himself fighting the Germans during the Battle of Mons. He certainly wasn't the first to die in that war, but he was the first to have it sentenced upon him.

Mac paused the conversation. It was time to put the birds to bed. Almost like clockwork the budgerigars hopped on to their higher perches around four pm, and that was the cue to their beloved owner to cover their cage. In a ritualistic fashion, he slid a tea-towel over them. It was one that a friend had sent him from South Australia, bearing that state's emblem bird, the piping shrike. Mac wouldn't see his birds again until dawn the next day, but at least a glance at the cage would still bring him pleasure and evoke memories of the kookaburras, magpies, and honey eaters that used to frequent his back lawn in Streaky Bay.

Craig was starting to become impatient for the end of the story, simply because nothing he had heard so far had given him the slightest idea of its conclusion, and certainly he was no closer to understanding white feathers. His Father would be home soon and he eagerly wanted more knowledge so as he could properly judge the level of cowardice he perceived his Dad to have.

Now that Mac's birds had ceased their chattering for the day and were falling asleep under the cover of a tea-towel, the old digger turned his attention to his pipe. He had taken up pipe smoking while convalescing in England. His friends back home were a little bemused when he wrote to them, telling how he had had a Craggy Root. It was some time before he let on that it wasn't what was meant by the Australian vernacular, but a brand of pipe made by the Rattray family. It was named after the wild Scottish coastline, and was one of the first made by Rattrays after they opened shop in Perth in 1911. His tobacco of choice was Black Mallory, which he liked as much for its bold black tin. There was a row of twelve on the high shelf of his scullery.

Craig winced a little as the Mallory fumes headed his way. He had hated anything to do with smoking ever since he was given a Senior Service cigarette by one of his friends,

after school. Craig was sick for three days because of the inhalation and told his parents that it was a stomach upset.

Once the air had cleared a little and Mac's tobacco had settled into a slow burn in his pipe, he took up his story again.

"Not long after the Battle of Mons broke out, and things were starting to go the way of the Germans, young Highgate was let out of prison and sent up to the front lines."

Craig reluctantly stopped Mac's flow, "What do you mean prison?"

"Well," said Mac, "he and a few mates from the Brighton platoon had ended up in gaol because they had been found up on the South Downs, when they should have been preparing for embarkation to Belgium."

The South Downs were a range of hills that ran along the back of that area of Brighton and Shoreham, where Private Highgate was born, and often the favourite haunt of lovers and picnickers.

A sympathetic tone entered Mac's delivery, "I don't think that young Highgate and friends were really deserting, but that's the charge they threw at him and earned him forty-two days in Dover Military Prison."

Although luck didn't help Private Highgate in the end, it did go his way initially when the top brass decided he deserved another chance, and sent him off to Mons.

"However," said Mac "not long after landing there and being given his Lee-Metford." "His what?" interrupted Craig.

"His rifle, British-manufactured weapon that actually took over from the old black powder varieties of the 1800s. Effective enough but only had an eight-or ten-round magazine.

"Anyway young Highgate decided that he wanted to go and join the same company as his brothers, so he scarpered."

"Did he join them?" asked Craig.

Mac took his Craggy Root out of his mouth and shook his head.

"No, that was his downfall. He met up with a Belgian landholder who persuaded him to work for him on his farm, which was doing quite well given the demand by the troops around the area. Highgate worked there for quite a few months, but developed a false sense of security. He wandered into Bruge on market day, and was jumped on by the military police."

Craig, while enjoying the story, was still wondering about the connection between all of this, and how Mac was involved and more urgently, what it had to do with white feathers.

Mac continued, "So this twenty-year-old disgraced private was charged with desertion and imprisoned to await court martial. Again, I don't think he meant to desert the army, he wasn't quite right in the head and just took opportunities where he found them. Sadly, the trial went against him and he went back to prison to wait his punishment. He was given a special jacket to wear which had a white feather sewn into it."

Craig suddenly renewed his interest in the story. At last Mac had mentioned the words white feather. So any time now, he thought, he would find out why he found one in his school desk.

Mac looked across at the covered bird cage as he related to Craig that the white feather symbolises cowardice, coming from the old practice of cockfighting. Any cockerel displaying a white feather in its tail was considered a poor fighter. Mac also explained that purebred gamecocks don't show white feathers, so a cockerel that sports one, is inferior and not wanted by any bird keeper.

"And young Craig," Mac looked into the boy's wide eyes. "Women used them to shame men into enlisting. There was an Order of the White Feather which encouraged women to give a white feather to any man, not wearing an army uniform.

"History shows that there were many mistakes made by the act of giving a white feather to a man out of uniform while there was a war on. And the worst offenders were mainly women."

Mac leant in toward Craig and fixed him with a serious stare. "You must be very careful when you deal out such symbols, to make sure you have got the facts right."

Craig's thoughts came back to his Father, whom he had little doubt was a coward. Mac continued in his cautionary tone, and told Craig the story of a man from Worthing in England who was on a bus in London, and because he wasn't in a uniform, a woman hit him with her handbag and thrust a white feather at him, saying that he was a coward and should go immediately and join up.

"The man then did something that I don't really approve of but can understand the thinking behind it."

Mac paused, annoying Craig who was eager to know more.

"He reached out and hit the woman, and although not really hurt, she was shocked as she fell to the floor of the bus. The man pulled the bell cord to tell the driver he wanted off at the next stop, then waved the feather at the woman as she cowered in fright."

"It seems that Private Ernest Atkins was on leave from service on the Western Front and was having his uniform de-loused, before returning to the war the following day.

"As he waved the feather in her face, he told the woman that he would gladly take it back to his comrades and it would forever represent the mean-mindedness of some people back home upon whom the fighting forces depended for support."

Craig's mouth hung open as he heard also that the soldier was charged with striking a civilian and spent seven days in jail before going back to war.

Craig spent some time digesting what he had just heard and ran it through his mind as criteria against which he placed his Father's behaviour. Yes, he thought, Mac is right to say be careful, but he could think of no other explanation than that his Father was a coward and hadn't signed up to join other Leith Fathers and husbands from Easter Road.

"OK, hang on a bit while I shake at the Shank," said Mac. Craig's mind was quickly diverted by the expression Mac had used,

"What's that?" he queried.

Mac smiled as he replied, "I'm off for a piddle."

Craig knew full well what Shanks meant. Many times he had aimed his own piddle at the name stamped on the back of the toilet bowl, in some ambitious attempt to spray the letters off! The Shank referred to was the manufacturer of bathroom porcelain known as Shanks. On a holiday to Paisley once, Craig's Father pointed out the first shop that John Shanks had opened in the

High Street. Shanks then moved to a new factory at Barrhead where he had found success. Apparently the factory employed around 1000 people and Craig remembered thinking that was a lot of people concerned about peeing.

SIX

Mac came back into the room, and for the first time since the two of them had sat down and begun to talk, he seemed eager to tell the story. For Craig's part, he felt a little more informed about white feathers and was starting to understand that by finding one in his school desk, it meant that he was not alone in his thoughts that his Father a coward.

The two of them had been talking close on two hours, and Craig sensed that his Mother would be wondering where he had got to. Also he was keen to get back because he wanted to be there when his Father came home (from the war) and, too, there were some home-made bridies warming in the oven.

Mac Penfold, although keen to get his story out, was hesitant because what he was about to tell the young lad was still raw and sensitive for him.

"Desertion and cowardice in the face of the enemy is considered so seriously by the army, that there is only one punishment." Mac was unsure of whether to continue filling young ears with stories of crime and punishment and death, and even inhumanity. But, his young friend well understood that a world war had not long finished and of course knew that it was far from the first such conflict. The press was full of stories of restitution and recriminations and revenge. Craig would have seen pictures of German and

Japanese officers being marched to their deaths as punishment for some atrocity or another.

"I had finished training at Aldershot and was just enjoying some leave, when I was called in to the captain's office along with four other guys from the same unit." Mac seemed to be transported back to that event, his eyes never blinked once as he fixed his stare on Craig.

"We were told to go back to our rooms and pack enough personal stuff for two nights, and of course prepare our rifles. We were to be ferried out at midnight for a boat trip. All they told us was that it was a war zone we would be heading for."

Mac had only been in the army a short while, but was well aware that you don't ask questions and the most often used words were, 'Yes sir.'

So along with four others he was driven to Dover and put on board the Taranaki, which had been converted to a Q ship not long after the outbreak of war. The German Navy knew them as U-Boat-Fallen (U-boat traps). They were made to appear an easy target in order to lure U-boats to the surface, so as to land an easy shot.

Their code name came from their home port of Queenstown in Ireland. They had the appearance of old steamers and even if they had been torpedoed, the damage would have been minimal due to their construction. Wooden panels hid a healthy arsenal of ammunition and weaponry which would be trained on the U-boat as it surfaced. The Taranaki had successfully destroyed U-boat-40 off Eyemouth earlier in the year. Mac found himself being secreted aboard at midnight, heading for France.

"There was no U-boat activity that night, so the ride over was smooth and fast, and I had the chance to look closely at my fellow travellers."

When Mac studied their faces, he detected a familiarity. He had seen them before and slowly his mind allowed itself to gradually reveal where.

As he had told Craig, he had excelled at weapon training, especially on individual targets. His scores had been in the top ten, and it was believed that growing up on a farm on South Australia's west coast, had much to do with his success. While others spent time with heavy iron traps, Mac was content to sit patiently and pick off individual rabbits as they left their burrows. He had been allowed from an early age to use firearms, and had become adept at quick reloading.

After training one day at Woodside Army Camp, near Adelaide, there had been a special parade held to award ten recruits who had excelled. Five of them had either 99 per cent or 100 per cent scores.

As Mac sat there on his midnight cruise to France aboard the Q ship, he started to realise that the four other men with him, were from that top five group.

So many questions surfaced but uppermost was "why were five men being ferried secretly across the ocean, late at night, heading for a war zone, when hundreds of armed soldiers were making their way on big troop carriers in broad daylight, heading for the same war zone?"

While that clandestine trip on board the Q ship Taranaki was taking place, with at least five soldiers not knowing where they were going or why, another soldier from the British Expeditionary Force was under no delusion as to why he was in a locked room in a disused fort in the French port town of Dunkirk.

Nineteen-year-old, Private Highgate had only been in the army twelve months before the start of the war. His military record was abysmal. He had spent 42 days in Sussex military prison for desertion. His comparatively light sentence was due to his medical report which suggested that the effects of a fever had resulted in an altered state of mind. He was certainly vague and easily influenced but not considered dangerous or intentionally rebellious.

However, following his despatch to France, his superiors felt less sympathetic towards him and grew intolerant.

So when young Highgate was found working as a gardener in Chateau de Goulaine, the proverbial book was thrown at him. He had simply walked out of camp, innocent of thought and oblivious of the danger he was walking into.

When apprehended by the military police, he was asked why he was working at this chateau.

"My Mother sent me here," he responded.

"When I told her I was going to France, she said to try and find the place where they make butter white sauce."

"You're not here for a pleasure trip soldier," growled the sergeant.

The look of innocence on Highgate's face failed to impress the arresting soldiers. "What made you think you could just leave the army and take up gardening,

particularly when there was a war on?"

Highgate's response both surprised and flabbergasted the military policemen.

"All I did was walk out of the camp. No one stopped me so I kept going. When I saw the sign to this place, it reminded me of what Mum said. She is mad on cooking French food and likes to use proper stuff. She knew that this sauce was made here ages ago and wanted me to get the original recipe."

"Private Highgate, this is a bloody ridiculous conversation we are having," shouted the other MP who wore corporal stripes.

"There is a fucking war about to rage over this place, and you're walking around looking for fucking French recipes."

Both the corporal and sergeant were at the end of their patience, if indeed they had any to begin with.

The sergeant instructed the other policeman to cuff Highgate's hands behind his back, while he came within an inch of the young soldier's face and shouted at him.

"You are being arrested for desertion in the face of the enemy and you will be taken to Dunkerque to wait for a court martial."

The innocent look on Highgate's face started to fade as he realised that these men meant business. A look of fear took over in his eyes, and he started to shake ever so slightly.

The MPs went through his pockets, tossing aside cigarettes, a hanky, some coins and a piece of paper torn out of a notebook.

"Don't take that!" yelled Highgate, when the corporal held up the piece of paper which had some scribble on it. The response from the sergeant was swift and decisive. With his right hand, he struck the young soldier on the face, bringing blood to the surface of his cheek and down his bruised nose.

Because he was handcuffed, he couldn't do anything about the mess that was congealing, except shake his head. Huge tears started to well and a shiver ran through his body.

For the first time since joining the army, Highgate felt strong fear and helplessness The nonchalance that encouraged him to gaily walk out of the army camp and into a gardening job at the chateau, had vanished.

He was bundled aboard the military policemen's Lanchester, an armoured car which had only been landed at Dunkirk the week prior. It seemed as though Highgate would have the unenviable role of being its first customer.

The Expeditionary Force were pretty proud of being able to acquire this vehicle as it was the second most numerous armoured car in service after the Rolls-Royce.

Its original purpose was to pick up fallen air pilots, but the MP unit had used some bluff to acquire it for their purpose of picking up wayward servicemen and deserters.

As he sat uneasily on the bench in the back of the Lanchester, he did manage to look back at the chateau, which had been his home for the last few months. They had welcomed this naive young man who was willing to take on any work and seemed to revel in pruning vines and scything hay, used as mulch to produce their famous grapes. Highgate felt the happiest he had ever felt since leaving home, knowing that he had found the very place his Mother had mentioned. He was also pretty chuffed that he had managed to get the wine maker to write down the recipe for beurre blanc sauce as invented by the previous chef Madame Clémence Lefeuvre.

It was not known exactly how old the recipe was, but the history of the chateau went back to circa 1000 AD. The Goulaines had owned the chateau until 1858 when a Dutch banker took control. It it was actually the last in the Loire to begin making wine.

Highgate had prided himself in having learnt the rich history of Chateau de Goulaine, even though his reading skills were somewhat lacking. Now as he sat in the back of the Lanchester heading for Dunkirk, he watched the chateau slip away from his vision through the slit in the armoured car which was actually designed for the gunner.

Although uncertain of his fate, he had no idea that this was the last sight he would have of his previous home of six months.

Twenty minutes later, Private Highgate, handcuffed, was led out of the Lanchester and escorted to a stone tower situated on the end of the Dunkirk Harbour which was originally designed to store life-saving equipment. Highgate was shuffled inside and then pushed on to a mattress in the corner. He was told to turn around to enable the removal of the handcuffs. So tight had they been, he had almost lost all feeling in his hands. When the sergeant released the cuffs, Highgate flinched at the pins and needles sensation as his hands returned to life.

Then the MPs left him, slamming an iron door behind them. Before Highgate could get his bearings, the door opened again and the corporal came in and threw something onto the mattress, turned around and walked out again with another slam of the iron door. It was the recipe from the Chateau that he had written out for his Mother. He read it over and over, feeling that it offered some comfort from worrying thoughts.

Easy Beurre Blanc Recipe

2 teaspoons minced shallots

1/2 oz. (1/4 cup) white wine

1/2 cup unsalted butter cut into cubes

1–2 tablespoons of heavy cream (so sauce won't 'break')

salt

white pepper

splash of olive oil (for sauteing shallots)

SEVEN

It wasn't butter sauce that Mac Penfold was thinking about as the boat bounced across the channel to France. Although they had murmured between themselves, the five soldiers didn't discuss the purpose of their journey. That had still not been explained by the sergeant, who was snoring on the only bunk in the below-water main cabin.

All of the men were carrying their issue rifles but as Mac noticed, there was no ammunition. Why, when conflict was starting to make an impact on Europe, and these trained soldiers were in the heart of it, were they being ferried across the channel with weapons with no bullets? It didn't make sense, but then again all of them had had a few years of experience of the greatcoats-on-greatcoats-off mentality of the military top brass.

Mac wandered up on deck, leaving his all but useless weapon of war behind him. It was around four am and he was seeing the dim outlines of Dunkirk Harbour appearing in the growing light of dawn. He had never been to France before. In fact if it hadn't been for the war, he probably wouldn't have left the paddocks of Streaky Bay in South Australia.

His family farm had an expansive view of the ocean that marked the beginning of the Great Australian Bight. Not being a brilliant student at school, Mac did develop a love of history, and like his counterparts in Britain would have known the kings and queens of history. He had developed an incredible knowledge of the explorers who plied the early Australian coastline. As he stood on this creaky Q ship, 10,000 miles from home, he wondered what thoughts Peter Nuyts had in 1627 when the Dutch explorer first sighted Streaky Bay.

In the dawn light the hills behind Dunkirk would not be dissimilar to the range above Streaky. Mac recalled also that it was the English sailor, Matthew Flinders, who had named Streaky Bay because of the streaks in the water. The streaks were the result of the reflection of seaweed and light. At least Nuyts and Flinders had a vague idea of why they were there, thought Mac, unlike him and his four fellow travellers.

Mac's reverie was suddenly interrupted by Sergeant Snelling. He came on deck and ordered Mac to return to the cabin and tell the others to bring their rifles. They were to fall in on the stone wharf of Dunkirk once the boat had docked and the gangplank had been put in place.

Dawn doesn't hit the sky, it seeps into the landscape like an artist introducing a sunlike colour on to an otherwise blank canvas. It can be a time of reflection or romance but it can also be a time of dread to those who have something to fear.

It was a dawn that Private Highgate did not relish. A few hours earlier, he had been visited in his makeshift cell in the stone-walled edifice that was Dunkirk Harbour by his company captain and the unit's warrant officer.

As the men entered, the cell guard issued the order "Private Highgate officer in the room, be upstanding."

As he got to his feet, Highgate's otherwise naive mind started to throb with a sinister undertone. Until now, he had acknowledged to himself that he was in trouble and that some kind of punishment would ensue.

"Nothing I can't handle," he had thought "already done a couple of months in Dover and that wasn't really too bad. Everyone was too preoccupied with the war that was coming, to worry much about me." But when Highgate saw the look on the officer's face, he started to feel a little nervous. This time it was going to be different.

The stone-walled room that was the prisoner's cell was hardly big enough to hold the wire bed and the soil bucket let alone the man himself. So, when the two other military men entered, there was little room to move. They were so close to each other that spittle was easily exchanged when they began to talk.

Whether out of kindness to the young private, or a feeling of intimidation himself, Captain Wainwright ordered him, in a surprisingly moderate tone, to sit on the bed. What he was about to say was going to have an emotional impact on all in that room, most of all Highgate.

"Eric Highgate, Private in the British Expeditionary Forces, you have been charged and found guilty of desertion on two occasions. The first was dealt with in peacetime and resulted in 42 days of detention in Dover Prison. However, with this second offence where you were apprehended working at a private facility outside the property of His Majesty King George the Fifth, King of the United Kingdom and the British Dominions, and Emperor of India, you were an enlisted person in the British Expeditionary Forces during a time of war."

Wainwright paused both to give Highgate some time to understand the words and to give himself some needed courage to utter the next few words.

During the pause, Highgate kept his stare on the captain's eyes, now and then glancing toward the WO2, as if seeking some clarification. However, there was no clarification needed in the captain's next words.

"Because it was during a time of conflict, and at a sensitive time in the security of the British Forces, a specially convened tribunal comprising myself, Warrant Officer Price, Lieutenant-General Sir E. A. Alderson of the Canadian Corps presided over by Sir John French, commander of the British Expeditionary Force, deliberated over the matter."

Another pause from Wainwright, then the words that would reveal the young man's fate. "The decision has been made to confirm the charge of desertion upon you. At six am tomorrow, you will be taken from here to the parade grounds within Dunkirk Harbour, where you will face a firing squad and be put to death for your actions."

Although the captain had added the obligatory question on whether Highgate understood what he had just heard, he didn't wait for any reply. He and the WO2 left the room and the guard slammed the door behind them.

EIGHT

Dawn seemed to be different here, thought Penfold, as he waited for his comrades to join him on the harbour wall. He couldn't quite work out what it was. The colours were basically the same as an English dawn, and certainly little different from the many dawns he had experienced in his birthplace of Streaky Bay on South Australia's west coast.

Mac had led a very rural life as a young man, his mind keen to absorb as much agrarian science as it could. But there were always signs of a cultural artistic side, and he was often to be seen mucking about, as he called it, with colours on a canvas propped up outside the grain shed on his family property. He was a fond reader of publications that talked about art, although he was fonder of the actual paintings that were reproduced therein.

So he knew something of the work of Monet who had been entranced with the natural light he found in France. Penfold imagined that he was standing on the very spot where the master artist had propped his easel to capture a sunset or a dawn like Mac was experiencing now. He remembered reading somewhere that this Normandy harbour showed the rising of the sun, like few other French towns. Apparently there were no two dawns alike, thanks to the natural hues that evolved with each second of new light emanating from the sun as it rose to start another day for mankind.

Although the sight of a French dawn filled him with pleasure, he still had no idea why he was here. He and the four comrades who accompanied him still knew nothing, but it was wartime, the world was in the middle of a big conflict, so some rules were made up on the run. The 'need to know' concept was an integral part of army life. Penfold had learnt not to ask the why's and wherefores. The uncertainty was about to end.

As the dawn began to throw its light on Dunkirk, five members of the British Expeditionary Force were paraded on the town's stone wharf and were about to be addressed by Captain John Wainwright, the same man who had just announced a sentence of death to a fellow soldier.

The sergeant who had been with the men on the journey over on the Q-ship Taranaki, from Dover called the men to attention as the officer marched at a slow pace along the harbour wall towards the assembled soldiers.

As he arrived, the sergeant saluted, and in what Mac thought was a rare gesture, Captain Wainwright extended his hand and the men exchanged a hearty shake. As warm a greeting as this may have been, there were no smiles to accompany it.

"At ease men," ordered Wainwright. "This as you can appreciate is one of the most beautiful places in the world. For that reason alone, it is so unfortunate that it will soon be embroiled in the coming conflict. War is an ugly business no matter which way you look at it. While we can console ourselves that we are here to protect people of similar mind and cultures to ours, the truth is that we have come to kill."

The five men on the harbour wall that day had not yet fired a shot in anger, so it all felt surreal to them. All of them were expert marksmen, and knew their weapons thoroughly, yet it had not really hit home that probably the next time they fired them, people would die.

Then they heard the words that they were longing to hear. Words that would explain why they were here.

Captain Wainwright stiffened as he continued, "A short while ago, in that stone bunker type building along the sea front, the sentence of death was pronounced on one of our own. He is a young private whose naivety led him down a very dangerous path. The man is to be known as a deserter. Someone who has shown cowardice in the face of the enemy."

Wainwright knew in his heart that this was not exactly true. Highgate had not dropped his rifle and retreated. Highgate had not defied orders to kill or even shoot. Highgate, like many young 19-year-old men from rural England, had simply followed his fancy.

"Men, because this is the first time such an act has been encountered in this war, which is still young, much care has to be taken in how it is dealt with.

"The job ahead has to be done swiftly and humanely. History has to show us as being firm resolute, but compassionate and to have taken as much care in the execution of our duty as we could.

"That is why we have selected you five who have excelled in weaponry, who have been recognised as the best that this Expeditionary Force contains.

"It will be your task, gentlemen, to carry out the firing squad execution of Private Eric Highgate."

The dusk was starting to settle on Leith and the lamplighter was plying his age-old craft outside number 356 Easter Road. This was one of Craig's favourite times. In some of the streets in Edinburgh, electricity poles supporting modern street lights had made such an activity redundant. There were plans to electrify Leith's street-lights during the next 12

months, but for the moment, Craig was grateful that there was a gas lamp pole right outside his home. The fact that he was on the second floor gave him an uninterrupted grandstand view with the mantle at his eye level.

From Mac Penfold's ground-level rooms, the view wasn't so appealing, as one could only see the boots of the gas-lamp lighter as he shuffled along the road with his six-foot long lighting stick.

It was seeing those boots that reminded Craig of the passing hours and the need to persuade Mac to finish his story. He was anxious to be upstairs when his Father came home (from the war) as he was now more than ever in the mood to confront him. Through Mac's story, he had learnt that cowards were actually killed by their own, and he was unsure how he felt about that in regards to his Father. Mac's voice which seemed to be sounding more and more like his native Australian brought Craig's attention back to the moment.

"So we knew our mission. There wasn't one of us that didn't feel ill at the thought of shooting one of our own men."

"But this man was a coward, Mr Penfold. He deserved to die if he had deserted," Craig interrupted.

"But was he a coward, lad? Or just someone who had made a stupid mistake and it was convenient for the brass to have him shot as a coward. It would further establish authority, and serve as a deterrent."

"You don't think he was a coward do you, Mr Penfold?" asked Craig.

Mac turned toward him and fixed his stare.

"From what I learnt, Private Highgate was a stupid young fool and deserved severe punishment, but from where I stood, he was no coward. He no more deserved that white feather sewn on his jacket than anyone at the beginning of the Great War."

Craig started to think that his Mother would be none too pleased that he was talking about such things. She was anxious that her family try to get away from the death and destruction that had been blazing during the war just finished. She would also not want to know how much Craig's belief in his Father's cowardice had deepened since speaking with Mac.

Private Highgate had been breathing since his first gasp at birth 19 years and 12 days ago. Now sitting alone in his cell in France, he had started to wonder how many more breaths he would have between now and the time when a small piece of hardware would stop them altogether. His brain was doing something similar to an audit of the senses. He thought about his toes, it was his feet that would take him from here to the parade ground where he would feel them for the last time. He raised both his arms and studied his fingers. Ever since birth, they had brought sensory messages to his brain as he learnt about life in all its stages.

As he looked at them, he recalled all the messy things they had touched, he remembered the intimacy they felt when he made love, and he remembered how his hands had formed bonds with other humans through a simple shake.

These hands would no longer feel another's. They were only minutes away from performing their last functions. So were his legs, their last function would be to support him as he staggered out to face his fate. His hands moved up his body, feeling his stomach and thinking that whatever was inside it now, would be the last food that it would ever digest.

Feeling his shoulders slump, he realised that they would no longer feel the weight of an army pack, or a rifle. He remembered carrying his baby nephew on his shoulders last Christmas – that was the first time he had bonded with the young relative and it was the last.

His hands reached his eyes. Unlike the rest of his body, they would be the ones that actually stare death in the face. Highgate wondered if he would see the puff of smoke from the rifles as they delivered their blow.

Then his hands moved to his ears. Would he hear the sounds of birds or the water lapping at the harbour on which his place of execution was situated? Could it be really true that the last three words he will ever hear would be 'Ready, Aim, Fire!'

Will there be enough time between the final word and the explosion of the rifles discharging their deadly message for these ears to catch the sound?

Highgate's mind seem to calm a little once his 'audit' was over. It was if the touch of his own body gave him some comfort. It was only 19 years old so the toes, the legs, the stomach, eyes and ears that he had just touched, had every reason to believe that they had much more work to do and new experiences to have. The reality, as his brain knew, was that everything that made up Eric John Highgate of Shoreham was about to come to a sudden stop. He wondered if it would hurt, but then realised that pain is really in memory, so if he was killed at the exact time of bullet entry, then there would be no memory, so no it wouldn't hurt.

Highgate was surprised at the calming effect all this thinking and reasoning was having on him, as he sat awaiting the sound of heavy footsteps to approach the door, under which he detected a ray of pale sunlight. Dawn was here.

Because he had been given a stripe just before he departed on this mysterious mission (although the mystery had now passed), Lance Corporal Penfold was put in charge of the four others and ordered to march them the 500 metres or so to the ancient wooden doors that led on to the parade ground of Dunkirk's harbour-based fort.

Little had been said between the men since the details of the task ahead had been revealed. Each one could only guess at the feelings each held, and it would be an easy guess.

Penfold was feeling particularly uneasy. Because of his newly gained rank, he had been given the details behind Highgate's death sentence.

For the life of him he could see no evidence of cowardice. The sergeant, who had accompanied the five members of the shooting party across from Dover, had been present at the deliberation that went into the decision to execute Highgate. He too was at a loss to see the justification, and felt that the decision was in the interest of man management and morale, and political expediency. Neither of which were reason for the putting to death of a fellow human being. Yes, he had technically deserted the camp, but it wasn't the white feather type of cowardice that he had committed.

"Being the beginning of the war, it was felt," stated the sergeant, "that a standard of behaviour had to be established right from the start."

NINE

It was 5.45 am when the small party of British Expeditionary Force marksmen entered the gates of the parade ground and made their way to what looked very much like a bird hide. There was enough room for each man to extend their elbows to comfortably rest their rifles on the gunsight. As they entered, the riflemen were relieved of their issued firearms and given a similar weapon which was loaded with a single bullet. The rifles were a long way from the automatic weaponry of later wars.

The rifles used in World War I were developed between 1886 and 1903. The diameter of the barrel fluctuated between 6.5 millimetres and eight millimetres. The magazine contained between three and ten cartridges, although it typically had five. The weapon featured a manually operated locking mechanism located at the end of the barrel. In the rifle's loading action, the empty case was ejected, a new cartridge placed in the chamber and the weapon cocked for the next shot.

There would be no need for a second shot. All they had to do was fire the preloaded single bullet, aiming at a piece of white paper placed on the target's chest.

One of the men asked why it was necessary to mark the target like that. "Probably a case of dignity for the young fella as well as to avoid need for a messy clean-up. You might feel tempted to fire at his head."

"Well wouldn't that be quick and effective?"

"Guess so Private, but do you want to wipe his brains off the back wall?"

That response laid a heavy silent cloud on the shooters, as once again they had cause to ponder on the task ahead. As the men settled into their positions within the hide, Captain Wainwright explained the process that was about to occur.

"Each of your rifles has been loaded with one bullet. At the order AIM, you will centre your sights on the white paper and nowhere else. Your rifles, except for one, have been loaded with a blank bullet. None of you will know which rifle contains the killing bullet."

This had been established as a psychological move. It was believed that not knowing whether it was their bullet that had killed the target, would relieve the shooters of any feelings of guilt or responsibility for the soldier's death.

While they awaited the arrival of Private Highgate Mac thought through that belief. Ironic that he had enlisted to fight in a war that would see thousands of people die, some of whom from his rifle, yet the authorities had this rule to alleviate as much anxiety as possible following the death of one person, and a coward at that. What made them think that soldiers would feel more guilt for carrying out justice than they would by committing the mass slaughter that was inevitably ahead of them?

Mac also had some concerns that what he was about to do was in fact, justice.

His reverie was disturbed by some movement in front of him. A door in the wall of the parade ground ahead of the hide opened, and two uniformed personnel walked out, carrying a chair between them. They placed the chair a foot or so out from the wall, ensuring there was enough space for someone to move around the chair, should it be necessary. The two soldiers both looked toward the hide and with gesticulating arms, seemed to debate over whether the required 16 feet between rifle and target had been established.

Having satisfied themselves that all was in order, they left the parade ground through the door they originally came through.

Mac noticed that the door remained open. It was as if he was watching a stage play where things were done for effect. The open door would indicate that there was more to come, and he didn't have to wait too long until something did occur.

The two soldiers re-appeared but this time they did so in regimental fashion. They marched to where they had been previously and positioned themselves either side of the chair. As in the theatre, this was a further clue that something else was about to happen.

Private Highgate hadn't slept. What was the point, he thought, all it would have done would have given him a few moments of escape from the tension that he felt . He decided that he would rather experience his bodily sensations such as breathing, while he could.

The only clue he had that dawn was breaking was the sliver of light easing its way under the door. The shivering of his body belied his thoughts. He actually felt a reasonable level of calmness but alert to danger. He thought of the beliefs some held regarding trees which shivered when they sensed woodmen approaching with saws and axes. Thinking of trees brought his mind to a tree on the Downs near Brighton, where he used to take his nephew kite flying. Most Sundays, during school holidays, would see him waiting to collect his nephew at Lewes Station from the London train. Then they would change to the Lewes Line which took them to Glynde. Then the walk to the top of the Downs, via Heyshott where they stopped for a lemon squash at the Unicorn Hotel. The publican there turned a blind eye to youngsters on the premises as long as they kept to the outdoor area. It was a favourite spot for Highgate and his nephew, because they could see up to the highest point on the Downs, and watch the kites of those who had climbed up earlier.

They had a favourite tree under which they had a picnic consisting of gob stoppers, sherbet dabs and those cigarette-shaped lollies. In fact, their menu depended heavily on what they had managed to shoplift at the Glynde shop, while the shopkeeper was distracted.

That was the tree that Highgate was thinking about so deeply that he hadn't noticed footsteps on the cobbles outside and the unlocking of his door. He quickly gathered his thoughts back from the South Downs to the reality that standing in front of him, framed by the dawn light of France, were two soldiers ordering him to stand. By the time the trio had entered the parade ground, all vestiges of kites, trees and family vanished from the condemned man's mind. He was now confronted by a hut-like structure about 10 or 15 feet away and opposite that, adjacent to the parade ground wall, a chair to which he was being led.

It is reasonable to suggest that up until now, Private Highgate had been in a state of denial. While knowing that he was under sentence of death, and having been incarcerated in Dunkirk for almost a week, he hadn't really accepted the reality of the situation. Now, that had all changed.

As the early morning light became stronger, he noticed movement in the hide that he was facing. Gradually he began to recognise the glint of rifle barrels, which removed any denial from his mind, he was here to die. Strangely, uppermost in his mind was how unfair all this was. He wasn't a threat to society, nor was he a danger to anyone around him. He had just wandered off from camp one day. How unfair.

Fairness it seems is not a feature of natural law. Animals don't recognise fairness.

They don't act fairly toward one another, nor do they act unfairly. Animals don't fight fairly, they just fight. Cyclones have no sense of the damage they cause, they just blow as nature intends them to do. It is only humankind that has established this concept of fairness. They strive to play fair in sport, they purport to be fair in business dealings, parents see fairness to their children as a high ideal. Even in war time, rules are established that ensure fights are fairly fought.

When any of these criteria are deemed not to have been met, humans become traumatised. People in sport cry foul, business leaders sue and parents carry guilt while their children grow resentful.

Eric John Highgate, soldier from Sussex sat on a chair in a French fort, waiting to die and he felt very unfairly done by. In later years this unfairness would be the subject of attempts to lift the charge of cowardice, clear his name of any guilt and honour his memory like any other soldier whose life was lost in war.

For the first time since his sentencing, Highgate started to feel angry at the deal that fate had handed out to him.

That feeling, which was now mixed with a level of fear that he had never experienced, worsened as the soldiers with him, placed a blindfold on him.

"Oops, sorry mate, didn't mean to hurt you there!" said one of them as he caught Hardridge's hair in the blindfold knot.

Whether the ridiculousness of that apology to a man about to die crossed the guard's mind, only he would know.

Highgate sensed the men leaving his side, their footsteps resonating on the otherwise empty parade ground and then he heard the shutting of the door through which he had come, ten minutes ago.

It was now incredibly quiet. The seabirds still cried their famous call as they searched the morning tide for their sustenance, but other than that, Highgate heard nothing. The next sound he would hear would be the voice of the captain calling the firing squad to attention, and that event was now just seconds away.

Mac Penfold and his four companions heard the sea birds squawk also. Mac wondered why the European variety sounded so different from the gulls around Streaky Bay. Was there something about the sun in Australia that made the difference? Then he recalled his Father telling him one day when they were out rabbit trapping close to the water's edge, just at the start of the Great Australian Bight, that they weren't technically seagulls. They were silver gulls that frequented Australian shores. They were smaller than the gulls that you would find on the European or UK coastline.

His Dad also told him that even though they were called seagulls, they spend a fair part of their lives inland.

Mac felt conscious that here he was thinking about bloody birds when he was about to kill a human being, although because of the dummy bullet, none of the shooting party would know if it was their rifle that fired the killing shot. They had watched the guards bring out the prisoner and sit him on the chair with his hands tied behind his back.

The men discussed what was the real reason that hands were tied. One of them suggested, of course, it would stop him running away. Then another said "Wouldn't that be better for everyone, the guy and us?"

Mac queried him, "Well," said the soldier, "I would rather aim and shoot at a moving target than have it staring right down my barrel. And I am sure that guy would rather be shot in mid stride than sitting there waiting for a bullet."

"Speaking of bullets Corp," said another member of the small group, "Can you tell which one of these five bullets in five rifles is the real thing? Do the dummies look different from the real thing? I've never seen one."

"Well there is a different indentation at the end of the shell," replied Mac. "but we can't touch them, they've all been pre-loaded and we are not allowed to look. The idea is that you will never know if it was you who actually killed the poor bastard."

"Wouldn't it better if we did know," asked the other soldier, "instead of spending the rest of our lives wondering?"

Mac pondered on this, thinking that it was all to do with the individual and how they dealt with the knowledge that they were the one who inflicted the mortal wound.

He came back to his early dilemma that all of them who bore weapons did so in order to kill the enemy. So if this Private Highgate was a true coward and deserter, does he then become the enemy? If so, then what guilt would there be if your rifle was the one that ended his life?

His mind was brought back to attention by the captain who was standing alongside the hide, containing the five shooters. Captain Wainwright had drawn his sidearm and held it against his right leg as he assumed the attention position. The men knew that if for some reason, none of the bullets that were about to be fired, missed their mark, or failed to finish Highgate's life, it would be the officer's duty to carry out the coup de grâce by aiming the pistol at the private's head and firing a fatal shot.

Highgate stiffened in his chair. A cold shiver ran through his body as if his brain had warned all his working parts that a piece of hardware was about to come flying towards then enter his heart, ending their work forever.

"Shooting party!" shouted the captain, "Take aim."

Highgate calculated that his next breath would be the last. He had a passing thought that it could be considered cruel for the condemned man to hear the captain's orders and the sound as the rifle barrels scuffed the ledge of the hide on which they rested. Wouldn't it be far better and even kinder if he didn't hear the preparatory orders? Would it not be less stressful if it happened just suddenly and without warning? Then his mind immediately found its peaceful place, kite-flying with his nephew on the Downs, where the…

"Fire."

Five rifles sent five bullets straight toward the white piece of paper pinned to the chest of a soldier who sat in a chair, five metres away, blindfolded and waiting for death. Technically speaking four of those bullets would not reach the target. The other one would relieve Private Highgate of his earthly duties, and not one of his military colleagues, who aimed their firearms at his heart, knew which rifle held that bullet.

Mac Penfold's story of how he was used, to deal with cowardice in the army in 1915, absolutely mesmerised young Craig Erskine as he sat in Penfold's ground-floor room at 356 Easter Road, Leith, so many years after the event.

Craig thanked Mac and was about to go to wait for his Father coming home to their second-storey tenement. Now more than ever, he was anxious to confront his Father and deal with this cowardice issue. The level of seriousness had heightened, now that Craig had learnt that cowards in war didn't just receive white feathers, they were shot dead. Is that what should happen to his Father?

Mac's voice, although tired after the long narrative, burst through Craig's thoughts. "There's just one other thing I want to share with you. You know how they tried to save the five of us from guilt or stress through thinking that we had executed one of our own?"

Craig nodded, "You mean that if the shooter knew that he had the blank bullet, then he would probably be happier knowing he didn't kill the man?"

"Well, when I fired my rifle, there was a recoil," said Mac.

Mac paused, waiting to see if that fact had hit any fertile knowledge within the young lad's mind. The look on Craig's face told Mac that it hadn't. He had opened up to this young boy, in a way that he had never done with a colleague or an adult of his own age. However, now that the tale was ending, he realised that he would have to voice the words he had hoped could be avoided being spoken.

"My rifle hadn't fired a blank bullet."

"You mean that it was you who…?" interrupted Craig.

"Aye lad," Mac continued "I killed a fellow soldier for what the so-called King and Country perceived as cowardice and desertion. I took away his life, because he was late back to camp.

TEN

Craig left Mac's rooms and slowly made his way up the stairs to where his Mother was waiting for his Father. Craig's young mind was not able to accept that anyone who was a coward in war shouldn't be shot. It seemed to harden his resolve to sort out the issue with his Father.

Craig's mind was so full of what he had heard from Old Mac that he either ignored or didn't hear his Mother ask him where he had been.

He went straight through the kitchen, hardly noticing his Mother lowering the pulley that had held the family's newly washed clothes up near the ceiling, so as the heat from the stove would rise and help dry them. Under other circumstances Craig would have stopped to help with the pulley, but the lad's mind was totally focused on dealing with how to confront his Father. He took up his favourite position near the window that looked down on Easter Road to await the man's arrival.

Craig didn't have to wait long, but there was something different this time. His Father had company. Alongside him was another man who was shuffling rather than walking and looked incredibly sad.

Craig heard them come into the kitchen, and also heard his Mother breaking into caring mode as she helped the stranger sit on the kitchen chair, near the fire.

Craig didn't go in straight away. He wanted to eavesdrop a little more to try and make sense out of what was happening. He was surprised to hear the sound of the pulley being lowered, and wondered what that had to do with anything. So, he entered the kitchen.

What Craig saw puzzled him more. His Mother was offering a pair of his Father's trousers to this stranger who immediately burst out crying. He had never seen or heard an adult crying before. It was an unsettling sight and his anxiety levels rose. He was desperate to find out why this man was here and then he wanted to confront his Father over cowardice, before he lost his nerve – the coward of a Father who didn't go to war and take his chances like his friends' Fathers.

He recalled some of what Mac Penfold had told him about cowardice and justification and reason, but he didn't want that to sway his resolve.

Craig also noticed something different about his Father's appearance. He had never seen him dress like this when he left for work (or the war, as his Mother would say) or when he returned home. He must change at work, he thought. Looking closer at what Bill was wearing he noticed a slight similarity to photos of his friends' Fathers when they were in the 'real' war. Could it possibly be a uniform?

There had been no eye contact between the younger and older Erskine since Bill and this stranger had come through the door of number 356 Easter Road, Leith.

When it did come, Craig felt uneasy as a strange atmosphere had pervaded the kitchen. Nothing could prepare the young boy for what was to happen next.

His Father's companion continued to sob, between sips of the hot sweet tea, that Craig's Mum, Janet had prepared.

As he listened Craig learnt that this man was named Alenti from Poland and had been persuaded to join many others of his countrymen who fought with the allies in the war. They had helped defeat Germany in 1945. With the war now over Alenti was lost, alone and bewildered with nowhere to call home.

As Alenti raised his head after another sip from the mug of tea in his hand, his eyes met Craigs. The man's mouth flew open and his eyes widened and everyone in the room was shocked by the wild look that took over his face. As he jumped up from the chair, his mug of hot tea fell from his hand splashing the hot liquid over his legs.

It must have been a searing pain but it seemed to mean nothing to him. The Pole's hands reached out towards Craig whose anxiety levels started to rise.

"Moj chlopak, Moj chlopak!" the man cried as he lurched forward.

Craig had no idea what those words meant however he had worked out that it had a lot to do with him. The lad now had only one thought and that was immediate escape. So he leapt for the door and then the stairs leading down to the comparative safety of Easter Road. Close behind him was the enraged man.

'Moj chlopak, Moj chlopak!' he continued his cry as though a battle charge. Behind him came Bill and Janet, also with looks of desperation.

As Alenti's hands were about to land on Craig, Bill jumped on his back and brought him to the pavement. Amid all the confusion Craig remembered thinking that he had never seen his Father in this way. What he had just witnessed was a courageous act, something that he would not have thought of in terms of his Father.

A small crowd had started to gather on Easter Road and murmuring increased as two Military Policeman arrived, braking at high speed as their Jeep parked abruptly on the pavement. The men jumped out then withdrew their firearms from the shiny white holsters.

Bill by this time had fixed Alenti in a firm grip and the two men were positioned between the MP's and Craig.

The scenario that was working itself out on the pavement of Easter Road was reminiscent of an armed uprising. Craig's Father was applying a headlock to the Pole, military police were pulling up in their jeep, two corporals jumping out before the vehicle had halted, pistols drawn.

Janet Erskine's protective instinct was manifested by wide eyes and outstretched arms as she reached to envelop and shield her offspring from what was quickly developing into a serious incident featuring desperate men and their guns.

Craig tried to make sense of what he had become involved in. Only a few minutes ago, he was safe and warm listening to old Mac's stories of his native Australia and how he ended up enlisting in the British Expeditionary Force, over 40 years ago. Now Craig was at the centre of what some would call an international incident - not like his safe comfortable home where the most worrying thing was a faulty clothes pulley. Young Erskine didn't want this intrusion into his hitherto peaceful life.

The world's woes had come crashing into Craig's life and he laid the blame squarely on his Father's shoulders – this man who was too scared to lift a weapon in defence of his country. But as Craig watched it all play out, he became confused. He had never seen his Father this assertive, this violent. He was on top of the foreigner now, pulling at the man's hands like a police officer trying to handcuff a villain. His Father couldn't match the other's strength but that didn't stop him exerting what power he could to restrain the thrashing foreigner.

Erskine senior, saw this and in one of those scenes reminiscent of a slow motion movie, stood up and placed himself between the man on the ground and the MP.

"Get out of the fucking way!" the MP yelled at Craig's Father.

"Not until you put down that weapon," Erskine yelled back. "The war's over you know."

"Not until I get this prick under control, now move!" retorted the soldier.

Then one of those moments that had the potential to change everything: the soldier's weapon discharged.

The bullet, again in what looked like slow motion, found its way through Craig's Father's uniform sleeve and as Craig was positioned behind him, came straight for the young boy who felt its force as it clipped his ear, and made its way into the stone lentil of number 356. It drew some blood from his ear and knocked the boy over, on to the raw pavement. As he fell, he saw a look of sheer horror in his Father's eyes.

Erskine senior let go of the prisoner and ran to his son's side. "Janet, Craig's been shot!"

There was a combined intake of breath from the crowd that had gathered. Then silence. While it only lasted a second, it seemed like forever, before anyone responded.

Janet Erskine made her anxious way to where her husband and son were positioned on the pavement. She screamed as she saw the blood on Craig's face. "No, No, No!" she cried as she formed a trio out of her fallen son and her husband.

"For God's sake, Bill, what have you done?" Craig had just heard his Mother scream for the first time in his life.

Bill Erskine had not had the opportunity yet to assess Craig's condition but caught his wife's stare and returned it with a vehemence she had never experienced from him before.

"Janet, have some sense, it was that soldier who shot him, not me!"

Craig experienced another moment for the first time, his Father's concern and his Father's touch as he cradled him in his arms.

Craig wasn't seriously injured, beyond a graze on his ear. However, the blood flowed freely from a vein that was close to the surface, making the wound seem worse than it was. It would soon clot.

The boy had done a quick mental audit of his body and found nothing of concern. But he didn't want this moment to end. He and his parents had entered a type of cocoon, wrapped in each other against a common foe. It was a very rare moment for the three Erskines.

They were not a hugging family nor did they hold hands. Their relationship was devoid of any unnecessary physical contact, so Craig had grown up with the feeling of emotional detachment. Deep within him was an innate need for a family group, family love, family protection. But the need was not able to draw on any capacity to show it or reach out for it. That absence had made it easy to believe that his Father was a coward. But in those few mad, frightening moments, he had seen a gesture from his Father that contradicted the belief.

It may have been the instinctive act of a parent animal for its cub, but it was there. His Father had shown a fleeting gesture of courage and a feeling of protection and love that his son had sought for years.

Craig realized that at this point there was no time to dwell on the cowardice issue There was too much to understand about the present. Who was this stranger? Why did military police fire their weapon in a Leith street? What was his Father involved in and how is this going to end?

ELEVEN

In post-war Europe the sound of gunfire still made people nervous. The war was over but another conflict was beginning, a battle of settlement, forgiveness and, sadly, revenge.

The political settlement of World War II between Roosevelt, Stalin and Churchill meant that at war's end, the Soviets annexed Eastern Poland and incorporated it into the Soviet Union, while the rest of Poland became a puppet state with a communist government imposed by Russia.

The vast majority of Poles rejected this settlement and wanted to remain in the west where they could continue the political struggle for an independent Poland while maintaining their language, culture, and traditions for an eventual return to a unified Poland.

This historical fact had presented itself on the Scottish doorstep of number 356 Easter Road, Leith, through the abrupt arrival of a man who had been brought there by Craig's Father. He was called Alenti and he had been incarcerated in the Polish Resettlement Corps which had done little to resettle, and much to disrupt.

It seems that the leadership of this group was a moving feast. Its hierarchy changed frequently, mainly due to its leaders being executed or 'disappearing' from the scene. Alenti had only been with the Corps for a few months when his turn came and he took over from his superior who had been shot in front of his family. Was this promotion really a death sentence for Alenti?

How did this supposed hero of the revolution find himself chasing a young Scottish boy down tenement stairs in Leith, being tackled by the boy's Father and being shot at by military police?

The response to that question was to provide a very complex answer to the simple question, was Bill Erskine, a coward? Craig mused on the fact that his Dad's actions in the last few minutes may not have been those of a coward. He recalled Old Mac's story about the dubious nature of being judged a coward in military terms. If this all turned out to be factual, it could be Craig's Father who was facing a firing squad. Now that the adrenalin had dissipated, the emotion of fear had become uppermost.

At the end of World War II, Poland felt abandoned. The episode became known as the Western Betrayal. As the Polish armed forces had fought alongside the Allies during the war, they had expected some help in resettling themselves as a Free Poland. Many members of the Polish armed forces did not want to return to a country that was now under Communist control. It would not have bode well for them, that they had served with the Commonwealth forces during the conflict.

Alenti was one of those Poles who found themselves vulnerable to a more personalised clash with their fellow human beings following the war. During any such conflict, most people managed to form a bond to fight a common enemy. When that war finishes, it's as if the human psyche has formed a strong need to hate something, to despise someone, to keep on killing after the armistice has sounded.

Poland wanted them home, but under a new regime. Even their adopted land of Britain was not quick to embrace their ally. The British themselves were struggling to regroup following the major conflict. Many Britons began looking with a vengeful stare at almost any European with an accent – he or she wasn't considered 'home grown'. Their tone that did not ring of Celtic, or Anglo-Saxon origin.

Similarly, throughout the recovering continent, revenge and retribution were meted out to civilians who were deemed to have aided and abetted German and Russian forces.

Alenti represented a nation of Poles who were bitterly disappointed following the Yalta Conference which laid the groundwork for European Settlement. He was one of many who longed for their homeland but refused to live in it under this new government.

So they continued to look for refuge in Britain. Alenti began to come under the spotlight when he addressed several meetings around Edinburgh of this disaffected group. They met irregularly in a meeting room below the Camera Obscura in the Royal Mile.

The University, which were now the owners of the premises, were pleased to allow one of its ground floor rooms to be used for public oration. Alenti and his group were regular users and it gave him a perfect venue for his speeches, and calls to action for the Polish exiles following World War II.

The evening when he was made president of the Polish Resettlement Corps, Alenti concluded his acceptance speech by saying, "Those bastards Churchill, Roosevelt and Stalin, to whom we have given our lives, threw us out with the garbage as they carved up Europe between themselves. I was one of almost 160,000 stranded in British camps, ever hopeful of joining our families in Poland, and I will do so or die in the attempt."

TWELVE

While the machinations of Hitler and Nazi Germany prior to the major conflict that was WW2, were not unnoticed in Poland, Alenti and his contemporaries felt optimistic. They felt that somehow they would be immune from the horrors that were starting to emerge. So in a confident move, Alenti and his wife established a business in a bazaar in the Warsaw suburb of Praga.

Their shop sign boldly showed their trademark: 'guziki do opatrunków na bunion' which loosely translated meant 'selling all types of wares from buttons to bunion bandages'. Oblivious to any of the clouds of war, threatening his country's skies, Alenti travelled throughout Poland sometimes for weeks on end, scouring for saleable items. "I had a 1931 CWS T1 [Polish tourer] and I drove many kilometres." Alenti's eyes almost glazed over as he recalled his beloved vehicle.

One of his compatriots at the meeting he was addressing shouted out "and I know why, smartie! Those vehicles made anyone feel like an A-grade mechanic because you could virtually dismantle the engine and rebuild it, all with one size tool."

The crowd laughed good-heartedly and even Alenti smiled, which was rare for him.

Alenti and his wife Maja, had such high hopes for their business. They were a popular couple in Praga and were the 'go to' folk for just about any non-organic item of need.

"Maja very much wanted to start selling food. The bigos she cooked for family and friends had quite a reputation." Alenti felt himself salivating as he remembered the stew of sauerkraut and meat, to which Maja had added her own cabbage-type sauce.

"No one could work out how her sauce was not running off the plate," he continued. "No one knew how she made it thick enough to just lie on top of the bigos. It helped make it much more manageable for the eater who could avoid the need for any kind of napkin."

The young couple had a five-year-old son named Adalbert. That name meant intelligent and noble, and according to Alenti, even at a young age, he exuded an almost superior air. "It was as if he had some insight, some knowledge, a gift perhaps that gave him an edge over others." Strong as that edge was, it would do nothing to protect him from what was to follow.

Adalbert and his Father formed a very strong bond from early in the lad's life. He accompanied Alenti on his trips in the car across the countryside. Even his Mother, Maja, felt some envy of this bond.

However, Maja had her own bond going on. In six months there would be a companion for Adalbert, and Maja had strong hopes that it would be a girl.

Both Maja and Alenti had some concern about the Poland that their children would inherit. Following the end of World War I, the country became known as the Second Polish Republic, and was considered a hero at the Versailles negotiations. As prosperous as Poland was becoming, it did so at the whim of the countries and nations that were its neighbours.

With a population numbered around 35 million, Poland was the sixth largest country in Europe. Strategically, it was envied due to the access it had to the Baltic Sea.

Alenti and his young contemporaries developed a strong belief that Poland could emerge as something of a leader in post World War I Europe. They dreamt of new opportunities in a healed environment. After all, the Soviet and German governments had signed a Non-Aggression Pact towards Poland in 1939, so what could go wrong?

THIRTEEN

The mood of war had never really abated in Europe since the armistice in 1918. The mood slithered and slipped its way, like a wounded serpent, barely alive but seething with distrust, scheming and counter-scheming. There really was no surprise that it all started again in 1939, although few countries would have guessed just how it would start.

That year the Second Polish Republic ceased to exist. Nazi Germany played the overture to World War II in a symphony of invasion. Germany invaded Poland one week after the Soviet German Non-Aggression Pact was signed. Through bombing, tank warfare and artillery, a whole swathe of Poland was captured. Then commenced terror on a more personal scale. Towns were taken over by an army hungry for victory and the need to establish itself as a leader through world domination. It was attempted though at the cost of the individual through torture, rape and humiliation.

Thinking that their position on the other side of Warsaw, may well give them some type of protection, the people of Alenti's town of Praga, awoke to a frightening scenario: the sudden appearance of German troops in their streets; door-to-door searches by men who really did not know what they were searching for, other than to slake their thirst for blood and torture.

As part of the ceremony celebrating his appointment as President of the Scottish Division of the Polish Resettlement Corps, in 1947, Alenti's speech included details as to how he ended up as a member of the Allied Forces that fought against Germany.

"My brother lived on the other side of the river in Warsaw, and he rang me to warn me that trouble was on the way." said Alenti. "his call ended abruptly and those were the last words I heard from him. So I got my wife Maja and my son, Adalbert together and we headed out for our warehouse in the bazaar, to try and secure some goods that would help us survive what was coming." Alenti couldn't stop a shiver running through him as he relived the event.

"When we got there, around 5.15 in the morning, there was no sign of invasion. There was the usual rubbish left over from the night before, and a few dogs and cats out foraging.

Birds were busy too."

"I had backed the CWS up to the rear of the premises while Maja and Adalbert stayed in the front, gathering together anything that Maja thought would be necessary for our planned escape."

Alenti's eyes started to tear at this point as he recalled that was the last time he had seen his wife and child.

"As I was opening the rear door of the shop, I heard the roar of an engine as a vehicle careered into the square," said Alenti. "For some reason, I did not think of danger. I presumed it was my neighbouring trader who had decided on an escape plan too, and had come to his shop for supplies."

"But when I heard Maja call my name, I knew something was wrong," he continued. "I ran around to the front only to see a three ton Blitz troop-carrying truck moving off. And... and..." he stopped and stared into the hall as if reliving the episode.

"I saw Maja's arm waving from behind the canvas that covered the back of the truck, and suddenly Adalbert's face looked up at me from the truck. It was a look of sheer terror."

The Germans, as part of their terrorist campaign to conquer Poland, had arrested Maja and her son, as well as anyone who they found in the streets that morning.

This was the last sight that Alenti would have of his wife and son as the truck left the square and he knew not where it was headed.

Many of the ears that heard Alenti's address that night in Edinburgh's Castlehill, belonged to those who had trod a similar path. They were men who had lost their family in similar ways and women who had no idea where their husbands had gone. All they knew was of the hated grey/green coloured trucks that scoured the streets of Poland, like street sweepers. The difference was that it was sweeping up the residents of the towns and cities within the Second Republic of Poland, shattering lives, and bringing the stench of conflict with it, for the second time in twenty years.

Atlenti was confronted by a real dilemma. If he chased after the truck, he was likely to be swept up as well. If he stayed and hid, he would feel helpless as a protector of his family, and guilty that he had not done more to save them.

"I made my way home with an aching heart," he continued after a long pause. Within that pause, the atmosphere in the room changed to heavy sadness as each member of the audience remembered their own agonies.

Alenti's journey home was a challenge for him, because he never knew where he would encounter German soldiers. His home was across the Vistula River, so he slowly and cautiously drove his 1931 CWS T1 through the streets that he felt were safe. He turned off at the museum and the art gallery on Centrum

Sztuki, and started to gain some confidence as he saw no sign of military activity.

Alenti started to breathe easier as he saw the Stadium Bridge ahead of him. It was still early, but quite light as officially the sunrise was 5am, at that time of year. The fact that it was a Sunday, meant there were few people about. In fact it was doubtful that even the lamplighter would be doing his rounds today, if the Germans were active in the streets.

So much was going through Alenti's mind: what happened to Maja, how was Adalbert and also the big question, how did this happen? Hadn't there been a pact signed just a few days ago? How come German troops were here and had Poland been invaded?

Suddenly, as he approached the intersection of Wioslarska Solec, where he would turn on to the bridge, a sinister-looking vehicle crossed in front of him at high speed. This was followed by another which slowed down and drew alongside Alenti. He could see that it was another military vehicle with four armed soldiers and they were casting inquisitive looks at him.

Fear returned to Alenti's mind. He felt that at any moment a bullet would come flying towards him, and that would be it. The co-driver waved at him to stop, which Alenti did immediately. But he decided to keep the CWS engine running, as he imagined that he may need a quick getaway.

"Stoppen Sie ihr Fahrzeug und steigen Sie aus!

Alenti had no knowledge of German, but he could tell that they wanted him to stop and get out of his car.

He turned off the ignition and stood alongside the vehicle, "Nie przykro mi nie moge mowic p o n iemiecku nie rozumiem" he said, hoping that they could understand his Polish.

By this time, the four soldiers had alighted from their vehicle and were surrounding Alenti, pointing their rifles towards him.

One of them walked nearer to Alenti's car and without getting in, reached in through the window and turned the ignition. As the vehicle had been left in gear, it lurched forward, taking the soldier with it for a few metres, until the camber of the street, caused the CSW to move its wheels towards the kerb, and the tyres bumped into the pavement.

The soldier who had been taken by surprise by this, advanced on Alenti and struck him across the face.

"Your car should not be on the road, it is unsafe," he addressed Alenti who was surprised to hear the soldier speak in Polish.

"There's nothing wrong with it," said Alenti, "you turned it on while it was in...".

Another blow across the face from the Polish-speaking soldier.

This time, he drew blood. Although not broken, Alenti's nose was badly bruised and a crimson stream started to flow from his nostrils.

The other soldiers started to inspect the car closely, kicking the tyres and hammering on the duco. Alenti could not work out just where this was all going to end. Was this the sort of treatment that his beloved Maja had received?

The soldier who had embarrassed himself with the car, came within spitting distance, and indeed did spit into Alenti's face as he said, "Wie hebt du und wohin gehst du?

Alenti looked helplessly around him and the soldier asked him again.

"He wants to know your name and where you are going," the Polish-speaking soldier yelled at him.

"I am Alenti Pawlowski and I am going home after working at my shop." He decided not to mention his wife and child, just in case it angered them more and gave them reason to throw him into the back of their vehicle and take him God knows where. He would only answer questions but not volunteer any information.

"How far away is your house? the German asked. "About 10 kilometres across the river," replied Alenti.

The soldier translated that information to his colleagues and the four of them had a conversation. Alenti had no idea what they were planning, but he started to shake when he saw what they were doing.

"Stand over there Pawlowski, against that wall," said the soldier, motioning with his rifle.

Alenti stiffened. He had heard of executions that had taken place by the military against civilian populations, and he began to think that he was going to be the next one.

"For God's sake, no!" he pleaded. "I've done nothing to you! Why do this to me?"

Two of the soldiers came near and held Alenti's arms and dragged him off the road and towards the wall.

Alenti struggled and yelled, but his resistance was useless against their strength. They slammed him against the wall, and he immediately slid down it on to his haunches.

"Aufstehen, Aufstehen!" but Alenti could find no strength to stand up.

The wall against which they wanted Alenti to stand, was part of a 16th century palace which had recently been converted into the Bellotto hotel. It had a black iron fence along the front; each paling had been honed to a spear like point. The soldiers started to draw Alenti towards it. Is it possible he was to be impaled? The terror in his mind was explosive. This nightmare must end.

One of the soldiers lifted Alenti's jacket and undid his trouser belt.

"Boze pomoz mi" shouted Alenti, to which, one of the soldiers replied, "Your God won't help you. Save your breath."

With that, he grabbed Alenti's hands and tied the belt around them binding him to the fence so as he couldn't move. Then the four of them took some steps back and lowered their rifles from their shoulders. Alenti was cold with fear and utter disbelief that he was going to die in this way. He pulled and pulled at the knotted belt, but to no avail.

As he looked up he saw the riflemen take aim at their target and begin to fire. His eyes closed involuntarily and he heard a barrage of bullets leave their weapons.

He opened his eyes, wondering if he was dead. He saw the soldiers shouldering their rifles and laughing. Then he saw that their target was not him, it was his car. Their bullets had flattened the tyres, shot out the headlights and smashed through the windows.

The Germans started up their vehicle and drove off yelling at Alenti, "Enjoy your walk."

FOURTEEN

Once the German soldiers were out of sight, Alenti struggled again with the belt that kept him a prisoner of the fence. Then he became aware of someone coming out of the Hotel Bellotto. It was a man wearing Polish national dress.

He nodded at Alenti "Don't panic I will race in and get a knife to cut you free." Alenti was relieved that this man spoke Polish.

"Thankyou my friend but if you slide your hand down inside my boot you will find my knife there. It's an heirloom but I always carry it just in case." The man did just that and said, "Just as well the Germans didn't find that because I guarantee it would be used to cut your throat instead of this belt. As his new found rescuer moved towards Alenti corner of his jacket flipped over, and a gun was easily visible.

"Czy mówisz po angielsku?" asked Alenti's rescuer.

"Tak," replied Alenti.

One thing that he was proud about and grateful to his parents for was the education that they were able to afford for him. That included the ability to speak a form of conversational English. But he wondered why this man who was dressed in traditional Polish dancing costume wanted to speak English. It seemed incongruous.

The man shepherded Alenti into the hotel and showed him to an office behind reception, and shut the door behind them.

Introductions followed and it appeared that his rescuer was in fact an Englishman who went by the name of Jack Archer. Jack had been a staff member within the British Consulate, in Warsaw. Even though the Germans and Soviets had signed a non-aggression pact, British Intelligence noted some disturbing behaviour by the two powers, and advised its government to close up the embassy, and evacuate staff.

Archer, however was a senior intelligence officer and had been in the Warsaw embassy for quite a few years. He had considerable local knowledge and an insight into some of the political chess-game-like actions and could see where it was likely to lead. So he was ordered to stay behind in Poland to keep an eye on things. His cover was to be an entertainer who worked at the hotel. Hence the traditional dancing costume he was wearing. A lunchtime concert for the tourists in the hotel had just concluded and when Jack went to his room to change, he noticed Alenti being bullied by the Germans outside.

"I think that may have been my last dance," he told Alenti, "this lot of Americans leave on the Nieuw Amsterdam tomorrow, desperate to get home. Owners were a bit nervous their beloved ship will get scratched if war broke out. This is only her second voyage since launching last year."

"So you think war is coming?" asked Alenti.

"Yes, nothing surer, the only problem is to decide who is actually going to fight, Soviets or Germans. This whole non-aggression pact is a fucking sham," concluded Jack.

Alenti then told Archer about his experience earlier that morning when his family disappeared in the back of a German troop carrier.

"That's why the Yankee tourists are leaving Poland," said Archer. "It looks to me that they will go back behind their isolation curtain and turn a deaf ear to the explosions in Europe."

Alenti was starting to feel a little stronger after his ordeal with the Germans and decided that he would make his way home. It was a 10 kilometre walk but it wasn't the distance that would be the challenge. He feared that he may meet up with the German bullies again.

"Don't go home Alenti," ventured Jack.

"What are you talking about? Everything I own and know is back there."

"Everything you love has gone in the back of that truck, and it pains me to say this, but you won't see them again."

The words stung. Alenti just stood and stared at Archer, not being able to form any words in response.

Jack continued, "Come with me. I'm heading out on the cruise ship tomorrow to New York then to England. I understand your loyalty to Poland, but this place is going to get pretty ugly. If you really want to do something to hit back at those Jerries, then the Allies are forming a big reserve unit on the south coast. It will be ready to pounce if this crazy Adolf gets any crazier."

Alenti thought about his home across the river. He had only been away for a few hours, but it seemed that everything had changed. There would be no Maja to greet him.

No young Adalbert to run to him, pestering him to play. There would be nothing but painful memories. He also feared what life would be like in an occupied Poland being fought over by the Soviets and the Germans.

Jack Archer stood, waiting a response. Because of his diplomatic status, he would be able to take Alenti with him to New

York. Then if the young Pole agreed to join the British defence forces, he would have an easy passage to Southampton.

FIFTEEN

Craig Erskine's last sight of Alenti, following the fracas outside 356 Easter Road was of him being driven off in a jeep by two military policemen. Bill Erskine was also escorted away in another vehicle. Craig felt a pang of concern for his Father, although it was distant. They still had some unresolved business.

Alenti's last sight of number 356, was of Craig standing holding his ear by which a bullet, aimed for him, had skimmed, drawing a few drops of his Celtic blood.

He would also have seen the enquiring look on the young boy's face as he wondered, how he came to be here, what was the connection with his Father. Underlying all that for Craig was the thought that his Father was a coward.

The scene outside 356 Easter Road, Leith was quieter now. Spectators had gone back inside and no doubt, many a kettle had been put on the hob, and much discussion about the recent incident, was underway.

It was up to Janet Erskine to start answering some of her son's many questions. How to even start to explain that life was not as he had read in The Secret Seven or The Famous Five. In the Blyton world, there were always two loving parents to provide children's needs. A Mum whose headquarters were the kitchen and the laundry, tasked with keeping the home clean and putting a meal on the table. Father came home from work into the bosom of the family as did the children who gambolled their way home from school. There would always be a friendly policeman just around the corner who would take the villains away. Yes, Craig was about to learn the reality that dear Enid denied. Why not have Julian and Timmy the dog creeping up on the Germans who were holding Dick, Ann and George prisoners in a Poland just conquered by Adolf Hitler. Yes Miss Blyton, why not describe how those jolly red-cheeked children had been bundled into a nasty big lorry and whisked away, never to see Mummy and Daddy again?

Janet began her explanation as soon as they got back into the kitchen. The coal fire had gone out, and the pulley of damp clothes was still at half-mast. It had only been about an hour and a half since Alenti made his lurch towards Craig, resulting in the climax out the front of number 356.

Janet Erskine had to relate a very adult incident in understandable language. Craig asked her why Alenti had been so interested in him, and what did he mean by yelling out 'moj chlopak'.

"It means, 'my boy'", explained Janet. "His son was the same age as you when he was taken away.

"When your Dad brought him home, he saw you and it reminded him of his son. He wasn't going to hurt you. He told me that he wanted to hug you."

Janet's reference to his Dad brought Craig's mind back to why his Father was involved in all this and that whole question mark of cowardice that had hung over him. It still puzzled him and disappointed him that while other Fathers were shipped overseas as cannon fodder, his Dad just seemed to disappear up

Easter Road at eight am and reappear at five pm to carry on a peaceful life.

Craig's Mother was quiet for a while and spent some time re-arranging the clothes on the pulley, and trying to get some spark of life back into the cinders of the fire.

As she raised the pulley again, she let out a huge sigh that was heavy with sorrow. The sorrow was in response to her child's thoughts about her husband.

"Son, Alenti had escaped from Poland after his wife and son were taken away. He managed to find his way to England where he enlisted to fight in the war."

"Something my Father should have done too," retorted Craig.

Janet looked sympathetically at her son, but generally ignored the statement. "When the war ended, Alenti tried to return to Poland, but found it very difficult. He then tried to start a new life in this country, feeling that we would all be grateful for the help they had given us during the war."

Janet paused while she got up and looked out of the second-storey window, hoping to see her husband, Bill, walking home.

"Anyway, Alenti joined a group of people from his own country who were trying to get back also, but found it impossible because of the heavy communist influence that had taken over Warsaw.

"So many of the Polish soldiers who fought with the British Army were demobbed at the end of World War II, given some clothes and a guinea each, then left to their own resources, which were nil."

Craig's Mum continued with Alenti's story.

"He and a few others used to gather down at the Leith Docks, trying to beg, borrow and I would suspect, steal a boat to take them to Poland.

"But because there is so much suspicion and even hatred held towards anyone who is a refugee of any sort, fishermen and boat owners shunned them."

Craig sat at the kitchen table, as his Mother continued."It's been pretty amazing how Britain has gone into the rebuilding of all its cities,but there's a lot more work to be done within the people itself." Craig was not at all sure where his Mother was going with what she was saying, but he knew that by the tone of her voice and the sad look in her eye, that this was something she was passionate about.

Janet"s eyes caught the look from her sons' and held his stare. "You go for a walk up the street these days and you'll hear more than the Scottish accent coming out of people's mouths, but those people whose voices don't have a Celtic twang are looked on as suspicious and dangerous and some sort of threat."

"Yes," joined in Craig, "I did see a wee fight going on outside the grocers last week with three women yelling and screaming at this other woman who couldn't speak English." Janet paused. A little part of her had hoped that her son had never been exposed to this dark side of human beings. Now, listening to Craig, she knew that it was too late. Post-war life was not a comfortable experience at the best of times but if you were not seemingly 'native' then it was particularly challenging. Both Janet and Bill despaired over what seemed to be the fading of the welcoming Scottish character.. They each were witness to people from Poland, Italy and even France being either bullied in the shops, or shunned in the streets.

Craig prompted his Mother who had paused in her telling of Alenti's story. "So how did Dad and Alenti get together?"

"The military police still have jurisdiction over the dock areas and even airports and bus stations, where people can enter or leave the city.

"One night there was a raid on the docks and Alenti and his friends were rounded up," said Janet.

"And locked up in gaol?" asked Craig.

"Well no," said Janet, "Because they didn't actually belong in this country, and were officially in need of government approval, they were sent off to your Father's office at the railway station."

"My Dad's office?" Craig interjected. "So he has an office in the railway station where he hides from the army, so as he doesn't have to go to war? He's a coward Mum!"

Little out of what his Mother was saying was helping to restore any love or respect that Craig had held for his Father, even though there was no doubt he had rushed to protect his son from a flying bullet. But why would someone like Alenti end up in a coward's office?

SIXTEEN

Janet Erskine had longed for this moment when she could stop all the pretence and tell her son the truth about his Father. She had become tired of continually defending him against Craig's perceptions.

"Son, your Dad is no coward. The truth is that he did try to enlist but was excluded because of his rheumatic fever. They considered him unfit for duty."

This news hit young Erskine like a gust of wind. "What?"

"We couldn't tell you lad, because of what your Dad went on to do," Janet went on. "Dad was approached by the Red Cross which does a lot of welfare work, particularly in times of crisis such as the war."

As his Mum continued, Craig started to get the feeling that something was going to come crashing down on him, and it wasn't the pulley!

"Your Father was made a Commandant of the Scottish Red Cross, and one of his duties was to organise the placement of injured servicemen who had been evacuated from the war zone. In particular he had responsibility for men who were allies of Britain, while the war was on. Like Poland, where Alenti came from.So since the end of the war, he has been helping people like Alenti find the welfare they need."

Craig stood up and walked over to the window of number 356 and took up his usual vantage point, looking down on Easter Road, as he had done every night to watch his Father return home from the 'war'.

This time though he was in a daze. His Mum's voice came at him now with renewed energy. It was as though her thoughts had been officially liberated, and she was free to speak them.

"But, why all the secrecy?" asked Craig who was still staring out of the window.He could hear his Mother take a big breath before replying, and that made him turn to face her. "Son, it's a bit like what we were just talking about. Peoples attitudes following the war could be a wee bit unpleasant. Some folk didn't like the idea of government money and time being spent on non- British returned soldiers. They thought that they all should have been sent back to their homeland after the war, where that country's money could be spent on them, and not ours."

"But why did Dad bring that Alenti man here? Asked Craig.

"Well" replied Janet "Alenti has not been granted a visa to stay in Scotland, so he was arrested by the military police and was being held while arrangements were made to send him back to Poland."

"So how did Dad manage to get him here, and why did those soldiers turn up?" "Son," explained Janet, "your Dad did a very foolish thing, although it was done out of kindness. Alenti was being held at his office, so while the police went off to find the documents to ship Alenti back, your Dad brought him here. He was going to hide here while your Dad tried to get him a visa."

"So really, Alenti was an escapee from the police," said Craig.

Janet went quiet and Craig realised that while she was pretty proud of her husband, this latest move was taking her family into unknown territory which had resulted in that bullet flying past her son's ear and spilling some of his blood.

"Where is Dad now, Mum?"

"More than likely being held in custody and he will probably lose his commission. He could well end up in gaol, son."

Craig looked back through the window – the rain had started and dusk was falling. He was sure that he saw a figure make his way down Easter Road toward number 356. He was certain because it was a figure that he had seen every night as it came back from a day at the 'war'. This time it was different. This wasn't the coward that he saw every night. The perception of his Father was changing.

However, Craig needed some more pieces to complete the jigsaw.

His Mother ran to the window, confirmed it was Dad, then tore down the tenement steps and straight into her husband's arms. This was a sight that Craig rarely saw because they were seldom openly affectionate.

They were laughing as they came in the door of 356, but Dad's grin began to fade when he saw his son staring back at him. Craig was in a dilemma. Only a few hours ago he was ready to confront his Father over cowardice, and he had built up some courage and even excitement at having that confrontation. Now Craig had to consider the strong possibility that he had been wrong.

Bill and Craig Erskine had rarely touched each other and certainly not hugged or shaken hands. It just wasn't in their makeup. But that relationship was on the turn. Bill slowly lifted his arms and reached out towards Craig.

Craig was confused. He had never experienced a feeling like this. His Father's open arms were a challenging gesture, because it demanded a response, and Craig, slowly and shyly walked into his Father's arms, for the first time since he was a baby.

As the two of them began to warm to this new relationship, Janet had managed to get some flame going back in the clinker in the stove, and was toasting a few slices of the pan loaf. Thick slices pierced by a toasting fork which Craig's boyhood imagination had always thought of as Lancelot's sword.

She began to spread the butter which had been under the warmer for half an hour or so, and reached for the marmalade that landlady, Mrs Livingstone, had left for them after she had put away that scary Hoover monster.

While Craig's Mum's hands opened the jar of golden spread, and applied it to the warm toasted bread, the boy listened to his Father explain what had happened to Alenti when they had got back to Waverley Station, after the incident outside. He said that he was not impressed by the way he and Alenti had been manhandled.

"I know that I was very much in the wrong having brought him here, but compassion and forgiveness are not high on the emotional priority list in the forces in post-war Britain," Bill said.

"Were you scared?" asked Craig.

"Not at first. After all I had my Red Cross commandant's uniform on, and I would have thought that demanded some respect."

He paused for a moment and adjusted an epaulette, which had been torn during his encounter with the MPs.

"Then when they pushed the two of us into the holding pen at Waverley, I started to worry," he continued.

Craig sensed some anger in Bill's voice.

"They were very clever with the mind games," he said. "The holding pen was similar to that goal you see in the sheriff's office in those Hopalong Cassidy films. The two of us were sitting on the floor and beyond us on the other side of the bars, the MPs were sitting laughing and, within our earshot, talking about the possibility of Alenti being deported and put up against a wall and shot."

Craig sat bolt upright, and his Mother stopped spreading the toast. "And what about you Dad? What did they say about what would happen to you?"

"Well they were giving the strong impression that I would be hauled off to Aldershot for a few years."

This was scary stuff. Aldershot was a military zone of Hampshire county in England, where those guilty of a military offence during the war were being held. It was where some of the captured Nazis were executed, so any suggestion of some imprisonment there, was a high cause for concern. Craig also recalled Mac Penfold's story of the firing squad in France.

For the first time in ages, Mum spoke up. "Would we have known that that had happened to you? We had no idea where you had gone when the police took you and Alenti away."

Bill didn't answer, probably because he just didn't know.

Not a word was spoken for a few moments between the three of them in that kitchen at number 356 Easter Road, Leith. All that could be heard was the whistling of the kettle as it bubbled away on top of the Rayburn. They were the only rooms at number 356 to have a Rayburn, the brand which had its origins in the early 1940s and was famous for the fact that the stoves were made out of 70 per cent recycled material such as old lamp posts, manhole covers and older stoves. Bill Erskine was secretly proud of the fact that his family had one in their kitchen.

Craig's words brought them all back out of their silent thoughts. "But how come you got out, and what happened to Alenti?"

SEVENTEEN

If silence could be weighed, then a heavy mass of it hovered in the kitchen of that apartment at number 356. Bill Erskine's eyes were engaging his sons, but no words were forming in his mouth. He looked almost pleadingly at his wife.

"Tell him Bill. Tell the lad what you did at Normandy," she encouraged him. "Normandy," interjected Craig. "Isn't that where Jimmy Baxter's Dad died when he was coming off a troop carrier?"

"Aye, you're right son," said his Dad, "it was."

"Do you remember that time when I was away from home for a few days a couple of years ago?" Craig did remember. It was about the first week of June, when the school holidays were on, and he was disappointed that yet again they couldn't go to Arran for their annual beachside break.

Another reason for remembering was the Army jeep that pulled up outside number 356 and his Dad getting into it and driving off.

He also remembered his Mother changing the subject each time he raised a question about where Dad had gone.

"Well," continued Bill "I was taken across the Channel to help coordinate a rescue mission to bring back someone important."

He reached inside his uniform jacket and brought out a wallet that Craig had not seen before. This wallet held no money, instead there were some photographs. One was of him sitting at the window of number 356, the other was of his Mum, and the other two were images that Craig didn't recognise. One was of about 16 US soldiers in a landing craft all with hauntingly worried looks on their faces and most were in a crouching position, as if avoiding something terrible. The other photo was of a landing craft empty save for three figures. They were all in battle uniform, one was holding a camera down by his side. He was standing next to someone who Craig later learnt was Field Marshal Montgomery the leader of the Armed Forces of Britain. The third became recognisable only after Craig had held the photo and peered at it closely. This man held neither a rifle nor a camera but he did wear an armband, white in colour with a huge red cross Yes, this man was Bill Erskine, Commandant of the Scottish Red Cross and the setting was June 7, 1944 at Normandy and more precisely at a beach they called Omaha.

"Dad," Craig's mind was racing, "how did you get there and why were you there?"

His Dad looked again at the photos and picked up the one with the soldiers crouching before disembarking into a hail of bullets.

"This photo is probably the most important photo taken while the June 6 landings were happening. It was taken by the man I was sent to save."

"But why was he saved when a lot of others were fighting on?" asked young Erskine. "Robert Capa is his name," said Dad, "although that was a cover name because of some of the highly secret photos he was taking of the war. "He was actually taking a photo of one soldier, at the exact time the soldier was killed by a sniper."

Dad offered up the photo of the men in the landing craft again.

"This photo has been declared the best taken of the D-Day landings, because it captured the true feelings of the soldiers. Look at their eyes." Craig didn't really want to, it was too chilling.

356

"But why did you have to go and rescue him?"

"He had been injured by one of the many bullets pouring down from the hillsides at the landing sites. It was thought by the Operation Overlord hierarchy that it was vital Capa's photos got back to England to be published, and that Capa himself receive some medical treatment for his injury."

The pieces started to fall into place for Craig. His Father was chosen to accompany the rescue party and treat Capa's wounds, while he was smuggled back from Normandy.

Craig's mind was spinning, trying to make sense of all that he was learning from his Father. Yes, his Father who was the man perceived by many, including his son, of being a coward. This is the man who received white feathers. This was the man who was reviled by those around him, who had relatives killed or injured in the war.

Yet, this man, Craig Erskine's Father, had crossed the English Channel and landed on the famous Omaha Beach, facing German bullets pounding into the sea around him. This man bore no weapon. All he carried was a medical kit, which he used to patch up another human being who had been shot. This man was no coward.

Craig reached out for the other photo which included Capa, as well as an army General, and someone else whom Bill hadn't yet mentioned.

Something drew Craig to look closer at it and, although he couldn't see his face, he recognised the man's stance. He recognised the way he tilted his head. It was the same man who had tilted his head at Craig, when he saw him just a little while ago, outside number 356. This man was Alenti Pawlowski.

"Yes, son," reassured his Dad. "That's Alenti, he was one of the guards sent on the rescue mission with me. You remember that his wife Maja was taken away by the Germans? Well she was the sister of Capa's wife."

Later, it was learnt that Capa's wife, Gerda Pohorylle, a German Jewish refugee, met Capa in Berlin where he was studying journalism at the German Political College.

When the Nazi Party banned Jews from colleges, he and Gerda, who adopted the name Taro, escaped to Paris. Capa who had also changed his name, taught Gerda photography. It was she who helped him form the pseudonym Capa. During the Spanish Civil War, which Capa was covering, Gerda was tragically killed in Madrid. She earned the unwelcome distinction of being the first woman photographer killed in wartime.

Maybe it was just for his skills, or maybe the authorities thought getting Capa back to work would ease his emotional pain. Capa was sent to Normandy with the troops, to cover the landing. That was where he met Bill Erskine who ministered to his wound, and Alenti who had accompanied the party to protect them, as best he could. Alenti must have done well because the three of them arrived home in Dover two days later, and Capa survived his wounds at the Dover Hospital.

"So, Dad, what has happened to Alenti, and how did you get out of custody?" "Pure luck, I think," he replied, "Alenti and I were in that lock-up for hours and we were awoken to the sound of camera clicks and flashes happening in the outer office. Then the door opened and in walked Capa."

Capa had apparently been at Waverley Station to take pictures of returning refugees and returned prisoners of war. He must have received quite a shock when he saw his two 'saviours' sitting forlornly in what passed for a secure location, in the Red Cross station. His notoriety and the respect that authorities now had for him, following his D-Day activities, had inadvertently made him somewhat of a powerful man in the office.

Apparently, he made the appropriate phone call and Bill was

set free. Alenti, however, was detained further, pending his application for a visa to stay in the UK.

Alenti had had his town invaded, his wife and son abducted, his country and culture wrecked by the Nazis. He was drafted into fighting for a nation other than his own. Also, he was sent into hellfire to render assistance to a man taking pictures of a war, and now he has to take on a different fight to seek shelter and protection and welfare in the nation that used him in their hours of need.

There were still many questions in the young man's mind but he felt that they could wait. However he did wonder why it was so difficult for people such as Alenti to stay in Scotland. His Mother told him "So many of the Polish soldiers who fought with the Expeditionary Forces were demobbed at the end of the war,here in the UK. They were given clothes and a guinea each then left to their own devices. Their resources were nil."

"But why can't they stay here? I don't understand" said young Erskine.

Janet paused before answering. In her heart she carried some shame that her country had treated Alenti and many others as disposable equipment. No longer of any use.

"In order to stay in another country to the one that you were born in, you have to apply for permission for what they call a Visa. Alenti's application was denied and Dad was helping him appeal the decision to deport him."

There it was. Like a stinging slap, Craig felt the impact of truth when it confronts you. What he had been thinking all this time was certainly a form of truth. It was Craig Erskine's truth. A truth that he had adopted on his own influenced by perception.

Life returned to a degree of normality at number 356. Janet Erskine worked out how to effectively dry clothes on a pulley, without the aid of a male. Craig went on to study International

Law at Edinburgh University. Bill Erskine, the coward, doesn't exist anymore. Craig admitted to himself that he never existed. A perception obliterated by Truth.

Alenti, like many others continued his search for a home in a post war world.

As the 72 year old Craig Erskine turned away from his childhood home, to return to Australia, he paused at the gate. He had just recalled something that had brought sheer irony into the story. In 1958, Craig emigrated to Australia on the P&O ship SS Strathaird. Once the ship had left Colombo on the last long haul to Perth, he took out from his cabin luggage a large envelope that he and his mother had decided never to open, in order to avoid revisiting the site of old wounds. Now with nothing but himself and a wide open ocean, he felt it safe enough to do so. The envelope contained several official documents pertaining to the application for a Visa for Residency in the UK. Stamped across it in bold letters were the words VISA DENIED. However the thing that had almost taken his breath away was that the vital document that could have avoided so much pain was called VISA 356.

The taxi that was to take him to the airport for the flight to Adelaide, performed a U turn on Easter Road to allow Craig to easily gain access to the back door. As he did, he turned to look at his childhood home for the last time and noticed the sign with the number 356, slip sideways off the rusty screws that had long held it there, against the dank grey wall.

Or maybe that was just perception.

The longhaul flight from Edinburgh to Adelaide via Dubai would give his mind plenty of time to ponder on the rest of this extraordinary story. It was a story that combined intrigue with disappointment and a surprising twist to his constant battle between perception and truth.

WORD FROM THE AUTHOR

This is a work of fiction, strongly based on historical facts that came out of the First and Second World Wars. Some of the characters were real.

My late Father was a Commandant of the Red Cross in Edinburgh in post war Scotland. His duties were assisting returned defence personnel in resettling after the Second World War and that included men from European countries who had been allies during the conflict and now,in many cases, were wandering homelessly around the UK. He also had the unenviable task of encouraging an established British culture to start accepting other cultures. He shared many anecdotes with me and I have used them as a basis for this story.

Private Highgate was the first soldier to be shot for desertion and cowardice in World War I. His family are still trying to have his death recognised as legitimate as those of the many millions who lost their lives in defence of their countries.

Robert Capa (assumed name) was a war-time photographer whose own story is exciting as any secret agents in the second world war. His photo of troops on board carriers riding the waves of Normandy has been honoured world wide as the definitive portrait of the D-Day Landings. The reference to his wife Gerda is accurate and she did lose her life while doing similar work to Capa's.

356 Easter Road, Leith still stands today and is home to quite a few residents living in rooms and apartments, as did the Erskines in this story. It was also my first home after being born in Scotland.

What follows now contains a fictionalised version of a fact that for years lay locked in strict confidentiality. A well respected International Institution lay at the centre of a disturbing event.

PART

TWO

PROLOGUE

According to a 14th Century saying "all truths are not to be told."

Each century has buried within it many truths that were never told. During years of conflict which every century has experienced, truths were left untold because knowledge of them threatened a feeling of national and international security. Some truths remain untold within families and it could be argued that if they are not told then they are not known. Their existence does not depend on their telling.

This story began with the dilemma for a young Craig Erskine when he learnt about truth and perception. He believed his Father to have cowardly tendencies then realized that his belief was born from the perceptions of others. His Father's courage was hidden because truths had not been told.

As the story now continues, Craig learns that while perception could well be replaced by truth, doubt often walks behind.

ONE

Alenti stood staring at the macabre spectacle before him. Smashed, gnarled metal and timber from which emanated an angry heat. A heat that in a bittersweet fashion had once gently pushed the giant train along the track to its final destination, a station called Auschwitz.

Irregular spurts of steam erupted from various parts of the wreck spiralling rapidly into the Polish sky as if it wanted no part of the tragedy. The once horizontal railway track was now pointed like a giant gnarled finger towards the same sky.

Hesitatingly he let his eyes move from the mangled wreck of the engine to the mess that was the carriages it once pulled. They were more like giant boxes on wheels with a severe appearance that more matched an industrial scene than anything to do with humanity. Those boxes had been full of unwilling passengers being ferried towards the rest of their lives, not knowing that there was not much of life left for them.

Then his eyes sighted the first evidence of human presence protruding from the torn timber of the wrecked wagons. Alenti, to his horror, recognized it as the foot and lower leg of what he presumed was a young boy. He pulled back part of the timber and in an instant felt frozen in time, as if a sleeve of ice had enveloped him. The leg was about the only thing left intact on the young body and a rivulet of blood flowed down from the lad's innards that had burst open when the wagon had been smashed up against the swollen mess that was once the train.

Alenti's eyes then travelled further down the line of broken wagons and saw body after body hanging loose, oozing blood and entrails. His stomach churned and he gagged at the sight but what was worse and even more horrifying was that each body he saw had the same face. The lifeless eyes were staring directly at him.

Lying alongside each of the boys' bodies was a fully grown woman also dead and also staring back at him. Their arms tightly wound around the children in their last Motherly embrace. The line of broken wagons stretched as far as Alenti could see, each having burst open on impact, spilling their mangled human contents onto the ground.

All their faces were staring at him and he began to shake uncontrollably because he recognized every single one of those agonized faces. Alenti was looking at all that was left of his wife and son, their agonizing fate replicated in each of the overturned wagons.

Suddenly the locomotive gave out its last steaming breath with a resounding wail like a banshee which coincided with a thunderous crash of its metal skeleton as it came to its final resting position on the mangled track. It was finished.

The noise woke him with a start, almost throwing him from the bunk. As he jumped that chasm between dreaming and reality, he screamed in horror at the scene that had just played out in his troubled mind. As much as he hated the makeshift holding cell he was in, he was greatly relieved to find himself back in Edinburgh's Waverley Station, and almost hugged the Military Policeman whose job it was to guard him.

Corporal Glaister was having none of that. "Shut the fuck up!" he yelled. "and get back on that bunk or I'll tie you to it."

Glaister's words brought Alenti back to reality. "Sorry, bad dream." He uttered.

"I don't know how you could bloody well sleep anyway." Glaister's voice softened slightly. "Of all the places for me to serve my last week in the army. There's not a minute's peace with all those trains puffin' in and oot, and folk goin' up and down those fuckin' steps." The holding area that had been especially constructed was in fact the Deputy Station Master's office at Waverley. Alenti knew the premises well because he had met many of his fellow members of the Polish Renew Movement there when they held meetings in a disused railway carriage.

The noise that had awoken him was from the arrival of the overnight train from Kings Cross in London. Before the war, competitive companies had raced each other to provide the fastest trip between England and Scotland and even reached an unexpected journey duration of just under seven hours. However, that all slowed considerably during and immediately after the conflict. The journey by rail between the two parts of mainland Britain slowed considerably mainly due to the amount of passengers who for a myriad of reasons felt the need to head north. This was particularly true of people from southern England.

People from Brighton to Cornwall who for four years had lived with the threat of German invaders arriving at their nearest beach, given their proximity to Europe. Maybe they thought that the Highlands offered them some security in the event of another major conflict. Many pondered on the irony of the English looking for a haven in the Highlands of Scotland.

The locomotive companies also experienced a passenger increase due to the many returned service personnel searching for a home. Many of those fares offered little profit raising revenue for the companies, given the Government's gesture of one free single fare anywhere in the UK that they wished to travel. This was seen quite begrudgingly as 'small potatoes' in return for their contribution to the Allied victory. Many of them were in a similar situation to Alenti's, in that their preference was to return to Poland, but their native land was still undergoing political unrest because 1945 did not bring the end of conflict to Poland.

It did bring an increase in the level of heated debate over how Europe would be settled in the Post war era. That debate occurred between the UK, USA and USSR. The main heat was on the issue of what to do with Poland. It was under Soviet occupation following the expulsion of German troops, but the Communist ideals curried no favour with many Poles who bemoaned their own style of government which had been in exile during the war.

The world may have been officially at peace in 1945 but Poland doubted that peace would ever return to their streets.

Alenti returned to his bunk although he was now wide awake. The pigeons of Waverley station had been awake a lot longer than him, even though his was a fitful sleep, domineered by visions of his lost wife and child. Waverley station was no longer a place that opened at 6am and closed at 9pm when the last train of the day steamed to a halt alongside the platform. It had become a 24hour operation as trainloads of passengers were disgorged, many of whom were set on finding new homes in a country of people that were unsure whether they really wanted them to find those homes.

"Corporal" Alenti sought to gain the attention of the Military Policeman who was appointed as his minder.

Glaister, with his boots on the desk, lifted his eyes from the magazine in his hands and raised an eyebrow in his prisoner's direction.

"I have been here two days now and no one has told me what is happening. Can you?"

The reluctance felt by Glaister in responding to Alenti was obvious in his body language. He slowly lowered his feet to the ground, turned over the corner of the magazine and placed it on the desk then sauntered over toward the cell.

"Listen Mr. Polish person, it's no fir me to be tellin' you what'll happen tae ya and ye ken what? I really don't care. This is my last duty and in the mornin' I'll be off as well. My job is to make sure you don't slither out of here. Whit I can say is that a fella frae the Red Cross will bring ye some provisions and all ye need to get ye on the road. So when I shut the door behind ye, that'll be it fir you and me , unless of course ye go chasin' wee lads again."

The mention of the Red Cross and the unwelcome inference about 'wee lads' reminded Alenti of what had got him into this situation in the first place.

"Will that Red Cross person be Mr. Erskine?" he asked.

"Dinna ken, but do you really think he'd be wantin' tae see ye again sae soon?"

For all the drama that had taken place on Easter Road, concerning the Erskines at number 356, Alenti didn't think that they had parted on necessarily bad terms. He did have the urge to see young Craig again to make a personal apology for the scare. And his Dad, the Commandant of Red Cross in Edinburgh had been one of the kindest officials that he had dealt with.

Since being incarcerated, Alenti had noticed that his sense of hearing and smell had been heightened. Probably a survival instinct coming to the fore. This time it was the smell of the

Corporal's morning coffee, brewing on the hob that was causing his nose to itch. He felt that he knew the answer but was still compelled to ask.

"Corporal, may I have coffee?"

The look on Glaister's face can best be described as astonishment. It came as a surprise to him that this Polish refugee felt that they had a relationship that allowed such familiarity.

He poured coffee into his cup, all the while holding Alenti's stare then took a noisy slurp and returned to reading his magazine, saying nothing.

Out of sheer curiosity, he glanced over the top of the magazine and saw a dejected look on the Pole's face, as he slunk back to his bunk. Glaister had come from a domestically violent background in Glasgow for which he was actually grateful because he felt it had given him what could be described as an emotional strength that knew little pity or sympathy for fellow human beings. Most of his younger life had been spent dodging Fatherly backhanders and leading gangs in the Gorbals, so empathy for his fellow man was an unknown concept. In truth, he saw it as a weakness and a threat to self-survival.

But as he watched Alenti lie back on his bunk in a defeated looking pose, something struck a chord within him.

TWO

Alenti was lying with his back to the main room staring at a featureless wall. He hated the feeling of rejection that had swept over him, even though it was only over a cup of coffee. It reminded him of where he was on the social ladder of life, a beggar. Whatsmore a beggar that was more often being refused than having wishes acquiesced.

His alert sense of smell indicated a stronger waft of coffee, but he dismissed it as imagination as if he was being mocked by his own senses. The sound of the iron gate to his small prison, being opened made him turn around. Corporal Glaister was standing holding a cup of coffee, extending it to Alenti. There was no sound from Glaister as though he didn't have words for a situation such as this. He didn't know how to react to the enormous smile that appeared on his prisoner's face. As Alenti reached out to accept, there was a momentary touching of hands. Skin to skin contact that briefly connected captor and captive.

"Dziękuję bardzo" said a grateful Alenti. "I am sorry I mean thankyou very much"

Glaister stood for a moment looking at his charge. He hadn't really taken much notice or interest in the man. Looking after Alenti was always just a job to do, he never thought of it as looking after a fellow human being. For a brief while, he took in the look of the man and saw someone not unlike himself, being forced into this situation by circumstance. Just like the Pole, Glaister would much rather have been somewhere else, such as on his Grandfather's farm near Inverness, than spending four years of his life in a state of conflict.

The corporal walked back to his desk and sat down with Alenti's file. He had only given it a cursory glance when the Pole was locked up, as he really wasn't that interested. The latter part of his war service was as a member of the liberation forces that released the victims of Monowitz Concentration Camp, many of whom were Poles. This was understood to be a sub camp of the more infamous Auschwitz and was named after a village in the annexed portion of Poland. The fact that the Germans didn't build this camp until late 1942 made Glaister think that there must have been an expectation that there would be a need for such a facility for quite some time to come. Monowitz was partly built through private enterprise as a manufacturing centre for synthetic rubber, using mainly Polish Jews as slave labour.

It was the first time that the private sector, such as it was during a world conflict, was involved in constructing a place of harsh imprisonment, torture and death. It went against the common belief that mainstream Germany knew nothing about the extermination function that such camps provided. Glaister was also told that the respected Krupp armaments manufacturer established a plant near Monowitz to capitalise on the provision of cheap labour. They paid three Reichsmarks per day for unskilled workers.

As he studied the details of Alenti's file, Glaister thought that maybe his Polish detainee could be considered lucky because by being here meant that he had missed the fate of so many of his compatriots who ended up as fodder for the furnaces of the various German operated camps.

As he continued reading he realised that Alenti, through the capture of his wife and son knew the feeling of loss, anger and fear. It was highly likely that they had ended up in a facility such as Monowitz.

Comparative quietness descended on the station as the hands on the famous Waverley Clock met at five minutes to 11. It was usual that at this time each day, the noise that had been generated by the steam locomotives overnight, had abated. Even the pigeons had flown to wherever it was in Auld Reekie that they went each day. They would return around 4pm to commence their roosting for the approaching night, bringing with them bird chatter that would mingle with the sound of the steam locomotives ferrying more people into Scotland's capital city. Like many such centres, Edinburgh had taken on the role of a city of refuge.

Corporal Glaister had fallen into a light sleep once he had finished his coffee, so he suddenly jolted when the main door of the office swung open and three uniformed men entered. Two of the men wore the same uniform as he did, bearing the epaulets of the Military Police. The third was from the Red Cross, Midlothian Section, and he was carrying a canvas bag.

While the MP's approached Glaister's desk, the Red Cross officer made his way over to where Alenti was lying on his bunk, inside the iron railing compound. He was startled when he heard his name being called. When he turned around, he was met with the compassionate smile of the Red Cross officer. He also observed that the Military Policeman were ensconced in conversation with Glaister and he noticed that they were looking through his file.

"This is the day you have been looking forward to Alenti" said the man from the Red Cross. He had introduced himself as Taylor.

"You mean I can leave?" asked Alenti. "I can just walk out of here now?"

Taylor's face straightened slightly "Well to a great extent, yes you can. However there have to be some rules to be adhered to."

"Taylor, I have known nothing but rules since I was old enough to know right from wrong." said Alenti.

It came as no surprise to him that there would be rules concerning his future. Not the everyday rules that apply to others such as traffic rules and taxation. He remembered that when he and his wife first started their business in Poland, there were rules that said what they could and couldn't sell. There were rules that dictated when they could and when they couldn't trade. It had been German rules that had robbed him of his family. Then in the Army there were rules that dictated where he would go and who to salute. He had witnessed how the rules of conflict were nothing more than a lofty ideal. A myth.Yes, Alenti knew all about rules and he knew that they would shadow him for the rest of his life.

He looked up at the kindly Red Cross officer; "And what do the rules say about where I can live? I have nowhere to go, I barely have enough money to catch a tram and I don't have any clothes apart from these" he brushed the dusty coat that he had now thrown across his shoulders. It covered the brace and bit overalls under which was a torn T-shirt. Thankfully the overalls were of a tough material so there were no holes but his feet were bare within a battered pair of boots. Edinburgh's November winds would mercilessly find any weakness in his garments and bring him grief.

Taylor welcomed this opportunity to beam some more.

"Alenti, you have been allocated a cabin at Tyncastle Park out to the west of the city.

It will have all you need in the way of furniture and of course heating. There will also be clothes in the wardrobe and food in the cupboard."

Alenti's spirits started to rise a little at this news. He hated being in this state of homelessness that had overcome him after he was discharged from the British Army. It was in direct contrast to being an enterprising businessman in Poland, until the German occupiers forced him out. Although he and many others had been reluctantly recruited into the British Army as allied support he actually gained more self-respect and a sense of achievement when he was made Corporal. He brought his mind back to what the Red Cross officer was saying and waited to hear the nature of the sting in the tail, he was sure there would be one.

"As you well know Alenti, you were denied a 356 Visa, and there is nothing we can do about helping the government to change its mind and let you become a citizen."

Alenti detected a patronising air as if Taylor was suggesting that it wasn't really all that bad. Here it comes, thought Alenti. I'm going to have to be handcuffed and have leg irons applied each time I go out. "Tell me Taylor, what is the catch?"

Taylor looked away from him while saying "You will have to vacate the cabin and leave the country within three months."

THREE

Tynecastle Park, one of Edinburgh's major football fields, had become a refuge ground for returned defence members with temporary cabins built around the perimeter and canvas tents across the main playing field. Due to the high demand there had to be a strict rotation policy. Each person or family had only 12 weeks residency. During that time they had another opportunity to apply for a visa that would enable them to stay and hopefully become citizens. This was seen as somewhat of a joke as when people made their application,they were not told that it would take longer than 12 weeks to process, so many of them were asked to leave not only Tynecastle Park, but the country, even before their request for a visa was considered. The authorities said that they could keep applying for a visa but in effect they would be homeless after 12 weeks. Government funds were low, following the war so the refugees were not offered any help toward the cost of their fare back to their country. The result of this was evident in the city's streets. The often pristine clean and some would say posh Princes Street would become home for those ejected from Tynecastle.

Alenti's cabin at Tynecastle was adequate. The allowance he was given was barely enough to cover his food needs, There was certainly nothing left over for clothing or even medication should he fall ill. There was a narrow verandah around the outside of the cabin which allowed residents to sit in fresh air. Nothing was uniform though with bits and pieces of furniture obtained from varying sources. Some were old bamboo or cane outdoor settings that had seen better days. Others were rusty pieces of aluminium with cracked Laminex tops. It gave the camp a look of despair as if the camp was as much a refuge for old furniture as it was for human beings.

There was an ablution block located just a short walk from his cabin. It was an extension that was built at the site of the original toilets for the grounds presenting a less than salubrious impression. Residents were responsible for cleaning the facility, resulting in poor hygiene and a high potential for disease. Alenti consoled himself that at least the water was hot, and that had its own special healing quality. Also, his cabin was situated on a slight rise which afforded him a view that overlooked the grounds and in the distance he could see the western district of Edinburgh. He cast his mind back three days. By comparison to the Waverley station cell he'd been incarcerated in, this had a touch of luxury.

Sleep had been his friend for those three days. He had not realised just how exhausted he was and this respite meant he could lull himself into a state of security and relax, without the adrenalin rush that happened each time he heard a door open and a uniformed figure appeared before him.

There was still enough warmth in the late Autumn sun that made it pleasant enough to sit outside. He had been apportioned what had once been a glorious outdoor setting made from cane. It had long lost its sheen and the glass top on the table for two had a huge crack across it. There was a chair for a second person, but Alenti had had no meaningful conversations with anyone since Corporal Glaister back at Waverley, so he doubted if he would ever see anyone sitting opposite him. He didn't really mind because he had a lot to think about. His priority was to plan the next phase of his life.

He preferred taking his shower in early evening as there were few people wandering around the camp. Alenti was on one hand desperate for company and friendship but on the other was a little wary of the other residents.

He craved news from Poland and had even written a letter to his wife's Mother in Warsaw, hoping to make contact with the only family that he had. But how could he be sure she was still alive. From the bits and pieces of news he received, he knew that his country was still struggling for political survival, and he wanted to be there. He wanted to be part of a revolution of thought and if necessary would take up arms.

As he approached the ablution area, he noticed three people talking near the entrance. As he got closer, he noticed that one was a woman. Their conversation petered out as he got nearer. He said good evening to them, in English but they said nothing and shuffled their way out of the doorway and looked away from him. Alenti found that a strange reaction as since he'd arrived at the camp, it struck him how everyone at least acknowledged each other, even if the communication ended there. He couldn't tell the nationality of the three because the level of their speaking voices was low, and he heard nothing but indistinguishable Mumbles.

There was no one else in the block when he entered which pleased him allowing for free choice of the showers. He took the one where there was a bench against the wall, making it easier to store his toiletries and towel.It was a warm evening so all that was needed for him to disrobe was to take his shorts off and place them on the bench along with his singlet.

As the water warmed, he could feel the stress of the day wash away along with the dust and dirt that had accumulated on his body. The feel of warm water was comforting and as well as cleansing, he felt renewed. His spirits had been down for a few days as he could see no future for himself, even though he was out of jail and away from the disapproving eyes of Corporal Glaister. Although he was out of prison, he knew that there were many challenges ahead of him and he only had less than three months to establish permanent residency of the UK or beforcibly returned to Poland, where he had nothing but his national pride, and that wasn't going to fill an empty stomach and keep him warm.

He hadn't been in Poland for over three years, and he had no idea what post war conditions would look like. Would his house still be there? He had heard that some Poles had lost their homes to returned defence force members and in lots of cases, squatters and vagrants filled the streets.

"Enough thinking for tonight" thought Alenti. Tomorrow he will start to search for his future. His thoughts quickly returned to the warmth of the water when that warmth disappeared. It was replaced by an icy splurge similar to being immersed in an icy pool. He immediately reached for the taps, fumbling to find them in the dying light of day that was eeking through the windows. Stepping quickly out of the shower stall, he quickly grabbed his towel and began wiping the icy droplets from his skin. While still damp, he slipped his shorts back on, collected his singlet and headed for the door of the ablution block.

Due to the dimming light of the day he hadn't noticed that the door to the block, which was usually open all of the time was firmly shut and he banged his head and his toe at the same time as he moved to pass through. He was knocked to the ground by the force of his body's collision with the iron door. His bag of toiletries scattered its contents across the floor.

As he struggled to his feet, he felt that he was not alone. He paused in his efforts to get up and listened to see if he could detect anything. He could. It was the sound of human breathing, and his eyes fell on three pairs of human feet, standing in front of the door. As his eyes travelled upwards, he saw legs, arms, shoulders then the sight of three faces staring down at him.

Alenti had faced fear before. Many times before as on invasion day in Poland when his wife and child were abducted. He had felt it in World War Two's trenches, in Europe under enemy fire on the sands of Normandy, and more recently on Easter Road in Leith when he attacked young Craig Erskine. Now it was as if the cumulative fear effect from all those incidents had gathered themselves in that ablution block. He began to recognise the three people as those who were loitering outside the entrance when he came in.

The woman leant down grabbing him under his arms and pulled him upright.

Although a warm evening, Alenti shivered but it had nothing to do with the weather. One of the men reached down and collected the singlet that he dropped and quickly wrapped it around Alenti's mouth tying it tightly behind his head. He winced as the action hurt when it twisted his hair. While the woman opened the door, the third man held him in a headlock and the trio walked towards the old scoreboard, where a fourth person was waiting with the door to the shed below open.

Alenti had difficulty walking without stumbling but it was obvious that his captors didn't care as long as they all kept moving. As they reached the door, the waiting man stepped aside as the others bundled Alenti through into a large room that sat under the main scoreboard.

It was lit by two lamps suspended from the ceiling. The light emitted by the two lamps supended fron the ceiling was faint but he was able to see chairs stacked in the corner alongside a large wicker rectangular shaped basket that held sporting equipment. A basketball hoop pole stood alongside but there was no netting where the ball would have been targeted. Alenti, knew that the scoreboard complex existed because he saw it every day from his cabin. He did not know that there was this expansive room under it.

The last of the day's light was weakly finding its way through the dirty windows, mixing with the feeble electric powered light that dangled from the ceiling. Between them they cast an eerie looking sheen across the room, highlighting the dust particles as if they were imps in the air, dancing mischievously around the empty hall.

Three of his captors stood idly by as the woman walked over to the stack of chairs, selecting the top one and walked back towards the group inspecting it as if deciding whether or not it was strong enough. She placed it firmly in the middle of the group, so firmly that the noise reverberated throughout the hall. The two men who had manhandled him from the ablution block gestured to him to sit on the chair. They also removed the singlet from around his mouth. Alenti moved his tongue to generate saliva which made him cough as though he was choking. The feeling soon settled and he looked around him, studying his captors, trying to make sense out of what had just happened. The man who had met them at the door of the scoreboard complex slowly approached the group around the chair. Alenti felt that there was something familiar about this man. There was something so familiar about the way he was walking, and the way he held his head. Many people had moved in and out of Alenti's life recently so he couldn't work out if he knew this person from the recent war activity or was it further back from that. There had been many meetings of the Polish Restoration Committee in the rooms beneath Edinburgh's Camera Obscura where he had made many acquaintances, but Alenti found it difficult to separate any individuals. There was something so familiar about the stance of this man. Alenti felt apprehensive. He had met this person in association with danger. The man approached him and Alenti detected a slight smile on his face, or was it a smirk?

"Witam Alenti, to było od jakiegoś czasu mój przyjaciel", the man spoke in an unexpectedly kind tone and the sound of his voice, strengthened Alenti's recognition, but he couldn't work out who he was or where he had met him.

"You say that it has been some time since we met, so was that in Poland or somewhere in the war." He asked.

The man walked over and selected another chair from the stack and walked back placing it in front of Alenti.

"And why have you kidnapped me? Why all this?"

The man responded, this time in English. "You think you have been kidnapped? Are you worth anything, Alenti?"

It was obvious now that although he had been addressed in Polish this man spoke perfect English leaving no doubt that he was of British stock. The fact that he was bi-lingual helped narrow down the list of possible identities but Alenti was still at a loss.

"Look, just let me go, I think you may be mistaken, I didn't come here to find trouble and there is no one that would pay any ransom for me."

"Alenti, let's leave the kidnapping theme out of it, it just doesn't exist. No one is holding you hostage or for a ransom."

The man twirled the chair around and sat on it with its back toward the front. Alenti thought that all that was needed was a baseball cap on his head backwards, and this familiar stranger would become like an American gum chewing lout. Only the rich sounding Anglo Saxon voice belied that image. "Why, then did you jump me , gag me and drag me over here, and who the hell are you, have we met before?" The man took a long time to answer. It was only at the urging of the female who had been standing behind Alenti all this time, did he respond and he did so in a serious tone of voice.

"Alenti, if we hadn't met before then it's highly likely that you would not be in this country right now. It was only a matter of time before we met again, and you could say that you have a debt to pay and now that I have found you, it's time to settle the bill."

He stood up and took a step closer to Alenti, while reaching around to the back pocket of his black military styled jeans. This movement alerted Alenti, and the alert changed to alarm when he saw what was in the man's hand. He was grasping a knife and held it aloft as if taunting Alenti with either torture or death. In the midst of his fear he still puzzled about who this man was, everything about him was familiar and it seemed as though he may well be the last person he sees while alive. The man lowered his hand and brought the blade closer to Alenti, who automatically shirked in response to the move. Two thoughts came to him in a rush. One was that he wasn't restrained on the chair, he could actually stand up and leave, so why wasn't he tethered? The other thought was about the knife which was flashing before his eyes. But he wasn't thinking about how much it would hurt as the steel met his flesh. Instead Alenti recognised the knife. It was his.

FOUR

The year that Craig started at University was the final of the Churchill years. Having a young, enquiring and even rebellious mind, Craig found himself tempering much of his criticism of the then Prime Minister when he learnt that the same man had been Britain's leader during much of the Second World War. The young Erskine was surprised at the criticism levelled at Churchill in the years following the conflict and he often discussed this with his Father.

"Why did we throw Winston out at the election Dad?"

"I think we brought him back too quickly the last time," said Bill. "A grateful nation forgot that it had given all the thanks it should to a wartime leader and it was time to find someone more attuned to a country in need of some after war care. He was a reminder of a time we all wanted to forget, war."

Craig then suggested that given Churchill had been a strong and decisive leader, then it would be beneficial for the country and the world, that they continued with more of the same. "Anyway, he deserved another term at least."

"Deserved?" exclaimed his Father.

"You don't use electoral office or re election as a reward son. 1945 was the end of a war but the start of rebuilding and reforming and learning, and a PM, noble as he was leading his country through a long period of conflict, isn't the man for that job."

"So you think the UK is ready to move on?" asked Craig.

"Son, I think that we learnt little about the human character following the 14-18 conflict. Many of the politicians who are making decisions today were in fact frontline soldiers in that conflict. As a frontline soldier you carry out orders, you shoot where you are told to shoot and when to shoot. You kill when you are told to kill and you leave your own thoughts and I'm sad to say your moral compass at home, because they really wont serve you well on the battlefield. So in 1939 those soldiers had become the decision makers in Whitehall, sending a new generation to their deaths."

Craig walked over to the window of number 356 and looked down on Easter Road. He couldn't count the many moods through which he had viewed this scene. From a child perplexed about what status to give his Father, to a university student confused as to why a second war had happened at all if they had already been through it only 20 odd years earlier.

"The last two conflicts have been worldwide wars. It wasn't just Britain against Germany or Asia, it was the world at war with itself. Maybe in the dance of war, countries and cultures chose the wrong partners." Said Bill.

"Sure, but we aren't born knowing how to dance are we? Asked Craig. Somebody has to teach us and to use your metaphor ,we have lots of people on the dancefloor of the world but few of them are using the right steps."

"Yes, maybe some of them just shouldn't be allowed on the dancefloor in the firstplace,it is not a place for them they are just taking places that are better filled with those who dance the purest." Said Bill.

"I think we are getting lost in our own euphemisms Dad!" smiled Craig. "We can afford that luxury because we won the war and history is often written by the victors. I wonder how the Poles will write the history of their war. One thing Churchill did was get the Poles such as Alenti released from those camps and enabled them to get home again after fighting for us.

"Maybe," said Bill "but then when they got home they found out that while they were fighting for us, their homeland was being ravished and looted by the Soviets who would like us to think they were Liberating nor Fighting."

Craig came back to the kitchen table and sat down with his hand on the newspaper that he hadn't read yet.

"So Father dear, I ask again, do you think the UK is ready to move on?"

"I think the world must move on and do it quickly" responded his Father.

"Does that include Germany? Has it been able to throw off the horrors of the Third Reich?"

Bill walked over to the window of number 356 and paused before responding.

"You know we came to hate the term Third Reich but really they were only words that translated to Third Realm. The hatred which I remind you wasn't total throughout Germany, came from within their vision, not as a result of it."

"Dad, are you saying that it could have worked?"

Father and son locked their gaze and in a silence heavy with thought there was formed an agreement not to take this conversation any further.

FIVE

It was Sunday morning, Bill and Janet had just returned from church. They had chosen the South Leith Parish Church, mainly because of its ancient history which reached back the 1400's. Craig had always questioned his parents choice of church which he felt suggested that historical prestige played a bigger part than faith when they were selecting a place of worship. The church had a strong connection to St. Mary and Henry V111 who had actually ordered the destruction of Leith. It had also played a part in the siege of the town. Craig had never developed a strong faith in Christianity, or religion generally. That which he had learnt at Sunday School and the Boys Brigade, had been severely challenged by what his historical research was showing him. Also he found it difficult to reconcile what was happening with people such as Alenti with the tenets of the Christian faith. In deference to his family, he attended most church services but he battled with the urge to stand and cry 'Bullshit!' at the pulpit. It was now agreed that he would stay at home rather than risk embarrassment to his family.

It was also agreed that he would devote some attention to the midday meal and have it ready when his parents came home. He had had some success at cooking but also some failures. His piece de resistance was Roast mutton with potatoes cooked in duck fat.

Unfortunately today's efforts were somewhat of a disaster given that he had used some olive oil because supplies of duck fat had dried up at the local grocers. He had overdone the amount of oil resulting in an overcooked piece of sheep being served for lunch. He smiled when he recalled the biblical story of the sacrificial lamb.

"I have told you Craig not to use such a light oil on aged meat." his Mother's voiced emanated from the kitchen. "And what the dickens have you been doing with this pulley?"

Craig had been trying to fix the running wheel on the pulley. There was no difficulty in raising it to ceiling height, but it wouldn't lock in and stay there, so he had left it lying on the table, meaning to return to the task later. "Well it's because of that bloody thing that the meat burnt. I got tied up in trying to free that darned wheel thing that I forgot to check the oven."

Mother and son glared at each other while the burnt meat crackled in the background and the pulley mechanism lay in a meaningless pile of screws rubber wood and rope. Then almost as one, they broke into laughter.

Janet said "You know son, we can't be that badly off if all we got to worry about is a burnt roast and a collapsed pulley!"

Craig agreed and asked where his Father was. Before his Mother could answer, Bill came up from the cellar with a scuttle full of coal which would keep them warm for the rest of the day. "You know Dad," said Craig " You would be the only one I know who would go down to a coal cellar, fill a scuttle and bring it back upstairs, without a single black mark on your face or hands."

Bill smiled as he filled the stove and shut it down to let it quietly burn away for the next few hours. Although miles apart in political beliefs, they had developed a mutual respect. It had been a long time since one of Craig's smiles had been directed at his Father.

Janet had finished salvaging the edible bits from Craig's attempts to roast a leg of mutton and set the table. "Bill, are you staying in this afternoon?"

"I'll be going out later for a while, I have to make sure that Alenti has all he needs." The mention of the Pole's name, jolted Craig. "Alenti? You know where he is? You still seeing him? I didn't know that."

Bill Erskine looked at his son. He was inwardly chastising himself for mentioning Alenti. He had intentionally not mentioned that he was still involved with the Pole following his visa refusal. He nodded in preference to saying anything.

Craig continued, "Where is he? Why didn't you mention him before this? I thought he had been bundled off back to Poland. I didn't think that you would ever see him again."

His Father acknowledged the fact that perhaps he should have said something earlier. It had been two years since the incident outside and all discussion regarding Alenti within the family had ceased. Craig became involved with entering University and life had progressed away from war related matters to the plans and hopes for a brighter future. The shadow of conflict had now changed to a brighter glow of promise and potential for a post war Scotland, although a shadow still remained manifested in war crime trials, appeasement, and sadly retribution.

"Can I come with you when you go to see him?" asked Craig.

The answer came decisively and quickly. "No. You are best not to get involved son. Besides I am not going to see him, I am just going into the office to put his file back in the right place." Bill tapped the voluminous folder on the dining room table as he spoke.

"But you won't tell me where he is?" asked Craig.

"I would rather not Craig, I don't want to start it all up again, and I think you would be best not to go there."

Craig was taken aback. "So you know what's best for me do you? Dad, all that stuff that went on with Alenti is what I am studying right now and it's where I want to make a difference. It's a perfect opportunity to see what's happening up front. If I had known he was still around then I would have sought him out much sooner. You were wrong not to tell me, it was me that was shot you remember?"

"I'll never forget that day as long as I live, Craig. And I also know when to leave things alone, they are now all dealt with and life goes on."

"That's the attitude that got this country into the mess its in now. Find a quick solution but fuck the consequences, what did you and your cronies do with him anyway, or did you wash your hands of him the day he was locked up at Waverley?"

"Craig, that's enough!" Janet had come into the kitchen where her husband and son were talking. She had become worried lately that old animosities were arising between them again. The family had enjoyed some pleasant times together since any perception of war time cowardice had been put to rest.

Bill raised his hand in a sign of peace. "Son, I hadn't mentioned anything to do with Alenti, because it reminded me of a very sad time between you and me."

"Ok," said Craig "but remember that avoidance therapy seldom works. Just not talking about an issue doesn't make it go away, in fact it is likely to make it more entrenched."

Bill's intuition told him to say nothing, and he quietly admired his son for his positive attitude to the challenges of life, and this assured him that he was well equipped for whatever fate had in store for him.

During the family's lunch, matters of war, politics and escaped or recaptured detainees were left to rest. The weather seemed have been restored to daily discussions. The strength of the November sun was starting to weaken and the shortening days were playing an overture to the expected darkness of the approaching winter.

University exams would soon be over and Craig was looking forward to some time away from books and more time in physical pursuits such as travel. Visits to the Soviet Union and Poland and even Prague were on his to-do list and even before his Father had inadvertently mentioned a reference to Alenti, Craig had planned to find out more about what happened to the Polish returned ally who had burst into their lives.

Once, the lunchtime dishes had been done, Bill announced that he was off to the office with Alenti's folder. Janet had promised Mrs Livingstone, the caretaker, that she would help with the little allotment out the back from which tenants enjoyed picking vegetables.

With winter approaching, there was much to clean up after summer crops and a bit of preparation for the bitter bite of frost. Craig said that he wanted to get some exercise so he wanted to walk the length of Princes Street non stop. He did admit that achieving that would be difficult because in that two mile return journey there were many temptations in the shape of shops and markets.

He watched as his Father lifted the file on Alenti into his Red Cross attache case put on his overcoat and leant to kiss Janet goodbye. "Not sure when I'll be home, but it will be before dark."

Bill glanced at Craig who was standing rather wistfully by the window. "You want to walk with me as far as Princes?" he asked.

"No thanks," said Craig "I'll be a little while yet."

Janet wasn't aware of any reason for tension in the room but felt that something was happening between her husband and her son. She detected it in the stare that Craig gave Bill, and in his tone of voice.

As Bill shut the door behind him, Craig turned back to the window to watch him head up Easter Road. It brought back the memory of watching a similar scene from his childhood when he watched his Dad 'going to the war'.

Bill Erskine cut a lonely figure on Easter Road. Buses were still running on a restricted timetable and given that the post war economy meant few families had reached the affordability of a car, there was little traffic and there were only two vehicles taking up kerbside parking for the whole thoroughfare.

Craig genuinely hoped that his Father wasn't offended by his refusal to accompany him as far as Princes Street, but seeing as Bill was not inclined to see any reunion with Alenti, Craig decided upon some investigative work, by following his Father.

He looked across at his Mother who seemed quite relaxed sitting alongside the kitchen stove with plenty of coal in the scuttle. "Think I might go for a walk, before it gets too dark. Might help that mutton digest!"

Janet resisted the Motherly urge to tell him to dress warmly and be safe. "Ok son, enjoy your time."

When Craig closed the door behind him, she went over to the window and looked down at him heading up Easter Road. He seemed to be moving quickly for someone just out for a stroll. She noticed his head slightly bowed against the wind and his steps quickened as he stepped off the pavement, as if he could move quicker on the road. Janet went back to her seat by the fire curious to know what was on her boy's mind.

SIX

Craig strained his eyes up the length of Easter Road to see if he could see his Father.

Something made him suspect that Bill was going to see Alenti and that it wouldn't be at his Red Cross Office. He realised that he would have to resort to some subterfuge if he was going to find out the truth.

In the most part, Easter Road is a fairly straight thoroughfare although there is a slight bend at the southern end which Craig planned to use should his Father turn around. One glimpse of Craig would render the plan useless, and Bill would no doubt head for his office rather than to where Alenti was located. The road became part of Edinburgh's history from the mid 1770's being the main route from Leith to Edinburgh. Horse drawn coaches would run each half hour into the central business district Locals would be treading or riding in the wake of such figures as Mary, Queen of Scots in the 1600's and Oliver Cromwell almost a hundred years later. The road was one of the first in Scotland to be coated with that country's own invention, macadam. That road surface gradually replaced the cobble stone material which gives visitors and historians an inner romantic glow, but actually became cursed by locals, particularly those who couldn't afford the hire of a carriage.

This historical aspect of his home environment found no space in Craigs mind as he stealthily sought out each appropriate doorway into which he could escape, should his Father spot him. He knew that if his Father turned off before he reached Princes Street, then it validated Craig's belief that it was no Red Cross Office for which he was headed.

The next few steps would tell. Bill stopped at the corner of the street that would have taken him to his Headquarters, and Craig hurriedly concealed himself behind a bus shelter that gave him agood view of his Father's next movements. Bill had only stopped to change his brief case over from one hand to the other and straighten his coat.

The next step that he took told Craig what he wanted know. Instead of heading where he had told his family he was going, Bill headed straight ahead onto Princes Street.

Sunday was generally a quiet day in Edinburgh's famous retail precinct and Craig followed his Father as he crossed the road to the bus stop outside Waverley Station steps. A small crowd had gathered around the busking piper dressed in the full regalia of the Buchanan tartan. Craig seemed to remember that their family could claim some allegiance to that particular clan. Their territory used to lie on the eastern side of Loch Lomond and Craig always wondered if there was a castle there that he could one day lay claim to. As a child he had been dressed in what was known as the Modern Buchanan and he never felt comfortable in it. He much preferred the hunting version of the same tartan which didn't have the yellow hue of the Modern. The "modern" was not seen as often as the Campbell or MacDonald or Stuart, so he was surprised to see the piper dressed in it.

His Father had joined the small queue waiting for the bus, so Craig remained within the small crowd applauding the piper and felt embarrassed because the only money he had on him was enough to pay a bus fare. He felt guilty at enjoying the music without paying the piper.

Three of the familiar coloured Maroon and White buses pulled up at the same time and Craig recalled being corrected when he called the colour red. As a young adult, he could now understand how that was wrong, and as a student he later learnt not to call it maroon.

The colour was officially known as Madder from the plant of the same name which produced the pigment that became the livery of Edinburgh buses and trams. His mind had been so engrossed in recalling all of this, that he almost missed seeing his Father board the number 25. He quickly moved behind a lady who was pushing a pram and managed to hide from sight as he slunk on the bus behind her, helping to position the pram.

Bill Erskine had taken a seat on the lower deck of the bus which indicated to Craig that this wouldn't be a long ride. It was hardly worth while climbing the circular stair to the top deck for just a couple of stops. Craig positioned himself at the foot of the stair near where the conductor stood so as he could pretend to be climbing up, should his Father spot him as he alighted.

"You should tak a seat lad, we dinna allow folk to stand here it gets a wee bit crowded when others are gettin' on and gettin' off." The conductor's voice took Craig's attention away from watching the back of his Father's head, fout rows up the lower deck of the bus.

Craig didn't want to tell the conductor that he had no idea where he was heading and certainly didn't want him to find out that he was following his Father. "I'll be getting off soon so it's not much point in sitting down and I'm looking out for some friends who are waiting for me at the stop."

The conductor was still concerned about the safety issues of his passengers but realised that Craig was not going to shift. "You realise that we have only another 3 stops to go laddie?"

"That's a short journey," said Craig, "where is your last stop?"

"We turn around just after Haymarket station then go past Tynecastle before coming back up onto Princes Street again then head down to Leith."

Craig hurriedly said, "Well there's no way I'll be going to Leith, that's where I've just come from."

"Weel if it's Tyncastle stadium you're after then you best get off here at Haymarket cause we're no stoppin' at the grounds."

At that point, Bill Erskine stood up from his seat and walked towards the back of the bus in order to get off at Haymarket.

Craig quickly turned his back and made to look as though he was going up the stairs. When the bus stopped and his Father got off, he quickly nodded at the conductor and got off also being aware to the possibility of his Father turning back and seeing him. Craig recalled having been in this part of town a couple of times before when his uncle took him to Rugby being played at Murrayfield which was just across the railway line from Tynecastle. He had never developed much of a passion for football or rugby but when asked he always said that he was a Hearts supporter, so he thought it coincidental that he was in the heartland of the Hearts of Midlothian. This team had just established its base at Tynecastle Stadium.

His Father had taken a turn onto McLeod Street and it became apparent to Craig that he was heading towards the Stadium. While the grounds were unmistakably where sport was played Craig noticed it had an almost military air about it. Two army personnel carriers were parked at the entrance and two uniformed soldiers seemed to be presenting a challenge to any intended visitors. As

Craig turned into Gorgie Road, he noticed his Father had stopped at the entrance to the grounds and was talking in what he thought was a familiar fashion with the two soldiers. In the background he could see just a glimpse of the green playing field most of which was obscured by rows of canvas tents and transportable cabins. The place had been used as an army depot in the last year of the war. Craig's senses were being assailed by the aroma of the Gorgie Fish n Chip shop. He remembered being there with his uncle and had learnt that when ordering your meal, you ran the words salt and sauce together "saltnsoss". It was up to the customer to ask or you simply got nothing extra on your chips. It had been a while since the 'sacrifical lamb' at lunch and he hadn't given any thought to food since, such was the intrigue involved in pursuing his Father.

While watching a reflection of the Tynecastle gates in the chippy shop window, he noticed his Father finally moving on into the grounds. Craig moved quickly so as not to lose sight of Bill, but he did wonder what type of approach he should give the guards when undoubtably they would challenge him. Looking again at the reflected sight in the window, he noticed that security at the gates didn't seem exactly severe. Although he was sure the sentries were armed in some fashion there was no overt display of weaponry, and the guards looked as though they were enjoying the conversations with people coming and going, as they checked their credentials. He hoped that he would be able to capitalise on the sentries casual approach. The only credentials that Craig had were related to the University, including an identification card showing his address and the types of study he was enrolled in.

As he negotiated the traffic while crossing the road, he had concocted the story that he was researching the effects of

International Law on migrants and refugees, and he wanted to talk to some of the families who were in the camp about their lives and resettlement. In reality, he thought, this would be highly appropriate research for him and he may be able to use his findings as part of a thesis. The settlement of migrants was certainly a current topic of interest.

Craig's anxiety levels started to rise as he approached the gates of the stadium. He noticed that the sergeant that approached him was wearing a sidearm, which was usually reserved for commissioned officers. Given that Scotland was now in its 8th year of Peace, young Erskine thought there may have been a deliberate attempt to de-empathise the importance and significance of weaponry. A pistol may be less conspicuous, he thought, but was still a killing implement. The sergeant didn't have to put up his hand to halt Craig, the soldier's poise and stance were enough to discourage anyone from approaching further.

His voice belied his gruff appearance, not really what Craig had perceived. "Hello there young fella', and whit be yir business here?" the sergeant's question almost lilted itself across the divide between the two men.

Craig explained that he was studying International Law and wanted to meet people who were living in the camp awaiting the outcome of Visa applications or in some cases, deportation.

"Aye, it's a terrible bother we have gotten oorselves into." said the soldier. "You'd think we'd get on better seeing as we was fightin' on the same side."

Craig was again surprised at how his perception of this conversation was so far from the truth. This rough and ready soldier seemed to convey a sympathetic and empathetic approach to those inside the compound. He saw another chance to further convince the sergeant to let him pass.

"I would be happy to chat with you when I come out and get some of your thoughts and how you think we should be going about dealing with this. Can I see you later?" Craig had cleverly started to move beyond the gate as he was talking, as if there could be no reason in the world why he should be refused entry.

"Oh, I dinna ken hoo the boss would like it, but I'm that fed up aboot it a' that it wid dae me guid to hae a natter. Talk to you later lad" The sergeant then moved on to deal with a supply truck that had pulled into the stadium.

Young Erskine tried not to look amazed at how easy it was to get through the front gate. So while his mind was racing with excitement, he measured his pace and looked as nonchalant as possible. He likened it to rubbing his tummy and patting his head at the same time. All quite possible, but needed total focus. Craig moved past the pillars at the front of Tynecastle, just in time to see his Father approach one of the cabins on the field's perimeter. Fortunately there was a pathway running along the back of the cabins which allowed him to get closer without drawing the attention of anyone on the other side.

SEVEN

Bill Erskine opened the unlocked door of the cabin and entered. A radio was playing quietly from the small kitchen area but Alenti wasn't there. Bill rightly assumed that he was at the ablution block. He placed an envelope on the green Laminex topped table between a plastic ashtray containing a butt and ash from earlier use, and a jar bearing a torn label. There was enough of the label left to show that it once contained imported Ryba Smazona. This was the Polish food that he missed the most. Alenti had said that it wasn't so much the particular food but the way it was cooked. The best Ryba Smazona or fried fish he missed was cod.

Bill looked around the cabin as he left. There was a single slat based bed in the corner of the main room and it was made with the pillows underneath the quilt which was in typical European fashion. The view from the front door was of four long rows of tents stretched out across the playing field where not so long ago the grounds had become Scotland's first all concrete stadium with a capacity of just under 54,500. There was quite a fuss when safety requirements were enforced and only 49,000 tickets were sold for big matches. The Hibernian Football Club which had its headquarters in Leith, accused their rivals Hearts of Midlothian of conspiring to restrict the numbers of tickets available to Hibs. fans. Easter Road on a Saturday night following a derby match, was no place for a Hearts follower to be, especially if Hibs had lost the game.

Craig had been watching his Father's movements from a vantage point behind the cabin, and he thought how ironic that it had taken all this time for Father and son to even be in the same football ground together. Craig's uncle had been the one to take him to the nearby Murrayfield where he attended his first ever rugby match and that extended to football, each time his Mother's brother visited them. Bill hadn't lingered for long on the patio surrounding the cabin before he made his way towards the gates again. Craig waited until he had turned a bend in the path which would have restricted Bill's vision should he turn around.

Craig mustered the courage to enter the cabin. The envelope with Alenti's name on it proved to him that Alenti was still in the country and disappointingly, that his father had deceived his family again. Craig quelled the resentment he felt. He was in the home of the man whose actions almost took his life, the man who'd formed a close relationship with Erskine senior, unbeknown to his family. He picked up the envelope and found that it was sealed. It would take too long to steam it open so he decided to tear the envelope and take out the letter within. He had reasoned that Alenti would not have known that the envelope existed so all Craig had to do was write his name on the folded letter then dispose of the envelope.

His thoughts were in a maelstrom, on one hand wanting to meet the Pole yet on the other hand wishing to stay hidden until he had digested more of the story. The letter would not take him long to read then he would fold it, write Alenti's name on it and return it to the table, remembering to take the discarded envelope with him.

Alenti,

Do not move from these grounds. The stadium will be de-commissioned as a camp in two weeks. If there is no re-thinking on your Visa, you'll become an illegal resident and marched out of here with your belongings. I think they will take you to London, probably Tilbury and put on first ship out. They think I am here on Red Cross business, let's keep it that way.

Don't say anything about me to anyone.

Falcon 69

Craig put the letter down on the table, folded it in half and took out his pen and wrote Alenti's name on it, and repositioned it. Then he stood for a few moments with the machinery of his mind running at full speed to find some explanation for the contents of the letter. Why did his Father ask that their connection be kept secret? If it wasn't Red Cross business he was on then what business was it? What is Falcon 69?

He left the cabin and settled back in his vantage point to await the Pole's return. He found it hard to get thoughts about his Father's visit and the note that he left in Alenti's cabin, out of his mind. It seems that Bill Erskine had been busy on the Pole's behalf. Why did he give the impression that he had nothing more to do with him after the incident on Easter Road? Why was no one to know about their connection, not even the guards here?

As Craig's eyes scoured the grounds, he noticed a figure emerging from a door behind the scoreboard on the other side of the field. The figure was approaching Alenti's cabin at a quickened pace while looking around as if searching for someone. As it drew nearer to the cabin, Craig noticed that it was a woman dressed in military style camouflage clothing.

She entered the cabin and looked in each of the three rooms collecting their contents and placing in a cardboard box. The wardrobes were emptied of Alenti's clothes and each drawer checked, although the man's private possessions were almost non existent.

The woman noticed the note that Craig had returned to the table, unfolded it and read it.

"Yes!" the woman exhaled a loud whisper, placed the note on top of Alenti's clothing which she had stowed in the cardboard box. She then moved to the front door of the cabin and looked cautiously toward the gates of the stadium. Confident that the guards were paying no attention she picked up the box and left through the back door of the cabin.

Craig was pretty confident that she would be making her way back towards the scoreboard end, so he started to follow her while maintaining a reasonable distance and using each of the perimeter cabins as shelter from her sight.

As he neared the scoreboard site he noticed some activity. There was a vehicle parked near the scoreboard service door. He immediately identified it as a shooting brake. He recalled seeing such a vehicle dropping his Father off from the city sometimes. Craig's young mind had only identified the word 'brake' with something that you can "break". The Brakes of the 1940s-50s were powered by internal combustion engines based on a horse drawn vehicle with a heavy drag chassis. They were known as Shooting Brakes based from the Dutch expression 'brik' for cart and later that was how wagons in general were described. They were very popular with hunters because they allowed easy transport of weapons ammunition and spoils of the hunts.

By this time, the woman that he was following had reached the scoreboard and disappeared from his sight through the door in the service section below the board.

The only cover that Craig had now was a giant oak tree and luckily a healthy profusion of leaves managed to hide him from sight. He heard the voices coming from below but could only identify a few words of English. The rest were spoken in a foreign language he couldn't understand.

The sun was starting to dip further down the western sky and the reasonably slow pace of Sunday traffic was easing in Edinburgh. Craig had been silent and still for about half an hour at his tree based vantage point. This was enough time to give some sense of security to a couple of chaffinches which landed quite close to him. He couldn't work out if their activities were related to the mating urge although he did notice a cup like nest nearby.

Memories of the school classroom returned when he recalled one of his teachers, Mrs Halpin who held an extraordinary knowledge of nature. She had been adamant that her pupils knew that it was the female chaffinch which built the nest. Indeed as he looked at the dancing pair in front of him, he did notice that the lesser coloured one kept darting to and from the nest with pieces of straw in its mouth. From that he deduced that this was the builder in the family and that it was the brightly coloured male that spent more time preening himself.

His attention to the birds was distracted by some movement at the scoreboard building. As he looked, he noticed a man dressed in camouflage similar to the woman he had followed earlier, slowly backing out of the door. Craig looked closer and had to put his hand in his mouth to stop a loud intake of breath as he saw a stretcher appear through the door and another man at the other side. On the stretcher was a human figure lying very still and the two men were carrying it towards the vehicle that now had its rear door open. Craig leaned further forward and in so doing, alarmed the two birds which had come to trust him and not see him as a threat. They fluttered away and Craig was worried that the activity would have alerted the people on the ground, but he then realised that not many people would be attracted to a couple of fairly common birds, cavorting in a tree, so he continued his stretch forward. The figure on the stretcher had its face turned towards where Craig was ensconced and through a parting in the foliage he immediately identified Alenti.

EIGHT

Only those who have died can really attest to the fact that a human being's life experiences run through their minds like a fast speed movie just as that life is ending. While some theories attest to this Alenti felt that he was about to have that very experience, a rerun of his life's story as he watched the knife that was hovering above him in that room under the scoreboard at Tynecastle Stadium.

The fear of a death that was so unexpected took prominence over any emotional experience that his mind was recasting. The faces of his wife and child whom he had lost in Poland at the beginning of the war did surface briefly and he felt an overwhelming sadness that his death would remove any hope of either seeing them again or discovering their fate. He was also consumed by the thought of the pain of a sharp knife entering his body and the puzzlement over why this implement that was wielded over him was so familiar. A smile crept over the face of the man that was wielding the knife.

"This is one hell of a way to return lost property Alenti." he said to him.

"Did you not wonder where it had gone, and more importantly remember where you last used it?"

Like air escaping from a balloon, Alenti felt the atmosphere changing. Just a second ago he felt sure he was about to die, then as a smile appeared on his adversary's face, he felt a rush of recognition washing over him. This man was not about to kill him, he was not going to die. As Alenti's mind relaxed its fear, his mind then revealed to him where he had seen both the man and the knife before.

It was Jack Archer. Alenti had met him following an altercation he had had with some German soldiers on a street in Warsaw. Jack was an intelligence officer with the British embassy and was masquerading as a Polish entertainer performing cultural treats for tourists.

Alenti also remembered that Jack had been dressed in Polish National Dancing Costume. The Germans had bullied Alenti and had shot the air out of the tyres of his vehicle then tied him, using his own belt, to the railings outside the building in which Jack worked. It was Alenti's own heirloom knife that was used to cut him free, and in the excitement that followed, he had left it behind with Jack.

Jack had persuaded him not to return to his home, not even to collect clothes and effects. He explained to Alenti that there were probably Germans living there and Maja and their son would not be waiting for him with tea on the table. Jack managed to get Alenti passage on a cruise ship to the USA then together they went to the UK. As a result, Alenti became a member of the allied Polish forces when the second world war broke out.

Jack returned the knife to its sheath and offered it back to Alenti who, with shaking hands, accepted it. It represented a piece of lost familiarity. For the first time since leaving his Poland he felt an emotional connection to something tangible. Such a feeling had deserted him while he was concentrating on the fighting and staying alive. His survival instincts had overwhelmed him excising all others from his psyche. This knife was the first object that linked him to something within his soul. The touch of the knife was like a lightning rod sending a bolt deep within him. Alenti now felt stronger, almost at peace with himself.

It was a reminder that he belonged to something much stronger and far removed from the battlefields on foreign lands and from the aimlessness and solitude he had experienced once that conflict had ceased.

Because he was so deep in his reverie, Alenti hadn't noticed what his so called captors had been doing. Although technically they had captured him, he no longer felt under threat. In fact the relief was mixed with anger at why they had seized him in the first place. If indeed they had meant him no harm, he wondered why the clandestine approach and what did they intend doing now.

As the leader, Jack, approached him, Alenti noticed that he wore the Red Cross insignia on his sleeve, something that he hadn't seen before.

"Alenti, we must move quickly now to get you out of here, and the only way we can do that is to carry out a patient retrieval. We're going to stretcher you out in the brake outside that has been made to look like an ambulance. So, my friend we are going to have to wrap a bandage or two around you, cover you with a sheet and put you in the back, Let's hope they won't inspect us too closely when we reach the gate."

"But why the mystery?" asked Alenti, "aren't I free to come and go anyway?"

"Yes but this time, you won't have your shadow with you." Alenti puzzled over this.

He had no idea what Jack was talking about.

"You do know that each time you left the front gate, someone was tailing you?"

"I had no idea." said Alenti. "But why would they bother?"

Jack was surprised at the naiveite of his newly found friend. It was apparent that Alenti had no idea of the interest that the authorities had in him. Jack knew very well that his own derring do attracted interest from governments of many persuasions. He had made the assumption that Alenti's exploits in Normandy as an ally of the UK and as a champion of the returned Polish defence forces at the end of the war, would have earned him a similar degree of government attention. Governments didn't appreciate loose cannons firing at will on their patch. Especially those who were disenfranchised, or rebellious, or held secretive information that could do harm to that particular government.

"Alenti, I can understand your hope that you will get back home one day, but look at Poland now after the vultures have devoured the carcase. Bits of your country have been chewed up and spat out in the direction of those who invaded you back in '39, and that was agreed to at a meeting that your own government wasn't invited to."

"But at least we have our own government again." said Alenti. "That's not to be sneezed at."

"Your own government?" retorted Jack.

"Different cloth maybe but same tailor. The Russians overran your place under the guise of chasing out the Nazis. And then when they are both chased out by the Allied Forces, the so called victors invited them to a carve up and you lost just under 180,000 kilometres and along with it you lost about 4.5 million of your Polish speaking people to the Communists."

Alenti couldn't take his eyes off this British soldier of fortune, and wondered at his knowledge.

"Then to add insult to injury, your guys set up your own government which is in reality a Communist government. Jees go figure." Jack leant in towards Alenti's face and held his stare. "You, my friend, are being watched because you and your so called Poles for Poland protest group are a threat to their existence. They don't want to see you step back on their shore and fuck up what they have managed to put together out of the remnants of what used to be a proud nation."

Alenti stood up for the first time since being abducted and his legs shuddered in keeping him upright. The woman gave him a supporting arm. Once he felt steady he asked Jack why he had to pretend to be an army medico and why Alenti had to be stretchered out.

"The only way you would be allowed out of here unaccompanied, or being shadowed is on a stretcher. The Poles have ordered you to be watched and they are to be told if you ever leave this shore.

"Jasna cholera" exclaimed Alenti. He wasn't usually a man who swore or cursed a lot and Jack, given his knowledge of the Polish language, was the only other one of the group who knew what Alenti had just said.

"You know, that sounds so much more meaningful than 'holy shit', maybe I'll use Jasna cholera from now on, much more effective." said Jack as he moved closer to Alenti. "If you are all supposed to be medics of some sort and you've come to take me to hospital, what am I supposed to have caught? What injuries have I got? How you going to pull this off?"

Jack took a deep breath before he replied, and Alenti noticed his chest swelling up as if preparing for something.

"Well, the story goes that there was a fight in the shower block and you came off the worse for wear. It's believed that you have a suspected broken rib, a black eye and badly bruised cheek bone. We will take you to Royal Infirmary where the Red Cross share a facility with the Army medics."

Alenti looked around and noticed that the other two had moved closer and were in fact encircling him. He turned back in time to see Jack's fist about to connect with his face. He felt searing pain as his jaw felt the force of the hit. His world turned black as he fell into the supportive arms of the so called medics, one of whom injected Alenti's arm with a syringe she had been holding behind her back.

As Craig watched from his vantage point at the oak tree, he saw the stretcher being slid into the back of the Brake. One of the men closed the vehicle's door and they all returned to the building under the scoreboard.

Craig paused for around a minute then made his way cautiously towards the vehicle. The sight of a human body lying under a sheet can be just as confronting as seeing a lifeless human body without covering. Craig experienced a feeling that he had never felt before, but that really wasn't surprising as he had never seen a dead human being before, so what he was feeling was terrifying and new. He realised that he couldn't stay in this position much longer because Alenti's captors would no doubt be emerging from the shed soon to carry out the next part of their plan. Craig took what he thought would be his last look at the shape beneath the sheet and another shiver went down his back. This time it wasn't in response to death but rather what he believed was a sign of life. There was movement under the sheet in the vicinity of where the man's right hand would have been. Craig knew that at times, a lifeless body would make some movements as the nerves and muscles inside, settled for the last time.

Then a hand and arm slipped out from under the sheet and lay a few centimetres above the floor of the vehicle. Young Erskine's first reaction was to run but he quickly overcame his fears and opened the rear door of the brake and jumped in. There was another stretcher lying alongside Alenti's with just enough kneeling space for Craig to fit while he gingerly reached out to touch the fallen arm. He got another surprise when he felt warmth in the limb. One thing that he was adept at was first aid, as his Father had arranged classes through the Red Cross, so he knew just how to feel for a pulse. Yes, he concluded, this man was alive. As he summoned up courage to lift the sheet from Alenti's head, the captors were coming out of the scoreboard shed , moving towards the vehicle. Fortunately for Craig, he was slender enough to fit under the corresponding stretcher and quickly toss a loose blanket across the bottom to hide his feet.

They were close enough now for Craig to discern what they were saying to each other. Jack, was asking the woman how far they could get before the drug she injected would wear off. "I'll check his BP and give you an idea." She said and proceeded to open the rear door of the vehicle.

Instinctively, Craig shut his eyes such as a child would do in the belief that no one could see them. The woman climbed in and sat on the stretcher under which Craig was lying. He felt her weight on his chest and when he turned his head toward the other stretcher, his view of Alenti was framed by the woman's khaki covered legs. He heard the air being pumped into the blood pressure monitor then after a few seconds, its slow release. The sheet covering Alenti was pulled back as the woman placed a thermometer under his arm. Craig realised that Alenti's captors would have known that he wasn't dead, that they wanted him to be alive and he could only wonder for what purpose.

While this was going on, Jack jumped in the driver's seat of the Brake waiting for the other two to join him. "What's the verdict Mon." Jack asked the woman.

"BP's 120/80 and temperature 38 degrees which is no surprise given what we pumped into him. You've got half an hour before he starts to come around." said Monica as she packed everything into the medical box which she slid under Alenti's stretcher.

Craig felt the pressure on his chest released as she left the vehicle by the back door, shut it and joined her colleagues in the passenger section.

On hearing this Craig thought about the note that his Father had left for Alenti which Mon (as he now knew she was called) had collected from the cabin and wondered if that would complicate anything. He also started to wonder how he was going to get out of the predicament that he was in and how the group would react should his presence be detected. His worries increased as he tried to think where this journey would end.

Jack shouted from the vehicle towards the scoreboard building. "Feargal, get your Irish arse out of there and bring it here where I can kick it!"

The order had the desired effect and the young guy from Cachel, soon appeared and started to lock up the building.

"There's no need to waste time doing that, we won't be back and once you've put yours and Mon's bag in the back here we won't need anything else out of it."

"O.K. Boss" came the response from Feargal, his words wrapped neatly in a Tipperary accent. He threw the chain and padlock inside the now deserted building, picked up the two bags and tossed them onto the spare stretcher in the Brake.

Craig couldn't avoid a loud exhaling of breath as the impact hit his chest.

Feargal and Monica both looked at each other when they heard the sound and their heads quickly turned around to find its source. But the thought soon faded as Jack said that they should prepare for getting through the front gate.

"OK, the next stop is sentry central, let's hope you were right about our friend's return to consciousness, Monica, otherwise it will be difficult for us. I'd like to have a plan B but we will have nothing but our wits, so I'm sorry it will probably mean me speeding through the gate and I can't guarantee that bullets won't follow."

Feargal was surprised to hear this. "Jack, I didn't see any of those guards with weapons."

"Oh Emerald Eyes," cried Jack. "They may not be visible but can you really imagine any British soldier helping to police a post war community full of so many nationalities, not having such a resource? They are under instruction to keep any weapons hidden so as the public perception will be that the UK is being kind and caring and welcoming to the so called new arrivals. Particularly Italians and Poles who fought with us during the war."

"And we aren't being kind to them?" asked a curious Feargal whose war time experiences had taught him a thing or two about human kindness and discrimination. He had also been the butt of so called Irish jokes and the few times he had complained he was laughed at further and told not to be so sensitive. He did actually spend some time wondering if they were right. Was he too sensitive? Is it possible to be too sensitive? The woe of the failed joker becomes apparent when they declare that their audience is sensitive. Many jokers know that they are taking risks when their mirth is generated out of someone's weakness or skin colour but when is it right to do so? As he waited for Mon to get her bags and put them in the Brake, his pocketed hand felt the outline of the object that had been with him since just before the end of the war. It reminded him of an extraordinary lesson in human relations from his time in a fox hole in France.

NINE

Feargal

His tour of duty with the Irish Guards had included dodging German bullets during the day and avoiding barrages from the Brits alongside whom he fought. He had been seconded to the British Army for training early in the World War 2 and shared their camp. The Brits called him the original Irish Joke. Yes he laughed when it happened and yes he adopted the 'sticks and stones' philosophy but something deep inside, his essence was hurt. He acknowledged that these same guys would risk their lives for him, as he would for them, but he slowly grew regretful of his 'Irishness' because they targeted that point of difference. Words were weapons also and they burnt deeply into wounds that no bandage could salve.

Feargal Brogan had never travelled out of Ireland until the war effort called him. He didn't realise that he would have to protect himself from the barbs of his own allies as much as bullets from the enemy. Although it was no comfort, he could see others suffering also.

He had been in a bunker alongside an Australian soldier and in quiet times they discussed the propensity for humans to seek out the differences between them and pick at it like you would a scab. You couldn't be overweight, you had to be described as fat, or skinny instead of slender. Slanty eyes for the oriental look and in his bunker mate Daku's case skin colour and culture.

Feargal doubted that this 'normal' looking young Australian with whom he shared a foxhole would have experienced cultural insensitivity.

"But you look pretty normal," said Feargal to the young Aussie. "What makes life hard for you?"

The digger replied "Things ain't what they seem mate, I'm an Abo."

The term Abo was a new one for Feargal. He knew very little about Australia except the fact it had its beginnings as a place the British used as a repository for the scourge of Anglo Saxon society. The general belief was that there was nothing of any consequence there until it was colonised by the British.

He heard tales of how the country had been tamed and, that the natives of that land were happy and grateful to the white colonials. Also there was the belief that the Indigenous dwellers wouldn't have been able to do much with the land and certainly not bring any wealth to it as what was happening under UK rule.

During a lull in battle, Feargal asked him "And to be sure aren't we in a similar boat? A rat ridden foxhole in the middle of the French countryside that's miles from our own, and doffin' our caps to an absent master. What unit you with?"

"33 Company RAASC based in South Melbourne, but that would mean nuthin' to you."

Feargal had heard of Melbourne being the place where the US General Macarthur arrived to take on the control of allied forces in the southwest Pacific.but his total knowledge of the so called far flung colony was pretty scant.

"Well if you're with the Service Corps , where's your wheels and how come you're sharing a fox hole with the Irish Giants?"

The Irish Rifles or the Giants as they were nicknamed earned respect for having been the only regiment that involved both their battalions in the Normandy landings, and they were also at Dunkirk. Feargal had never shared much of the war with anyone from his own Brigade because the Expeditionary Forces to which he was assigned were a mix of nationalities. You never knew who you would end up sharing your water bottle or dixie with under fire.

"I was driving a US Army Studebaker down from Dunkirk with load of Yanks who were going to put the pressure on those Kraut pricks and send them packin' back to Fritzland. We pulled in for a rest stop at that town back there where you lot were camped."

"That was the town called Lille." said Feargal. "We just been helping the Frogs to liberate the place and get the Germans out of there."

"Well it was too late for us." Said Daku. "I had just parked the truck and went for a piss while the Yanks were getting themselves ready to unload. I never had much time for the Americans but they didn't deserve that."

Feargal was puzzled. "Deserve what?"

"A fuckin' shell landed fair square on the Studi and took out everyone inside. There was screaming like I never heard before. Blokes running around on fire. The grass they fell on ignited and the wind picked up the flames and attacked the barn where I had been pissing a few minutes before. If I hadn't have got out, I would have gone up with them." Daku paused and Feargal noticed he was shivering, no doubt with shock.

"Bejesus mate, that shouldn't happen to anyone Did they look out for you afterwards?"

"You gotta be jokin'. I got hauled in front of the King Dick of an officer and told off for parking the truck so close to the barn.

Then I was just standin' around not knowing what the fuck I was doin' and a black guy from your country gave me a blanket and showed me where I could get some sleep. Funny he said nothin' just patted me on the shoulder and gave a look. He noticed my colour because my hat had blown off so I think he understood why they had treated me like shit."

Daku stood up, stretched then squatted back down in his foxhole position.

"So that's why you got me here Irish boy. The next morning they gave me a new kit and turned me into an infantryman."

There were no human beings closer linked and more bonded than the occupants of dug outs, bunkers and foxholes in the face of enemy bullets.

Feargal's good natured, steady as she goes Irish based attitude clashed with the aggressiveness of the young Aussie who always seemed to have some axe to grind and who found little to be happy about.

"I'm not here through fucking choice, you know." he responded to Feargal.

"Jees, none of us are to be sure you're not carrying that cross on your own, you're stuck here now and so are thousands of others just like us so get over it me boy!" said Feargal.

Suddenly the lad literally jumped on the Irishman and bundled up the front of his battle dress with his hands and brought his face within spittle distance from Feargal.

"You call me that once more you Irish shit, and my next bullet is going to end up in your skull, and I'll claim it was a German bullet."

"Call you what?" Feargal called out in alarm, this was a big surprise. The lad had his right hand pinning the Irishman's left arm to the ground and his left arm up under the chin. The face which was catching the moonlight as it dropped its beams into the dugout, was alive with bulging eyes and teeth bared in a vampirish grin.

Feargal brought his knee up to connect with the lad's groin. The Aussie screamed out in pain and released his grip on Feargal to quickly grab his genitalia in both hands and move away in pain to his corner of the dug out.

Feargal was relatively unhurt and quickly found his rifle and leapt up, standing over and aiming it at his adversary. "Where did that come from lad?" asked Feargal. "You're like a March Hare on a spring, leaping on its mate, looking for his first bonk of the season."

The young soldier was still holding his groin but the moaning had stopped as he stared up at Feargal, not totally sure of the man's intentions with the rifle.

Finally he found strength to talk. "I ain't nobody's boy." Feargal was puzzled.

"But you're an Aussie not a yank and you sure ain't black so what's the problem? We use that term a lot in Ireland but it's meant to be friendly. You sound as though the whole world is agin' you. Man up lad."

The young soldier fell silent and stared into the moonlit field beyond the defence perimeter they were guarding. When he did speak it was in a heavy slow measured tone.

"I am from Ngarkat country"

Something in the lad's manner made Feargal lower his rifle and squat on the ground before him. He sensed that a story was about to be told.

"I never knew that I was anything different to the others I went to school with until one day my Mother visited the school and when she left, the kid in the desk next to me said that he didn't know my Mum was a boong."

Silence fell again between the two soldiers until Feargal broke it. "You going to tell me what that means? What's a boong?"

The younger soldier replied. "When I went home, I asked my Mother and she just clammed up and was silent for the rest of the night. I didn't have the courage to ask her again because it made her so sad."

Their conversation stopped suddenly when a flare was seen far in the distance. The soldiers immediately grabbed their rifles and took up position in the fox hole and watched about 30-40 German soldiers sillouhetted in the glow of the phospherecense.

Their immediate alarm abated when they saw that the enemy was in fact retreating and not advancing. They were making their way back towards Berlin. It confirmed that the end of this horrific conflict was drawing closer.

Just as the light from the flares was fading, a corporal from Signals slid into the foxhole telling them that the emergency had passed and that the unit would be moving out in the morning. They would be heading back to Dunkirk for embarkation to Dover. This Dunkirk evacuation would be different to the last. This one would not be a retreat and the expeditionary forces would be in charge. However, the corporal warned continued caution as there could be some stragglers trying to catch up with their comrades ahead, so the men were not to relax their guard.

When the two were alone together again, silence returned. Nocturnal birds and animals that had been scared off by days of gunfire and explosion, seemed to be returning to their traditional grounds. Even the so called songstress of the night had resumed its sweet and melodic sound. Feargal recalled being told by his grandmother in Cashel that the song of the nightingale or nihtegale as it was called then, was the sweetest and the saddest sound on earth.

"Why sad, Granny?" Feargal asked her often to tell the story of St. Patrick and the Rock of Cashel, in the county of Tipperary.

"Maewyn Succat was a 16 year old Brit who was captured by pirates and taken to Ireland as a slave. And was it not that after five years of misery, his fate was to escape and find shelter in the Rock. Much of his succour came from compassionate folk and whatever he could scrounge. But it was never enough and while full of despair, did he not decide one moonlit night to climb the rock and throw his worthless little body from the very top. As he made his way upwards, with tears in his eyes, surely was it not the sound of a bird that made him stop."

Feargal enjoyed this part of the story and remembered his granny actually reaching out and closing his mouth which he had let drop open while listening.

"And was it not so" continued Granny "it was the first few chords from the nightingale that brought calm to the lad's soul. He paused in his ascent at a spot where a nest containing four eggs was stowed. The parent birds had been scared off by Maewyn's distressed wailing. Hunger pangs were stronger than his distress and he was driven to gorge on the eggs, shells and all. It was scarce enough to fill his belly but enough to sate his immediate hunger. He looked out on the plain to which he intended to plummet himself and believed that he was meant to find those eggs. His body and mind were meant to gain strength enough to garner some hope for himself. All the while the sweet strains of the songstress of the night played through his ears and delighted his soul."

At this point Granny usually poked the fire and Feargal imagined the flames were making the shape of the Rock and he even imagined he saw young Maewyn sitting on its outcrop.

He turned back to look at the old story teller to hear the end of the tale.

"When the young man awoke to a bright Tipperary sun he felt new vigour flowing through his body and made his way down the rock. And wasn't it with a Cashel farmer that he found work helping to shepherd sheep to the coast for shipping to Britannia and to be sure the captain offered to feed him in return. On arrival back in his native land he knelt and gave thanks to the Lord and offered his services to Him, in any guise that God would choose. He spent many a year in servitude for which Our Holy Church bestowed upon him a high honour. In the year 432, he returned to Cashel and baptised Ireland's first Christian King."

Granny always concluded by reminding him that the street they lived in was Aengus street, named after the King who had the great honour of being baptised by St. Patrick. Each time he heard the story, a young Feargal would go and visit the Rock and try to imagine how as a young boy, St. Patrick would feel as he scrambled up the rock, intending to end his life, then being redeemed through the simple sound of a birdsong.

And it was the sound of the nightingale's song that gave him some comfort as he lay in this foxhole in France alongside his angry Australian partner. He remembered also his Granny explaining the sorry aspect of the angelic song.

"It is a sad sound son, because is it not the male of the species that you are hearing. It is a cry for love for a mate falling on the ears of a fickle female. To be sure the bird is lonely and will remain alone until his call is received and he is accepted. He may never be. Think of that the next time you hear a nightingale my boy." Granny concluded.

The words "my boy" that ran through his mind brought him back to where he lay in a foxhole in France alongside someone whose soul responded differently to the same words. Both of them peered into the darkness which had deepened slightly due to cloud cover over the moon. There was a new lightness in their hearts now that they knew they would be heading back to England tomorrow. Dare they hope that war's end is in sight?

"What is your name?" asked Feargal. Up until now they had gotten by with grunts when it came to identifying each other.

"I am called Daku but I got Dak a lot when I was at school. Then when I joined up everyone here called me Kak yer Daks."

Feargal looked puzzled. "To be sure but would they not be callin'you that because of the sound of your name Daku, it's not because you're an Aboriginal for Christ's sake. Is it not a case of you being a wee bit sensitive?"

Daku's body language showed that the Irishman was on very sensitive territory once again as the young Aboriginal soldier looked back at the horizon as if he had seen danger approaching.

"Don't you know what Dacks are?" he said after a thoughtful moment. "No, what are they?"

"That's what they call your underwear in Australia, and when they found out that I was Aboriginal, they added Kak ya because that means shit and when people are scared or weak, they often say that they have Kakked their Daks. Shit themselves."

Feargal now understood that Daku saw this as another putdown to haunt his life. "But I've said it before you don't look brown, does Daku mean shit?" he gingerly asked.

Daku didn't react badly to the question probably because it gave him a chance to talk about his heritage. "It means sand hill.

Where my people come from is dry country and to survive they had to rely on other tribes to let them use their water."

Feargal was becoming so fascinated by this story that he almost forgot he was supposed to be on the outlook for enemy stragglers finding their way to Germany.

"How come your lot got such a bad deal when it came to tribal lands?" he asked Daku "This means they would have spent their lives dependent on others and going cap in hand just to get water to survive on."

Daku nodded. 'Our mob had a Being called Ngautngaut and he lived in the mallee scrubland. He went on the other tribe's land one day without asking, and when bent over the Murray River to drink, he was murdered. Ever since, our mob has lived in the shadows. Even though we got our land, it's pretty fucking worthless."

"What about school, where did you go?"

"Place called Bordertown." Answered Daku."When white fella was carving up our lands to settle themselves, they worked out areas called states, and Bordertown gets its name because it's on a state border. We were allowed into town for school and shopping and that, but come five o'clock we were bussed back out to our lands and not able to get back in until next day."

"And this was because...?"

"Because we was fuckin' black" answered a dejected Dak.

Feargal decided not to continue, he could see the effect it was having on his partner.

He reckoned Daku's age at around 19-20, about 10 years his junior but had an old soul within him that wouldn't settle.

He was jolted out of his reverie by gunfire and yelling off to the west of them. They both readied their weapons and looked around their perimeter. It was hard after hours of staring into dim light not to imagine that trees and bushes were actually German soldiers hell bent on annihilating them. Then the dilemma whether to defy orders and shoot first or be shot at. Whatever was happening to the west of their foxhole had died down now and the early morning chorus of birds took over, almost as though nothing had happened.

As Feargal looked at Daku who was guarding the other perimeter of the foxhole he thought what a lot of internal pain the lad was carrying. How should he act to avoid enraging him further? He wished the young fellow could hear the sound of the nightingale and find some peace.

Daku was eyeing the perimeter to the front of the foxhole while they were having this conversation and Feargal was looking southwards. The morning light was intensifying over this field in France which normaly yielded juicy high quality onions for the export market. All that could be seen were squashed rotting produce spread across what was once a most fertile field. The rotting corpse of what had no doubt been a loyal farm dog lay where it had received a German bullet in its groin. If only they had aimed a little to the right, thought Feargal, the dog would have known nothing of its death. Instead the animal would have bled to death as it lay in pain, trying to work out how bits and pieces of its body that were normally inside,were now strewn around. It would have crawled a few yards towards the back door of the house where it would have waited in unspeakable agony for its owner to explain what had occurred.

Feargal and Daku had inspected the farm while patrolling the area yesterday. Noticing the smashed up tricycle and broken doll lying in the corner of the yard, they deduced that the farmhouse had been home to a family. More horror awaited them as they walked around the front of the home. They saw what they took to be the farmer still dressed in his overalls and woollen jacket but with only one boot on. The naked foot looked as though it had been pulverised by some heavy piece of equipment and sure enough, alongside him lay a pitchfork the hook of which displayed pieces of skin and bloodstains were splattered on the shaft of the implement.

The sight that will remain with Feargal for the rest of his life was the eyes of the farmer. They were literally bulging from their sockets as the body swung to and fro on the end of a rope which had been hoisted on a hastily erected gibbet over the front door of the family home. As the body swung around, the two soldiers saw a yellow star emblazoned on the farmer's jacket. The bulging eyes were the natural result of the trauma a strangled body is put through, but Feargal wondered if it was a silent scream from the farmer, seeking some explanation for human horror inflicted on another human.

Feargal accepted the fact that he too was a killer. He had been fighting in this war for seven months and had no idea how many people had died as a result of his actions on the battlefield. Are the deaths that he caused any more justified? How does that really compare to the type of killing he was witnessing right now? Was this not sheer blood lust ? Does there come a time in a prolonged battle that we no longer fight for King/Queen and Country, we just fight?.

Feargal struggled to find justification for the death of this farmer whose blood now stained the Yellow Star. And there it is, he thought. He was a Jew. Whoever killed him saw the Jew and a French one at that, he did not see the man.

The trees and bushes in the onion field no longer represented retreating uniformed German soldiers. Daylight was intensifying and changing what resembled a soldier's helmeted head to an outcrop of gnarled timber on a dying tree. What once looked like a row of rifles pointing skyward now could be seen as an expanse of running bamboo which was conducting its own invasion. Feargal turned to Daku and pointed out an old Vendeuvre tractor which last night scared them as it appeared to be a German armoured patrol vehicle.

"I knew all along you Irish dickhead!" said Daku with a laugh in his voice. "I was just leading you on."

It was the first time that Feargal had seen even a glimmer of a smile on the young Aboriginal's face. Tensions between them were easing, and Feargal felt that Daku was starting to trust him, which helped the young chap to open up more in conversation. Maybe the nightingale had sung for him after all.

"Sorry again about what I said last night." ventured Feargal.

"No worries mate" was the response.

Feargal was moving around the foxhole in the early morning light, gathering his gear and preparing for what they had been told would be 'going home day'. Daku was still lying with his rifle pointed out to no mans land with a mixture of alertness to duty and pensive state of mind. "Daku, can I ask you what it is you don't like about being an Aborigine?"

In the silence, Feargal wondered if he had managed to penetrate the lad's pensiveness.

He then turned and held the Irishman's stare, before finally replying. "One thing is what you just called me."

"An Aborigine? But to be sure you are, are you not? "

"I am a Daku McKinley."

Feargal could tell that for all his young years, this man was crying for all who had gone before. He knew that ancestry played a big part in his life, so the hurt that his forebears felt when white man landed on their land with knives and firesticks, was still alive and burning within the young soul. He mused on the fact that when he was growing up in Ireland, he and his contemporaries would run around waving nationalistic flags, dressing in orange and green, but while it may have been based in history, they were doing it for fun. He couldn't honestly say he felt the pain of his great grandfather over religious or territorial invasions.

His childhood play wasn't contained to his own country either. He remembered being Geronimo and fighting his mates who were the US army, but it all ended in harmless hysteria when his make do wigwam collapsed and the plastic axe he threw about landed in the river and was swept away. Somehow he couldn't imagine Daku playing make believe war games between Indigenous Australians and the colonists from over the seas. Yet weren't Geronimo and the so called Red Indians involved in the same sort of conflict? Conquer, invasion, dispossession? And was not the greatest of all, dispossession? Was there any difference between the takeover of Aboriginal Country and what happened in the Wild West? He knew more about Wild Bill Hickock than he did about what happened in Australia.

"What do you think is the biggest loss your people have suffered because of the so called invasion?"

Daku looked at Feargal while he contemplated. If the Irishman hadn't known better he would swear the Aboriginal man was asleep with his eyes open. Had the young lad's mind gone to that Dreaming that they talked about? If so then he wished he could join him.

"Our Stories." Daku's tone of voice when he uttered those two words took Feargal by surprise. He didn't understand what he was meaning but he felt a sadness when he heard him speak. It matched the wistful look in Daku's eyes and even his body stance.

"Stories? What do you mean by stories, and how can someone steal them?"

"How did you learn about your family and about where you lived? You weren't born knowin' that."

"To be sure it would have been my Ma or my Granny and then teachers at school"

Daku stopped cleaning his rifle and looked at Feargal "And how did they teach you those things?"

"They told me, we learnt by listening."

"In other words they told you stories." Said Daku. "The difference is that our stories were told by our people who knew how to tell stories and those stories weren't about magic toys and wooden fuckin' puppets that wanted to be boys!"

Feargal reacted at that. "Hey from what I've heard your lot talk about Serpents looking like rainbows and huge long spirits that haunt waterholes, so what's the difference?"

"Jees, the Serpent is how we learnt about the river that runs through the land and gives it life. And if you've ever been to a waterhole you'll hear the spirit talk to you through the wind in the trees and moving the top of the water. Your white fella yarns scare shit out of your kids by talking about old witches slamming them in ovens and eating them." Daku turned back to his rifle and finish the pull through process smoothly and effectively. "Our stories and songs actually teach us things like when the Pelican or the Mallee Fowl is ready to eat."

Feargal loved his native Ireland but it didn't consume him as it seemed Australia did to Daku. The connection the young lad felt for country was like veins and arteries connecting to a heart.

"So to be sure this land of yours is really part of you isn't it? What do you want to see happen now lad?" asked Feargal.

"Truth telling." said Daku and resumed his sentry duty.

While the dawn heralded a sunny day, and birds felt secure enough to start singing, there was still concern about remnants of the German army skulking around, eager to fire a departing shot, so it was not a time to let their guard down. Daku stood up in the foxhole for the first time for at least three hours. He wanted to call out as he gave a long overdue stretch.

Feargal turned away from him to sweep the eastern side of the perimeter. "How you feeling now anyway? To be sure it will be good to get somewhere where there is hot water and a decent meal. We'll be due for some leave after this stint, you know. What do you think you be doing?"

Daku thought for a few minutes. "Sleep for a start, then I want to go for a long walk."

"I'm thinkin' that if I said walkabout, you'd jump on me again?" ventured Feargal. "You bet I would. What white man thinks a walkabout is, ain't same as for us. You think that when we're late for somethin' that we've gone off for a wander somewhere and don't really care."

"Not true?" asked Feargal.

"No smartarse. We get the call to go walkabout it means our spirit needs to go home."

Feargal thought about that for a while then said "I'm thinkin' that would be just a wee bit annoying for your boss or whoever you were supposed to meet up with. There's many a time that I've wanted to just up and leave, but you just cant do that."

Daku gave an unexpected reply. "You know what Irishman? You are probably right.

But an Indigenous heart finds it hard to ignore the call. It comes from country so why the fuck not?"

Feargal turned to look at him "Because you're part of the human race, lad, Begorrah if we all just took off when we felt the need, what sort of state do you think the world would be in?"

"Take a look at where I am" said Daku as he looked down on his Irish mate. "Sharing a hole in the ground, 12,000 miles from home, armed to the teeth and killing other human beings. I'm tellin' you none of this might be happenin' if we took more walkabouts."

Feargal turned around and resumed his sentry duty, and thought on what Daku had said.

By now, the sun was well on its way to establishing itself in the early morning French sky. Feargal actually began to feel himself relax. Sunlight was beaming on the back of his neck thawing the tense frigidity of the night. There had been no enemy engagement in the last 12 hours, and they were going home. What better reason would there be to relax.

To say that what happened next was a fusillade of bullets would be incorrect because in retrospect Feargal recorded perhaps four that found the foxhole and a hand grenade that exploded nearby. It brought nothing but earth and rubble from the field. He had immediately turned to face the source of the attack and saw three enemy soldiers a few metres to the south of them, using the occasional tree to hide their approach. He quickly despatched a shot at a figure that was not as obscured as it should have been. It met its mark and Feargal heard, with a degree of pleasure, an outcry and watched as a German infantryman fell face down in the onion field and never moved again.

"I got him Daks!" he yelled out.

One of the other attacking soldiers moved to the east, so Feargal considered it safe to leave him to Daku. He now concentrated on the third who was still partly visible behind the tree and moving around within his position as if looking for something. Feargal figured that it would be a grenade that the German was looking for. However he also figured that the soldier would have to stand up in order to throw the missile. He took the risk and waited. Meanwhile a bullet from the east pounded into the foxhole but again movements from Daku's position reassured him that that flank was well looked after and there was no use two of them using their energy there. Returning his attention to the front, he noticed that the soldier had moved and was nowhere to be seen.

"Shit!" he exclaimed. "You can't lose your attention for one bloody minute, now where is the bastard?"

The answer to that question soon arrived as Feargal saw out of the corner of his eye, the German soldier moving in from the west with a grenade in his right hand and holding his rifle in the other. The Irishman instinctively pressed the trigger on his self loading rifle which spewed out its contents. Fortunately one of the bullets found its home, but for some unknown reason, the dying soldier wasn't able to release the grenade from his hand, so it also found a resting place within the man's body. Similar to the previous grenade, earth and gravel fell into the foxhole but because the German's body had absorbed the blast, the fall out included skin, and body parts.

Feargal started to brush off the debris from his uniform and shuddered as he recognised what some of it was and realised that he would probably never rid himself of the stain. He turned around to talk to Daku, just in time to see the third German soldier approaching the dug out and was only a few steps away from where the lad was lying on guard. Instinctively, Feargal fired his rifle and as chance would have it, there was one bullet left after the spray that he had used a few seconds previously. There was a look of shock and surprise on the German's face as he clutched his hand to his heart area which was soon drenched in blood from Feargal's bullet. As he fell, just clear of the foxhole, Feargal looked at Daku who looked as though he had frozen. as he had never been so close to the enemy before.

"You can look out now Daks, the boogey man has gone." said Feargal as he scanned the countryside so as to avoid more sneak attacks. "To be sure I'm thinkin' its time for you and me to get going back to HQ. I'm always worried they forget about us out here on the outer perimeter. We don't want to miss that boat."

Although he had his back to Daku, the Irishman knew.

It wasn't the silence because Daku was a quiet lad and quite often didn't respond to conversations or questions. There was something else in the air. Feargal wasn't one for the supernatural but given his Celtic background, he always kept a little piece of his mind open to accommodate spiritual thoughts that had no explanation. This was one of those moments. Slowly he turned around and saw Daku lying in the same position, his hand on his rifle but his head on the side. A pool of blood had formed and was seeping into the soil beneath him. Feargal didn't have to look any closer to see that the lad's death would have been fairly instant. A fragment from a grenade had lodged in his neck, and it would have severed the carotid artery.

The young Aboriginal lad's eyes were open but Feargal didn't have any inclination to close them. Given the amount of spirituality and sense of country that Daku had, he felt it appropriate for the young soldier to keep his eyes alert, as if that may bring some comfort to the departing soul. Feargal was saddened by the death of his foxhole mate. They had shared some deep thoughts over the last 12 hours. They were thoughts that would never be forgotten by the Irishman. He was jolted into reality with the arrival of the signals corporal and two stretcher bearing medics. As Daku's body was laid on the stretcher for the journey back to HQ, Feargal reached out to touch the soldier's face and without letting the others see, he removed the fragment that had brought death to the boy. He felt that it wasn't appropriate for something so man made and inorganic to be a part of Daku, as his spirit started to roam and find a new home. That object became something of a touchstone that accompanied Feargal for the rest of his life. He wondered if there really was any great distance between his Granny's tale of the nightingale and the young fellow's serpent within the Dreamtime. Feargal recalled some of the words of Daku.

"Ah mate, I'm not really out there looking for something, its more a case of 'm looking for whatever is waiting for me".

TEN

Returning to Ireland and conducting tours of the Cashel Rock and Castle, would bring him claustrophobic frustration. Feargal enjoyed reading the works of the English author P.C Wren and often imagined himself within the plot of the book Beau Geste and the exploits of the Foreign Legion. However it wasn't the 'beautiful gesture' within the translation of the story's title, that attracted him. It was a craving for the life of a soldier of fortune. That craving was fulfilled, but it wasn't in the deserts of post war North Africa rather it was Europe that provided the backdrop for his adventurous pursuits.

Although he didn't have to stay in the army at the end of the war, Feargal saw it as a means of maintaining an income while he waited for either fame or fortune or whatever to reach out and welcome him on to another path of life with an unknown destination. It was as if he had reached a cross road where it made no difference whether he turned right or left, each would bring him the challenges he needed.

That intersection presented itself one Saturday afternoon while he sat in Rutherford's Bar on Drummond Street. He enjoyed the ambience of that pub because of its rich history.

The Edinburgh winds were a constant challenge to the landlord who seemed to be forever re- varnishing the exterior woodwork. Even though he celebrated the end of the Second World War by giving the bar a coat of varnish which he had somehow acquired with a nod and a wink from the army depot near South Bridge, the timbers always seemed to be crying out for more. Feargal enjoyed the fact that the hotel was a favourite drinking place of the author Robert Louis Stevenson. He suspected that the tourist information sign over the chair in the corner may have been placed out of convenience rather than fact that the bard had written part of Treasure Island while sitting there. However it was food for his adventurous soul and he always sought it out when he visited for a Scottish and Newcastle 60/- HeavyBeer.

Feargal preferred the brewed liquid to the distilled Whisky either Irish or Scottish. He often reminded those afficionados that beer had been produced in Scotland for about 5,000 years from bittering Celtic herbs. Then Scottish brewers surrendered their pride and imported hops from around the world, then exported back a quality finished product One Saturday afternoon, after he had finished his shift at the Q store near South Bridge, Feargal still in his soldiers uniform was in Rutherford's Bar having just listened to a commentary of the football match between Edinburgh's Hibs and Dunfermline Athletic. For most in the bar, it was a solemn event as the lower ranked team from Fife scored a two nil win.

Just as he indicated to the barman that he wanted another Heavy, Feargal became aware of a tall man standing alongside him. It was obvious from the man's weather beaten face and tanned arms, that he hadn't spent a lot of time in Scotland. The biceps showed evidence of either regular sessions in a gymnasium or a life of hard work either at sea or a more agrarian pursuit. The English accented voice took him by surprise.

"Interesting that while Scotch is a proud heritage product from this land, it was beer that that initiated a bonding with the so called Sassenachs south of the border."

The look on Feargal's face begged some explanation.

"I don't know if you are a William Wallace 'nae tak oor freedom' kind of Scot but although Fountain Brewery got underway with its own product in 1856 it eventually formed a union with Newcastle Breweries.It always made me smile when true blue Scots would toast their William with beer some of which has been manufactured in the same country that hung drew and quartered their beloved leader. I'm sure that if they knew, much of that brew would be spat out on the bar floor."

For all his love of tradition, Feargal could see the irony in that. He held out his hand to the stranger.

"Feargal…" The greeting was firmly received in a hand that Feargal would imagine could wield the heavy sword that Wallace once owned.

"Jack Archer… it's a pleasure to meet you. I can't help but notice you're a soldier.

How do you occupy yourself now that there is no war to fight?"

"Well after all the demobbing going on there's a pile of uniforms and equipment needing going through and disposing of. They offered me a Quartermaster's job for a couple of years and as I had had no better offers, I thought it a good option."

Jack looked into his glass of whiskey for a few seconds. "I don't know you very well , but I am feeling that you're a little frustrated with what's going on in your life?"

Feargal felt that this man was no bar crawler. He had started this conversation for a reason. It was only a matter of minutes before he found out that he was right, this man was on a mission.

"I'm thinking that maybe your skills could be better used than in an old Army and Navy store and checking off lists of returned items from a war that ended two years ago."

Jack indicated to Feargal's glass, "Another heavy?" Feargal nodded. He was intrigued.

Jack waited until the barman had filled the beer glass.

"I have a task you may be interested in doing. I have to warn you that while it's government sanctioned, any involvement by the British government will be denied and you could well be arrested and detained, or worse."

"Or worse? Queried Feargal.

"It's an occupational hazard for people like me who try to work just under the radar and as far as responsible authorities are concerned, I don't exist. If I am ever caught then I get thrown to the wolves, so to speak. The problem is that the war is officially over and there are signed documents stating that very fact, all signed by the appropriate people." responded Jack.

"Anyone detected working against a particular country once Peace has been officially declared, becomes an Enemy of the People. They are guilty of a capital offence that has International Sanction."

Feargal was quiet for a while as his mind dealt with the information that Jack had just given him and trying to understand it. It seems that whatever the job was, he would be able to handle it. What made it all dubious was the possibility that he may pay for it with his life but he reminded himself that he just spent the last 5 years or so within a bullet's breath of death. What could be different here?

As he continued to digest it all, his eyes fell on the mark on the bar counter of Rutherfords where Jack had put a freshly filled Heavy. When he lifted the glass, he noticed the wet ring that is usually left from such an action. Astonishment hit him at what he saw.

Immersed in the ring of beer, he saw what looked like the Barrack wall of Edinburgh Castle. As he looked closer he could see the protrusion that was the barrel of the One O'clock Gun which had been shot from the castle each day except the Sabbath and Christmas Day since 1861. He remembered hearing that the idea had actually been brought over from Paris. Ships at sea relied on it to set their maritime clocks. It had a direct sight line from the castle to the sea at Leith and the resultant smoke could be seen just ahead of the booming shot over the city.

As he watched, the sight started to fade from the ring stain on the bar and he realised that it was a reflection that emanated from the castle, through the glass shutters atop Rutherford's door and bounced off the mirror that the barman used to check on customers around the corner of the bar. Although his Irish background would suggest a strong connection to the ancient beliefs that surrounded his mystical homeland, he had little faith in omens or signs from above. But he had a dilemma and was looking for anything that would guide him to a decision, so he amusingly thought that the vision of the Castle on the bar top was a good enough decider. He turned to Jack.

"To be sure, I'm demanding the right to say no if I don't like the sound of the mission that you want me to undertake, but I will say this. If it be to my liking, then I am your man. I've had enough of old greatcoats and dixies."

Jack wasted no words in telling Feargal about the mission. He put it very simply but did not understate the danger and the possible consequences.

"There is a Polish returned soldier who has been in Edinburgh since the end of the War and has basically no fixed address. He wanders around from boarding house to abandoned houses around Leith docks area. He has been refused a residency Visa (V356) because of suspected political interference."

Feargal asked "What sort of Politics?"

"Well, he's has been somewhat of an activist trying to garner support for returning Poland to its pre-war status and trying to loosen the grip and influence that Russia has on it. He's been somewhat of a squeaky wheel and it's attracted the mighty oil can that is His Majesty's Government."

"I don't understand then why they don't pack him off back to his own country" said Feargal. "Just let him go."

"Make a lot of sense, wouldn't it Feargal? The problem is that there is a reason they don't want him to land on Polish shores.

"There's more to it. I actually know him because I bumped into him in Warsaw just before the war started after he lost his wife and son, I helped him come over here and enlist in the Allied Forces, and he actually turned out to be quite an ace operator. He was involved in a few clandestine operations in Europe and assisted in a secret rescue trip to Normandy while the landings were going on. Since then he has been active in trying to win support for returned Polish defence personnel because he felt that UK owed them some gratitude instead of being ignored and not looked after like their own people." Jack emptied his whisky glass and thought about a refill, but decided that he would finish his conversation with Feargal.

"Because of all his public speaking and and angst about how he had been treated the Department has been keeping an eye on him. Something rather unbelievable has happened. After struggling for years to get a visa to stay here, he has actually withdrawn his appeal against the refusal decision."

"Why the hell would he be doing that?" asked Feargal." To be sure if it were me I'd be battling for them to reconsider right up until the time they threw me in jail and deported me."

"Exactly, and that's why they have taken some extra interest in him." Jack decided on another whiskey.

"I'm working under a Major Sanderson from Intelligence who tells me that there is a lot to be told about this Alenti character. He suspects his reasons for no longer wanting to stay here, and why he's so willingly returning home once the Government sort out his passage."

"What could they possibly be?" asked Feargal.

"It is said that every man has his price." said Jack "Maybe Alenti will receive an offer that is so valuable that he find it hard to refuse. Just lately he has been seen around Edinburgh talking with a variety of people. Mainly men who the Department has traced back to an office in Falcon Avenue off Morningside Road."

Jack added that Alenti wasn't the only one.

"It appears that many returned Polish soldiers and pilots had been approached by this group. These are the men who like Alenti would like to see a change in the way their country is run and it is not the way that you might imagine from a country that has been thrashed by the Nazi whip so violently. There is a definite program of recruitment going on and the frightening thing is the connection it has to the horrors of the last war. Hopefully I will learn more in due course. In the meanwhile I have to find ways to extricate him from the camp and position him in a spot from which its easier to follow him around."

"But to be sure didn't the Ruskies send the Germans packing?" queried Feargal. "They sure did and the Soviets started to spread their influence allowing the Polish United Workers' party to have strong control over the country. In fact the new Poland became the Polish People's Republic, however there was still heavy Soviet connections which many Poles despised. I wasn't going to tell you this because it sounds both fantastic insane and downright frightening."

Both Jack and Feargal looked around the hotel to see how secure their conversation would be.

"We believe that there is an underground movement working with the now outlawed Nazi Party of Germany. Some Poles seem to see a post war Germany as an attractive industrial ally and are prepared to turn a blind eye to the historical fact that they committed so many personal horrors following their invasion in 1939. They seem to think that would a worthwhile price to pay for improved economic development."

If Feargal had been drinking his beer at the time he heard this, there would be an almighty spray and a choking fit. What he was hearing was atrocious.

"What the fuck? Get yourself out of here, man. To be sure isn't that the most ridiculous thing to say and how could that be possible? Weren't they all rounded up and hung or dealt with? So are you telling me that if this guy is allowed to go back to Poland, he will be used to drum up support for a second Nazi Party?

Jack nodded, " Yes it doesn't seem possible does it?"

Feargal took another gulp of his beer, wondering if he was being fed a line by this sandshoe warrior.

"Where is he now and what are you going to be doing with him?

"Well we thought that he had gone underground or was even killed but he came under notice in an incident on Easter Road in Leith. He had gotten some help from the Red Cross but fell foul of the law when he attacked a young boy in the street."

"Are you be telling me the truth here Jack?" queried Feargal. "This Pole attacked a local boy here?"

"Yes" said Jack. "It was explained away that he had mistaken the lad for his own son who had been taken away with his Mother by the Germans in Poland just before the start of the war. Anyway, he was locked up for a while then taken out to Tynecastle Camp to await decisions being made as to what to do with him. Our task is to retrieve him from there and from the do-gooders who want to send him back to Poland."

In the process of all that we also have to try and find out who the Mr Big of the recruitment group is. No one knows.

ELEVEN

The occupants of the Tynecastle Camp were used to the movements of people and cars and military personnel and vehicles. So the activity near the scoreboard where Alenti had been loaded into the back of the brake, went unnoticed. Craig Erskine lay under the stretcher opposite Alenti's unbeknown to Jack, Monica and Feargal. From the rear seat, Monica asked "So what exactly are we going to do with this guy?"

In reply, Jack gave her a quick summary of Alenti's experiences having escaped German invasion of his homeland, losing his family to them then serving as an ally at theatres of war such as Normandy for the so called Empire. Then being discharged onto Edinburgh's streets and told he had a month to get out of the country.

"He is now an illegal alien and will be arrested if he is found outside of this camp. Yet the irony is that at month's end he will be thrown out of this camp anyway"

"We have had him under surveillance for some time and we believe that he has been approached by a clandestine movement here to get him to work towards re-establishing the Nazi Party in Poland."

"As if he would do that," said Monica "those bastards captured his wife and son and they turned on the Jews and all but annihilated them. Why would he agree to help them?"

Jack agreed that it sounded an unlikely proposition.

"However it seems that its true that every one has their price."

"Aw to be sure, and they be paying him?" asked Feargal.

"Not with money." Said Jack. "Something that he would want far and above cash. It is an offer that he would find irresistible, and I'm telling you two now that even the purest of souls would find it so."

"Who has been in touch with him here?" asked Monica "Does the Government know there is such a Nazi support movement in Britain?"

"MI5 know that the Pole will be approached here and cajoled into making contact with the underground once he gets to Poland. They just don't know who is leading the push from this end. I also should tell you that the Big Brass don't really care if he makes it back to Poland and carries through his plan. They figure the world would put a big stomp on any plans to reawaken Hitler. However they do want to find out who the pricks are that are working underground here in the cause."

Jack turned around in the driver's seat, started up the motor and began the journey. From his location under the spare stretcher, Craig could hear every word. He also found it incredulous that Alenti would have anything to do with an attempt to resurrect the horrors of the past few years. He felt the motor slow down as they approached the gate and heard the footsteps of the soldier approaching Jack's side.

"O.K. what have we got here? Och. Aye you guys were called into to take Voytek off to the hospital. Have you got him on board?"

Craig momentarily wondered why Alenti had been called Voytek but concentrated on keeping himself concealed during what he was sure was going to be a search by this chatty Sergeant.

"Yes he is in the back but he's out to it." said Jack.

"Well I better tak' a look just in case he's got the family silver with him!" He laughed at his own joke so hard that he brought on a coughing bout no doubt exacerbated by the stub of a Lucky Strike cigarette that was stuck to his lower lip by some excreted saliva.

"Fucking yankee fags, they will be the death of me. Won them in a poker game but but now I've tasted them I'm wishing I lost the game. Taste like bloody tar."

In an effort to distract him while Monica went to check on Alenti, Jack asked him what he would have given to the Americans if he had lost."

Well the lads and me would buy up all that crap they call Spanish Shawl and put them in Players packets. Those yanks would have got one hell of a surprise when they lit up."

The soldier started to laugh and cough again then rolled a giant spitball and ejected it out of his mouth onto the ground. The sentry had started to walk around to the rear of the vehicle, while recalling replacing Players or Senior Service cigarettes with the more aromatic tobacco.

"Mind you," he said "The Nancy boys didn'a mind yon Spanish Shawl, right up their alley if you know what I mean." He followed the remark by running his hand down the front of his uniform and thrusting out his pelvis. That launched him into a paroxysm of coughing and spat up more phlegm before giving his face a perfunctory wipe with an army issue khaki hanky that had seen better days.

Monica had already opened the rear door of the brake and pointed to Alenti's stretcher. She had pulled the sheet down sufficiently to show the bruising on his face.

"Shite!" explained the soldier "He did get a rollickin' didn't he, any idea wha' did it?" Mon just shook her head, thinking that silence was the safest response.

Craig had almost forgotten to breathe and when he did, he exhaled slowly and quietly.

He could see the soldier's arms as he leant forward for a closer look at Alenti. Then he stopped breathing altogether when he heard the soldier say.

"Hold on a minute, what's this you got here?" and he leant toward the stretcher that was covering Craig. The soldier then got up into the brake and sat on the stretcher just like Monica had done before.

Craig's mind was racing. He had no idea how he would respond to the interrogation he was bound to receive when they looked under the stretcher.

The sergeant was more interested in a piece of paper on the floor of the brake than anything that may be under the stretcher.

"It looks like oor Wojtek has made some contact with someone and it dis'nae look like its anyone in this camp." The soldier unfolded the note and started to read.

Craig experienced rushes of confusion, fear and worrisome anticipation. This was the note that his Father had left for Alenti. It was the note that Craig had taken out of the envelope and left on Alenti's table. How did it get here? He had left it in plain sight in the cabin.

Monica picked up the bundle of Alenti's clothing that Feargal had collected as they stopped briefly at the cabin.

"It must have fallen out of this pile, Feargal just grabbed anything that the guy might need. By the way, why do you call him Wojtek?"

"Corporal Wojtek you mean?" replied the sergeant. He paused to discard of the sodden cigarette butt he had been lipping for at least an hour, and replaced it straight away with a Lucky Strike.

"He's actually an animal. A bear in fact that some Polish soldiers found in Iran when they were runnin' awa' from the Soviets. They all bit turned him intae a human, had him drinking beer and smokin'. They even taught him to do some military work and made him a corporal. He's up at the zoo here if you want to see him."

"Edinburgh Zoo?"

"Aye he was one of the lucky Poles that found a home here after the war. He's a member of the Polish-Scottish Association. You're allowed to go and see him, if you can bear it!"

Sergeant launched into another paroxysm at his own joke and coughed up more phlegm which was fired into the scrub behind the brake at impressive speed. Once he had calmed down, he turned his attention to the letter in his hands.

"Can we go now Sarge.? We got to get this guy some attention." asked Jack from the driver's seat.

"Weel, haud on lad." said the soldier. "This wee note here pits a different slant on things. It's obvious that Wojtek here is communicating with someone, and I'm no happy aboot what he's communicatin' aboot"

"What do you think it's about?" asked Jack.

"We got a note yesterday from HQ tellin' us tae be on the lookout for any strange contacts of visitors that these blokes might be receivin."

From where Craig was positioned, under the spare stretcher, he was able to detect an exchange of glances between Jack in the front seat and Monica standing near the rear of the vehicle. It was a look of tension or apprehension that lasted barely a second between the two but Craig saw it. He also saw the nod that Jack gave to Monica who, he noticed, still had the syringe with which she had administered a dose of tranquiliser to Alenti, half an hour ago.

The Sergeant looked up from the note that he was reading. "Ye ken this changes everything. I'll be wanting you to take this guy on his stretcher into the sentry station up there, and then your vehicle will be impounded while we tak a wee look at it. You four will hand over any weapons that you may have, and join me in the guard house where we will start havin' a wee talk." He was looking straight at Jack as he spoke, then added.

"Now I'm no wantin' ye to worry, I am sure everything is ok, but if I understand things correctly from what I'm readin' here then there's been some major interference at a fairly high level, and I canna' ignore it."

The soldier was about to move out of the vehicle when Monica leaned in towards him and asked if she could see the note. Hopping up into the brake she noticed a flash of his watch on his left wrist under his buttoned battle dress jacket and shirt.

"Do you mind telling me the time please?" she asked as the sergeant resumed his sitting position on the stretcher.

"Aye lass" he undid the button of the jacket, slid it up from his wrist then did the same with his shirt cuff, revealing the watch and an area of skin that was just big enough for Monica to target with the syringe that she had previously filled in case Alenti needed another dose. Having had some training as a nurse, Mon had prided herself on giving painless injections, however combining the skill of siting the needle and moving quickly unfortunately for the sergeant resulted in a painful entry into skin.

"What the fuck are ye doin? What is that you've just put in me?" he asked as he held his painful wrist.

Monica said nothing but moved forward to catch the soldier as he succumbed to the sedative, threw the bags off the spare stretcher and laid him out.

TWELVE

Monica

Her family were not what was considered hard party goers but the passing of an Old Year never went without celebration. Her grandmother who lived with them insisted on sweeping the floor and brushing the dust outside before any new year commenced. While midnight struck, the family eagerly awaited the arrival of the first footers. Each year when helping to greet them at the front door of their Aberdeen home Monica would peer closely to see if anything resembling a birthday present was among the traditional items such as Black Bun, whiskey and the vital lump of black coal. January the first 1939 was no exception. Now at the age of 20 she had grown up in a traditional Scottish household which meant adherence to events such as Rabbie Burns birthday, St. Andrews Day and Hogmany. Such celebrations completely usurped any thought of acknowledging someone's birthday should it fall on one of those days. Monica Haldane was born on January the first.

When friends realised that it was her birthday there were such conciliatory comments as "never mind, lass we'll get to your birthday later." or "oh I was so concentrating on getting' a nice piece of coal that I forgot your present, I'll bring it around tomorrow."

Monica wanted to shriek "But my birthday is today, not tomorrow and I want to celebrate it now!" but swallowed the words and hid her true feelings behind a smile. It seemed that her once a year day was forgotten in the midst of dancing the Dashing White Sergeant to the strains of Jimmy Shand on the gramophone, and the gorging on left over Christmas delights and the drinking of all manner of alcoholic drinks from Mead to Mulled wine and Green Ginger to Gin. She often felt ashamed for holding such feelings and how petty they were given that the whole world could erupt in conflict at any moment.

Though Monica didn't enjoy the taste of alcohol, she did enjoy Drambuie and cream and had enjoyed a few wee glasses of it during Hogmanay. That was her limit though when it came to intoxicating liquor and she had found that it created a distance from her peers.

However this also gave her resilience and a sense of independence and an inner strength that she valued highly. As the sun came up on the first day of the year that would see the world plunge once again into a major conflict, Monica arose without disturbing the snoring, coughing, farting and recovering bodies from the previous night and went for a run.

Her usual run took her from her front gate on Pitlochrie Place to King Street, turned right towards the Sports Village where she would have loved to have spent more time but found it unaffordable. As she turned right into School Road, she sighted the University over her left shoulder. What she saw made her stop. Monica was actually pleased for the excuse because she wasn't in her usual condition given the number of Drambuie creams she had last night. As she slowly brought her breathing back to a normal rhythm she watched as an unmarked yet unmistakably military lorry with a covered load pulled up outside the main gate of the University. It was followed by what she thought was a Land Rover or a Jeep, containing two soldiers. The men took up position at the front gate and Monica noticed they had rifles slung on their shoulders. The colour of both vehicles was dark green but there were no letters figures or numbers showing. Suddenly there was a fairly strong military presence outside the University of Aberdeen.

As it was only six in the morning on New Year's Day, Monica and the newly arrived soldiers were the only people on the street. The mid-winter sun dimly lit up the outer walls of the University and as the iron gate was opened by one of the soldiers, it caused an eerie outline of its shape to fall as a shadow on the bitumen driveway.

Monica could feel her heart rate starting to decrease and she knew that if she wanted it to stay high she would have to resume some movement. However, her curiosity heightened when she noticed that two other soldiers had alighted from the truck and opened its tailgate to reveal an object covered by a dark green tarpaulin. Her mind was working feverishly as to what it could be. The soldiers each manoeuvred the object over the tailgate and between them walked it in through the open iron gates and disappeared inside the Bursar's office which was located right at the front of the University.

Monica crossed the road and flattened herself against the University wall easing her way towards the gates. All the activity that she had witnessed previously was now centred on the building containing the Bursary. The sentries had moved to either side of its front entrance. Monica noticed that although their bodies were erect and still, their eyes were flitting quickly in 360 degrees. Her knowledge of the University quadrangle gave her an advantage over those searching eyes and she was soon safely at the window that looked into the Bursar's office. What she saw was to take her into a new world, most of which she failed to understand initially. The object that had been brought into the office had had its tarpaulin taken off to reveal a large crate. Reaching into it, the two soldiers pulled out an object that resembled like an oversized typewriter.

A year ago Monica was sitting in one of the classrooms of this University studying nursing. The workings of the human body certainly interested her and she was a keen student however she regretted that she had not been able to take up some other less stereotypical profession. Monica's Mother worked in Watt and Grant's department store which was renowned for being Aberdeen's most expensive store. While many would think that her Mother held some prestige because of her employer, she was only permitted to work on certain counters such as buttons and sewing implements. Anything beyond that she was directed to walk the customer over to a male attendant who would dismiss her and assume caring for the customer. Monica remembered her Mother telling her how she was spoken to severely when she was seen to be giving advice to a customer who had brought their fox stole in for repair. It was a service that set the store apart from the others and brought with it some prestige. Mrs Haldane had quite a bit of sewing experience having once worked in the Singer factory and made most of the family's clothes so felt that she had something to offer the concerned shopper. The customer was delighted when she was told that a little bit of what was called invisible mending would take care of the problem, especially when Mrs Haldane actually showed her where to do the sewing. Mr Bowman the floor walker had been at lunch when the customer had first entered the store so he was rather shocked to see a relationship well underway between the female customer and his underling. He was so incensed he picked up the stole as politely as he could and ushered the customer to his corner of the store. At the close of business Monica's Mother was chastised for not following company policy and referring customers to the male in charge. It cost her a shilling in wages, but created such a feeling of humiliation and anger, that she left the store's employ a week later.

Monica was determined not to find herself in a similar situation and be forced into taking on positions that were considered to be status quo for women. She would go where her skills went beyond calls for nurturing roles. The irony is that once the war got underway, women were evenutally seen as suitable for jobs previously considered as exclusively for males.

It was this societal behaviour that attracted Monica to human behaviour and she applied and was accepted into a new course at the university called Sociology. Unbeknown to many, the British Army had commissioned the University to offer such a course. There was little doubt in the minds of the Defence Forces Heirarchy that Christmas of 1938 would be the last peacetime Yuletide for a while. Only a few weeks prior Austria had experienced its first Christmas under German Rule, following the March invasion known as the Anschluss.

Those within the populations of Vienna and other cities who were Jewish began to suffer death, injury and imprisonment as the Third Reich started their annihilation of a demographic based on their faith. Jewish businesses were attacked and those that adhered to the Jewish faith were subjected to street violence. Hungary followed suit imposing harsh anti-Jewish laws and establishing two concentration camps. But it was knowledge of the depravity within those camps that eluded the rest of the world, including much of the German population. While maybe no one truly predicted the flashpoint to be reached in September 1939 there was no shortage of signs and indications that world peace was on shaky ground. An audit of the staff levels within Britain's Intelligence Corps revealed a glaring need for people trained to critically observe and understand activities underway in Europe and help provide a conduit of knowledge back to the decision makers in Whitehall.

As Monica watched, one of the soldiers who she could now see was a commissioned officer walked into the room where a younger man was studying the machine in front of him.

"Well Corporal, time is of the utmost importance here, I can't wait forever, what have you found out?"

"Sir, with all due respect to your ears, Enigma is fucked!" the soldier knew he was taking a risk using swear words in front of an officer, but the glee that showed on his face, also indicated that right then, he didn't care.

Monica could hear most of the conversation from her position at the window and her ears were alerted by the word Enigma. During her Sociology course, she had stumbled across documents in the University library that mentioned the existence of a cipher machine an earlier form of which had been developed in the First World War by the Germans. Now as the world seemed to be on an inevitable path and the Third Reich continued on their slow but determined march through Europe, Enigma became more technically refined and used widespread as a source of coded information.

Major Jack Archer dismissed the Corporal's choice of words as he himself was pleased and excited with the result. He and Corporal Macklin had just returned from Warsaw with a machine that was going to severely disadvantage Germany in the coming war. The Polish Ciber Bureau was set up in 1932 and for seven years secretly emulated the cryptograph which was the pride of the German Defence forces. The Poles had mastered the intelligence behind the device known as Enigma and had agreed to share it with the British and French government. Jack Archer had worked closely with Polish Intelligence for several years so he and his Corporal were seconded to Warsaw to gain an understanding of the machine and transport it to Bletchley Park Intelligence HQ. To avoid detection by Germany who were so far unaware that their cryptograph had been copied and was working against them, they travelled by cargo ship on a circuitous route from Warsaw to Aberdeen. It would then be taken to London on a truck owned by the National Fishcuring Company. The lorry made frequent trips between Aberdeen, Edinburgh and London so should arouse no interest.

"Kippers for the Kaiser, sir!" quipped Macklin.

"That's pretty clever young Macklin" responded the Major.

"Now put your flathead to work and get this thing working properly. We have to have it ready in two days. The Boffins at Bletchley are getting impatient."

Monica continued watching from her spot outside the window, as the corporal started to disconnect the wires and cords in readiness for packing the unit. The major left the room with instructions for Macklin to let him know when it was ready. When Archer moved away, it gave Monica a better view of the machine although the box she was standing on was barely taking her weight. She felt some excitement run through her as she realised the significance of what she was looking at. Through this machine, the governments of France and Britain had the opportunity to find out more about Germany's plans and intentions.

It was hard to know which gave her the biggest shock, the box finally collapsing beneath her and the subsequent thud of her rear end hitting the ground, or looking up at a uniformed Major Archer with a pistol in his hand.

"Don't move an inch" he commanded as he knocked on the window to alert the corporal to summon one of the sentries at the gate to come around and tie Monica's hands behind her back. Having winded herself when she fell off the box, Monica was in no shape to move so lay face down with only enough energy to try and spit out the earth and grass that had entered her mouth. She was also too frightened to move. She had never had a gun pointed at her before and in fact had never been this close to a weapon of death.

The soldier was none too gentle while tying her hands together as he placed his knee in the small of her back and tightly tied the rope around her wrists.

"Now get up slowly." said Archer. Monica lay still but not out of disobedience she wasn't able to swing her body into the right position to even try and be upright.

A kick to her legs jolted her and she became more entrenched in a state of fear. "Get up and stand against the wall." Archer yelled his command which made her flinch and she felt the beginning of tears welling up but fought them back as she didn't want to appear weak in front of the men. Finally she found enough breath.

"I'd be happy to stand up but I need some help to do it." she said trying hard not to let fear taint the sound of her reply.

Archer signalled to the corporal and the sentry to help her and they both grabbed her arms and pulled her upright and placed her against the wall. She noticed that Archer had replaced his pistol in his holster and was staring at her with his hands on his hips.

"I am not going to waste time with you girl so it is in your interest to answer my questions quickly and honestly, otherwise you will find yourself being put on that truck and taken away from here and I can promise you that no one will find you. Who are you and what are you doing here spying through the window?"

Monica had regained both her breath and her composure and now that the gun was no longer levelled at her, felt a little stronger with her confidence returning. "I think that it is you that should be telling me what you're doing here, I'm a student here so it's you that's trespassing."

Archer was silent for almost a full minute, then took enough paces towards her that brought him within a breath of her face. They were of similar height so it was a case of eye watching eye. Monica felt that she could see his soul through his brown eyes and she knew he was angry.

"I warned you," he said in what could be described as a loud whisper. "Answer my questions or so help me you will rue this moment. Who are you and why are you here?"

Archer put one hand on either side of her head and was so close that she felt the touch of his body against hers. But this was no act of love or lust, this was a threat of worse to come.

Monica's bravado started to waver a little although the thought of kneeing him in the crotch did cross her mind, but thought better of it.

"My name is Monica Haldane I live in Aberdeen and I am a sociology student at this University. I was out for my run when I saw you all arrive and I was curious."

Again Archer was silent all the while holding her stare and now she was starting to worry. It was as if she was in an embrace that was inspired as a friendly gesture but now was becoming inappropriately lingering. A smile or perhaps sneer was forming on Archer's lips and Monica began to suspect that he was enjoying this moment. Her knee twitched in anticipation of the message it expected from the brain to connect with his nether region.

Then as suddenly as it began it was all over.

"Untie her Corporal." said Archer as he stepped away from Monica. "Do you know what you saw in there?" he asked.

"It was either an Enigma or at the least a very good imitation of one. By the way your corporal was behaving I would say that it is working as required and telling you a little bit about what is happening in Europe, particularly on a military scale. And the fact that you are now packing it up, I would say you are about to freight it somewhere in the guise of cargo in the fish truck. What I don't understand is why it's here in Aberdeen."

Archer fell into one of his silences again and Monica swore she saw his left eyebrow raise in surprise. His lips formed a wide smile which indicated to her that he was pleased with what she had told him. She began to massage her wrists where they had been bound with their new found freedom her hands brushed the grass and dirt off her shorts and legs which were bearing the marks of her sudden fall.

"I am going to break a golden security rule here, but I want you to come for a walk with me, just around the University grounds."

"Why?" asked Monica. "I've just done a two mile run, I don't need the exercise right now, and anyway what would walking with you achieve for either of us?"

Archer smiled. He liked this fiery girl's attitude and courage especially under the circumstance of being confronted by a military presence in her home town at six in the morning.

"Well you would achieve a higher level of knowledge than you have now about what's going on and I may just benefit from some input from you, based on your apparent knowledge about what you saw in that room there. What do you think Enigma is?"

Archer started to move away from her, taking for granted the fact that she would agree to the walk.

"Well it's a cryptograph machine used mainly by the German government and it's believed that they use it to keep their expansion and military plans secret from the rest of the world. Britain and France have been trying to break the code for ages now with no success. Have you done it? How did you get hold of the machine."

Archer had gone through the University gates now and started the walk, confident that Monica would follow, and she did.

"How do you know all this?" he asked her when she had caught up with him. "My first assignment at Uni was to study how organised groups use their communication skills and how they relate to other groups that may be opposed to their philosophy. So we looked at encryption and I learnt that such a machine had been invented by the Germans during the First World War. I developed a bit of a passion for it and have been researching it ever since. But, I repeat, I had no idea we had one in this country so how did it end up here?"

Major Jack Archer was known as Mr Security around the Department of Intelligence based in Whitehall. He didn't have a lot of knowledge in cryptography, but he knew how to shield such matters from prying eyes and ears and minds. Although he had to admit to himself that this young student had somewhat slipped under his radar.

"Well as you rightly said, Britain and France have been struggling to counter the German ciphers and codes for years but it was the Poles who finally cracked it. They established a Cipher Bureau about seven years ago and one of their very clever people also took on the Soviets and broke their cryptography as well."

"That's all very well." said Monica "But you haven't told me how you got hold of that box of tricks in there, and why here in Granite City disguised as a box of fish.?"

Archer couldn't disguise another smirk. "You are probably aware that this year of 1939 is not going to be the most comfortable around Europe and there's been a lot of negotiating going on between Downing Street and Berlin. Now our Prime Minister tells us that he is confident that peace will prevail and all it needs is for Germany to maintain open communication and to stick to agreements. That's all very well for Whitehall but I'm afraid we military monkeys see it differently. It wouldn't surprise us if we are not slogging it out sometime soon."

"You mean another war?" asked Monica. The look on Archer's face needed no words to explain.

By this time the pair had crossed half the distance between the Bursary and the Assembly Hall, both privately felt a growing trust of one another, although Major Jack Archer had to remind himself that he was one of the heads of Intelligence in His Majesty's Service and that state secrets and familiarity did not generally mix well together.

"Suffice to say, that the Poles have decided to build up some protection for themselves following their stoush with the Soviets in 1921. They realised that they need to shore up protection measures with European allies, so that meant sharing Intelligence, hence that box of tricks, as you call it, is on its way to Bletchley Park who will be able to cut right into the heart of an over ambitious Germany if the situation worsens."

Monica's mind was spinning at hearing this. "God I want to be there."

"Think twice, then think again," warned Archer. "Things have gone fairly smoothly so far but we've got to get this toy to London yet and its possible that we there will be a challenge or two along the way."

"Such as?"

Archer stopped walking and turned to look at Monica. He had already decided to recruit this girl with her knowledge of human behaviour and a surprising knowledge of Enigma. However if he told her what she wanted to know, if she was going to join his team, her life would be in immediate danger the moment she crossed the line. He acknowledged to himself that it may already be too late, if his Intelligence was true, then what was going on at the Aberdeen University at dawn on a cold New Years Day, could well have been observed. She had a right to know.

"What we are doing today is a culmination of a fair bit of Intelligence effort between the UK Government, France and Poland. When the Poles took us into their confidence about Enigma, our boffins at Whitehall weren't happy about just accepting and liasing with the others without some type of investigation as to the merit of the idea."

Monica knew that she should head for home, her family would be awake now regretting the overindulgence of last night. However she was excited by what she was experiencing and could see a career opportunity ahead. "So how do you verify something like that?

"You go to the source." said Archer. "Germany?"

He indicated towards the Bursary where the corporal was packing the unit. "Young Macklin and I and an Intelligence Officer crossed over to Germany as representing the National Fishcuring Company looking for an expanded export market. What we were really doing was breaking into the Nazi's Cipher Branch. We wanted to get enough information to verify what the Poles were telling us. Fortunately the branch was in the same building as the department that purchase food and supplies for the defence forces. So we engaged in some selling of dried fish for the troops."

"But how did you get into the Cipher Branch?"

"As I said it was in the office next door so we managed to stay behind after our visit and wait until dark when all but the Chief Cypher had gone home. Then it was a case of knocking him out and smuggling him back on to our boat, then interrogating him on the way."

"Did he give you the information that you wanted?" asked Monica.

"In a fashion. He gave us enough to provide our Intelligence bods back here to sift through and work out the chaff from the seeds. We found enough to convince Bletchley Park to accept the Polish offer."

"But what happened to the German?"

Archer wondered just how much she could take and questioned the wisdom of telling her anyway. He decided to tell her.

"Well when we searched him before taking him on board, we missed a knife that he kept in his boot. When Higgins leant over him to question him more, that piece of German military steel made itself known to his chest."

Monica's hands went to her mouth in shock. "Higgins was your Intelligence Officer, what happened to him?" Archer just pointed his thumb downwards, and Monica bit her finger but felt nothing. "So where are they now?"

"We brought Higgins' body home and I didn't hear anymore. That's what happens in this department. And the German helped to feed the fish stocks of the English Channel."

Monica felt that she had never stood so still for so long.

Archer continued. "It wasn't a wasted trip. Although we have no names, we did discover through some persuasion that there is a Nazi cell working in the UK somewhere, gathering intelligence for Berlin. Mr Hitler is making all sorts of promises about his European intentions but we have our doubts that this year will end peaceably."

"You don't think that he will really invade us? It's a ridiculous idea." said Monica.

"Talk to the Czechs about that, ask Austria how it felt although Hitler would argue that Czechoslovakia was conceded to Germany to embrace and unite all German speaking people. And it was a powerful way to test the rest of Europe's reaction to his expansion plans. Austria, he would argue was going to happen anyway following a failed attempt in the First World War."

Monica shook her head "Oh come on. Can you really see German troops marching up and down Princes Street or the German flag draped over Buckingham Palace?"

"What I am telling you, is that there are one or two people currently laying some groundwork to help achieve just that and we believe that at least one of them is in a pretty powerful position in this town."

THIRTEEN

That first day of January 1939, Monica Haldane was recruited by Major Jack Archer and thus began a close professional relationship which weathered the storm of a major war that erupted several months later. Monica managed to adhere to a study plan enough to get through three years of University, gaining her degree. However she was never able to take up any meaningful employment in her field because of the amount of missions she was seconded to, working alongside Archer in espionage and Intelligence work

In 1945, Major Jack Archer became just Jack Archer, whom the military recruited from time to time for work that required some expert security knowledge, a lot of which was carried out under the radar of most governments.

Monica was often a willing participant in some of Jack's post war missions. As much as she was glad that unexploded bombs, acting as an liaison agent with the Resistance and some femme fatale espionage were all over, peacetime created a void in her life. So when he called, she seldom said no. It was such a call that found her assisting the snatch and grab of Alenti from Tyneside.

Feargal had stepped out of the vehicle to help Monica with the now comatose sergeant. "So boss, to be sure we have another problem here, What would we be doin' with his nibs here?"

Jack had already worked that out and turned the vehicle around and drove towards Alenti's cabin.

"Fear not Emerald Eyes, we will tuck him into bed in the Pole's cabin and he can sleep it off. By the time he has woken up, we will have delivered the other one, and our job will have been done."

Craig, who was starting to suffer cramps having lain so still for so long under the stretcher next to Alenti, realised that this could be a chance to escape. In fact as he thought about it he also realised that they would be sliding the stretcher out and carrying the soldier into the cabin on it. This would reveal him. He looked across at Alenti who was still out to it and decided to slide across under the Pole's stretcher, but he only had a few seconds to do it as the brake was pulling up outside the cabin. Jack had left the driver's seat to go and open the cabin door while Monica and Feargal slid the Scottish sergeant's stretcher out and carried it into the cabin.

Craig now had to decide whether to risk staying in the vehicle and finding out where they were taking Alenti, or get out now. Again he only had seconds to decide and act. Leaving now would make detection less likely so after checking where Jack and his team were looking, he painfully got out from under the stretcher and slid out of the brake, heading for the bushes that surrounded the perimeter of the grounds. Once hidden, Craig watched as the trio returned the stretcher to the brake and started again on their journey.

They made it through the front gate with no trouble from the other sentries.

"We've left Jock in the Pole's cabin." Jack told the soldiers. "He wanted to do some searching in the man's stuff."

The sentry waved them through. Craig watched them turn right out of Tynecastle. He knew they were headed to the infirmary building where the Red Cross had a special clinic so he wondered if his Father would be there. Anyway he had learnt enough for one day so decided to head for home and think out the next day's plan.

Craig walked back down Princes Street. Many of the shops, including C&A and Jenners were closed but lights were on to allow staff to prepare for the opening sale at ten in the morning the next day. This had been an exceptional day for him. It had begun with him tailing his Father across Edinburgh to finding the man who had traumatised him on Easter Road a few years earlier. Then he heard about the possibility that the Pole was involved in re- creating Nazi Germany in Poland. Craig actually wondered if Alenti was really aware of that fact or was he being used as some foil or dumb waiter. Also he wondered what the enticement was that Jack had spoken about. What would be strong enough to warrant the encouragement of a return to terror, especially in Poland? There was much for him to occupy his mind and too many mysteries to avoid exploring.

Daylight was dimming when he turned into Easter Road and he felt the early sting of the wind that was coming in from down in the harbour. There was a slight bend in the road which the early architects had followed strictly. Craig wondered if in some way it was their way of placing the three to four storey tenement buildings so as to provide a type of abstract tunnel for the wind to follow thus cutting down on the icy blast that was so prevalent particularly in winter.

Although his relationship with his Father at number 356 had had its share of challenges, he always felt a touch of comfort each time he turned this corner. It was his first home and as such formed a part of his core. As time would tell, Craig was lured by the spirit of exile that called so many Scots to travel the world and flourish where they became planted. He didn't know it yet but Australia would be that place of flourish and he wouldn't return to number 356 for 50 years.

One of the last remaining operating street gas lamps was close to the front door of 356 and as Craig moved further down the street, he recalled how as a boy he would look forward to the lamplighter's visit. There was something magical about this figure that would appear about dusk each night with a long pole or stick in his hand. When the stick touched the lamp some two metres above, light would erupt then cascade gently downwards as it gained energy until finally settling at the ideal brightness for the night. He remembered being a little apprehensive of the lamplighter and would never want to be outside when he arrived. The men were called Leerie and as time wore on, they were required less and less because timers were attached to the lamps. Leerie was only required then for maintenance. Their occupational demise was imminent and Craig hoped that the lamp posts themselves would be retained.

As he crossed the road he remembered a poem by Robert Louis Stevenson that his Mum would read him to try and calm his fears about the mysterious Leerie.

My tea is nearly ready and the sun has left the sky.

It's time to take the window to see Leerie going by;

For every night at teatime and before you take your seat,

With lantern and with ladder he comes posting up the street.

Now Tom would be a driver and Maria go to sea,

And my papa's a banker and as rich as he can be;

But I, when I am stronger and can choose what I'm to do,

O Leerie, I'll go round at night and light the lamps with you!

For we are very lucky, with a lamp before the door,

And Leerie stops to light it as he lights so many more;

And oh! before you hurry by with ladder and with

light; O Leerie, see a little child and nod to him to-night!

FOURTEEN

Craig was six or seven doors away from his home when he noticed a black Wolseley pull up outside number 356. The driver didn't get out but a minute or so later, he saw his Father emerge from their front door in his Red Cross Uniform and satchel. Bill got into the car which did a U turn on Easter Road and drove away. Craig hadn't seen his Father since earlier this morning when he saw him leave a note for Alenti in his cabin at Tynecastle.

Janet Erskine was sitting by the fire in the lounge listening to the BBC Radio and the latest episode of The Archers which the Light Programme repeated on a Sunday afternoon. This was the only time she actually sat down for an hour or so and indulged in a radio programme apart from Saturday football.

She looked up as Craig entered and watched as he took up the almost traditional position of backsides to the fire. Janet smiled as she wondered if this was an instinctive act from the male of the species as she had never seen women do the same. Janet seemed to spend more time tending the fire and maintaining the heat rather actually standing in front it, lazily enjoying the warm sensation. Craig had been much more help when he was a schoolboy than now when he was a University student. Bill seemed to be busier than ever being a Red Cross Commandant in Post War Scotland.

During the war itself, it seemed that he was involved in more Edinburgh based activities which meant he was at home often and was able to help with the domestic chores of everyday life. Now she had noticed an increasing number of calls for him to attend this or that crisis which often involved overnight stays. It wasn't rare for him to be called to London or even Paris for meetings or dealing with returned defence personnel from the Allied forces having difficulty settling back into a world of relative peace. He had even made a couple of trips to Berlin which concerned her as she had no idea how safe a place Germany now was. Janet had given up asking too many questions of Bill, it was as if he was still working under confidentiality agreements that surrounded his work during the war and it became difficult for her to find any satisfactory answers. So she had adopted the attitude that as long as her menfolk were safe, she would do what she could to support them. While she had an accepted place as chief of the kitchen Craig and his Father were doing less and less of the other domestic tasks. Her biggest regret over this was that it meant her personal time such as listening to the football on the wireless on a Saturday was becoming increasingly threatened and she had long given up hope that she could attend a game by her beloved Hibernian.

"Oh you're back then?" she said

Craig wondered if it was a Scottish trait that made some of them state the obvious. He just smiled not wanting to really tell her where he had been.

"Where's Dad gone?"

"He got a call while we were having a cuppa then he said that he would be picked up in about 10 minutes. Someone needed him at the Red Cross clinic at the Infirmary."

"Would that someone be Alenti?" asked Craig.

Janet's facial expression warned him that it may be wise not to get on to that subject. Her curt response was "That episode is over as far as this household is concerned.

I have no idea where that man is nor do I want to. I am also sure that your Father feels the same way, so no more please."

Given what he had gone through that day at Tyneside Craig was in no mood to leave the subject, there is so much unfinished business there, but with respect to his Mother, he would try and not mention it again to her.

He walked over to the window, remembering the number of times he had done that before as a young boy. Now, many years later, he was still looking down on Easter Road waiting for his Father.

FIFTEEN

Alenti awoke in the stretcher as it was being taken inside the Clinic at the Edinburgh Infirmary. His groggy eyes stared at the blue Midlothian sky waiting for his mind to tell him what had happened, where he was and why this was happening. From where he lay he couldn't see who was carrying the stretcher.

The sky scenes were now replaced by those of an austere high ceiling with a gas lamp suspended each 25 yards or so. None of those were capable of working anymore. They were just waiting to be removed leaving the task of illuminating Edinburgh's prime medical establishment to the new electricity that was making huge inroads into Scotland's way of life. The smell of antiseptic wafted in the air and his ears picked up the clanging sound of metal dishes and the type of serious murmuring amongst human beings that can only come from a place where their lives and deaths are intertwined.

Jack Archer strode down the hospital corridor ahead of Feargal and Monica who were carrying the stretcher. Jack turned right at the end and the colour of the walls changed to the green that is often seen in places where the serious parts of life are carried out such as Polish Hospitals. Alenti recognised it as the colour in the hospital where his Father had died in Warsaw, and remembering the stark cold surgical slab where he identified his parent. This thought caused him to tremble as he contemplated his own fate. Monica noticed the movement under the blanket but kept her stare focused on the back of Feargal's head as they manouvered around the corner in pursuit of Jack. At the end of the seemingly never ending passage way, Jack opened the door to a room which was used partly as a storage place for the hospital's iron lungs and partly as an office /clinic for the Red Cross to interview and process refugees and returned defence force members. As the stretcher was being carried through the door, Alenti sat up. The last time he had seen Jack, it was via the man's fist and as for Monica he remembered her face disappearing in a haze as she injected a sedative of sorts into his arm.

Feargal held out his arm to support Alenti as he struggled up from the stretcher which had been laid on the floor. Alenti quickly moved away from the Irishman once he was up although still wasn't steady on his feet.

"Zostaw mnie w spokoju, nie dotykaj mnie, gdzie jestem, czego chcesz ode mni."

"I have no idea what he's sayin' Jack but I can tell he's not pleased, to be sure."

Jack was the only one in the room that could understand what Alenti was saying. The last conversation they had in Polish was in Warsaw in 1939 when he bumped into Alenti who was trying to escape from a couple of German soldiers out to do mischief.

"Feargal, in a word he has just told you to fuck off. He does speak reasonable English so I suggest we just try and settle him down. He is obviously concerned at where he is and what's going to happen to him. What I know is that two Red Cross officers want to see him to ensure he is in good health. What I don't know is whether he is staying in Britain or shipping back to

Poland. Things are on a need to know basis and apparently I don't need to know."

Alenti was fully alert now. "Don't talk about me as if I wasn't here. Tell me why I am here and why did you kidnap me. Who ordered you to take me?" His lip had started to bleed just where Jack had hit him. "And why did you hit me?"

"Alenti, if I hadn't have done that, we couldn't have claimed that you had been beaten up by somebody else and we would not have been able to get you out of there."

"But why did you want me out of the camp?" Jack looked at Monica and Feargal. He contemplated how much to tell Alenti and wondered just how much he really knew about this.

"You must realise that you can't be politically active in a post war world without attracting attention. You have been spouting a lot since the war ended. Now is the time that most people want to forget about what happened during the war and you keep reminding them when all they want is to get on with peace."

Alenti frowned. "You talk about peace in a post war world. My country hasn't known real peace for a long time and any hope for such an outcome went 'poof'" He gesticulated to add punch to his words.

"As soon as Germany was dealt with and there was a little piece of hope that Poland would be restored, you and the Yanks and everyone else that felt badly done by, made decisions about what would happen to our country. Who actually gave you the right to do that? Hitler invaded us with tanks and weapons, you came in the name of Peace and split us up to suit yourselves, not the people of Poland." Alenti turned to look out of the window onto the corridor outside. As he stared into the empty space, a moth flew into the glass in front of his face and banged into it several times. "Poland is like this moth here." he pointed. "It has been attracted by the hope of the light that is shone on it, it is shown a glorious prospect ahead, but there is a glass wall that will not let the moth's dream be realised or its destination reached. Yet the light of hope still beckons while he bangs his head in failed attempt after attempt until he can't fly his wings anymore. Then he either sticks to the glass by his draining body fluids and lifeblood or falls to the floor to be collected by the dustmen. You, Jack and your American friends and those that you pretend to worry about in Russia turn from holding a torch to holding a brush and dust bucket when resistance has gone."

Jack seriously wondered if he would have to get Monica to charge up her syringe again. Alenti's passion could get out of hand.

"Alenti, America for a start wouldn't let Poland dry up like that moth. Its torch or beacon of hope has been a fairly genuine gesture of good will for many years and..."

"That is rubbish!" exclaimed Alenti, stamping his feet to make his point.

"You know, as a Pole, I have nothing to thank Germany for. I sure not enjoy the horror that Adolph Hitler brought upon us through his plans to swallow up Europe, but you know what Jack… when I sit down and think through what I did for you and the yanks. How I risked my life in a so called Allied cause and then at the end when I asked for help to re- settle, you turned your backs on us. Our Air Force practically won the air war for you. As much as you boast about the Battle of Britain and those fucking Spitfires you wave about like some triumphant warring symbol of a peace bringer, who was it that flew them? I'll tell you Jack, Polish pilots. Anyway my point is that even though Hitler is rightly condemned as a war criminal on a grand scale, I am thinking that his plan may well have worked if it had been given a proper chance."

Alarm bells went off in Jack's head, was the idea of a new world order still alive? "Alenti Alenti, calm down please. Listen to what you're saying man. You are glorifying the man who almost wiped out the Jews and built incinerators to do it. He wanted total tyranny, for Christ's sake at any cost."

"He didn't want to annihilate the Jews just to wipe them out!" shouted Alenti.

"He saw their capitalistic ways as a threat to Europe, he saw America being driven by sheer greed and capitalism, and in the driver's seat were those who adhered to the Jewish faith. He wanted to extend German borders to make his Europe as big or even bigger than the USA, so as he could resist the greed from the Western World creeping into this side of the world. He had to think big to act big. You all think he was focussed on Britain and Poland and France, his real fear and hatred was reserved for Capitalism and what the USA represented."

During Alenti's tirade, Monica and Feargal gradually moved towards Jack. Whether it was a conscious movement or a sub conscious feeling of threat or danger, not even they would be able to tell. But there was a sense of a need to form a group opposition to what they were hearing. The three of them from Feargal in his fox hole to Monica and Jack through their Enigma exploits had literally put their lives on the line to resist the abhorrent practices of the Nazi invaders. Yet here was someone they had also put themselves at risk to rescue, daring to sing praises of Adolph Hitler and the plans of the Third Reich. A very uneasy atmosphere had developed in that room. It was almost like the proverbial Mexican Standoff.

The lone antagonist standing alone in front of a line of three and silence fell between them.

Then the uneasy peace was shattered by the forceful opening of the office door and the entrance of three men, two of whom were dressed in British Red Cross uniforms and the third in a plain black suit and Trilby style hat. Jack immediately noticed Alenti's face light up at their presence and when one of the Red Cross Officers moved towards him to shake his hand, Alenti turned the greeting into a firm embrace.

"Oh Bill, Bill it is so good to see you my friend."

Monica asked Jack how Alenti was so friendly with the man and Jack briefly explained the relationship between Bill Erskine and the fact that he was the Father of the boy who was involved in a fracas in Leith that led to Alenti being locked up at Waverley then taken to Tynecastle Stadium.

"And it's great to see you again my friend. I am sorry that you have that injury on your face, I will ask Brian here to give it a once over with some soothing stuff from his magic case."

The other officer smiled and nodded and patted the case that he had brought in with him. Alenti's mood had considerably lifted since meeting up with Bill . It helped him feel more secure but still didn't understand why he had been forcibly transported here. Jack and the other two were still standing together and Jack was feeling that it was developing into a 'them and us' situation. He had no idea what it was but was aware that there was much not being said, and he was unsure of what was expected of him now in regards to the Pole. The brief that he had received from the Home Office was to extricate Alenti from the camp and take him to this clinic at the Edinburgh Infirmary for examination by the Red Cross. As his suspicions grew, Jack was wondering if he should ask for some ID from the three men that had arrived. He also wondered about the plain clothes man and what his role was. There were definite signs that this was a security issue of some sort, but he couldn't understand if it was Alenti who was considered a security risk and whether he was being protected or guarded.

The discussion that they had held previously worried Jack a little. It was strange to hear someone of Alenti's background speaking in favourable terms about Germany which had invaded his country and captured his family and the veiled respect he seemed to hold for Adolph Hitler. Could anyone in Poland seriously consider a re-emergence of Nazi politics? As Jack had told his colleagues earlier, his brief had suggested that Alenti was being courted and eventually some offer would be made that would be hard for the man to resist. Thoughts of 'pieces of silver' came to Jack's mind but there simply wasn't enough evidence yet that such a deal would be made. Anyway, he thought, is it really his concern? The details of what to do following the arrival at the hospital were a little vague so he wondered if he should refer to the department for more information.

Bill Erskine approached Jack and his team. "We will take him into that office and give him a medical examination and talk to him about any concerns he may have." It wasn't a request, it sounded more like a statement of fact with no permission required from Jack This convinced Jack to call the Home Office.

"Sure thing Commandant." said Jack although feeling uneasy using that rank title.

The Red Cross was certainly not a military organisation so there is no reason to expect them to follow the tradition of Captain, Field Marshal or General but he thought that the use of Commandant was questionable. It was all he could do to stop himself clicking his heels as he said the word. Alenti seemed quite eager to accompany the men into the office so Jack felt he had no reason to stop that going ahead. Anyway it gave him some space and time to make his phone call.

SIXTEEN

The phone line into the office was connected to the Infirmary's switchboard, so he had to ask the operator to link him to the Home Office. Once that happened he had to ask for Major Sanderson and because the Major was not in his office, Jack had to play a waiting game while they searched for him. As he waited he watched the activity in the office where Alenti was being examined. The look on the Pole's face showed an eagerness to cooperate and willingly undress so as medical checks could take place. It wasn't surprising that Alenti felt that way, he had formed quite a bond with Erskine through the drama over his son, and of course he had worked under fire with him during the war when they were part of the mission to retrieve the photographer from the D-Day beaches in Normandy. Jack easily understood Alenti's feelings having met up again with Erskine, especially after the last 48 hours during which he had been taken from the streets of Edinburgh, refused a visa to stay, imprisoned at Waverley Station and then Tynecastle Stadium camp. In addition he had been hit across the face by Jack, sedated by Monica and transported to this offshoot office of the Edinburgh Infirmary.

The man's mind must be in turmoil so the arrival of a friendly face would have been most welcome. Jack's thoughts were interrupted by a voice on the other end of the telephone.

"Sanderson!" There was no gentile quality to the voice as if the Major was incredibly annoyed at being disturbed.

"Major, hello. It's Archer here. I'm wondering if…"

"Who?" Jack's opening line was interrupted by an increasingly impatient Major. "Jack Archer, you recruited me to extricate a person of interest from Tynecastle to meet up with the Red Cross at the Infirmary."

"Yes." Was the perfunctory response from the Major. As nothing else came forth, Jack continued.

"I am at the Infirmary now and the Pole is being medically examined by the Red Cross and it hasn't been made clear to me as to what our role is now. Do we hang around, do we pass him over to the Red Cross, do we take him back to Tynecastle?"

The silence from the other end prompted Jack to say "Major, are you there?"

"Of course I am bloody well here. What were you told to do?"

Jack tried hard to keep impatience out of the tone of his reply, because he knew it best not to anger Sanderson's type of personality. "No, you told me that all I had to do was deliver him to the Infirmary but I am not clear whether I just walk away from him now or should I stay and keep an eye on him."

"Who is with him now?"

"Erskine from the Red Cross, one of his colleagues and another guy who says nothing and I know nothing about."

"Is he tall, slightly paunchy, beady little eyes close together?" Jack did a quick rethink.

"Yes that's a close description." Silence came again from the Major, then "He is one of ours name of Duthie. Officially he is a secretary of the Red Cross. Try not to get too familiar with him, keep it all low key, the last thing I want is an international incident particularly concerning the Poles."

When Jack looked up he saw that Alenti was dressed again and sitting opposite the two Red Cross officers. The third man whom he now knew was an agent of the Home Office named Duthie had actually come out of the office and was standing nonchalantly with hands in his pockets talking with Monica and Feargal.

"So what do you want me to do when they are finished with him?" Jack asked Sanderson.

"I want to know as much as you can find out about the conversation the Pole had with the Red Cross. And Archer."

"Yes Major?"

"Don't let that Polish squib out of your sight. It would not go well for you and your two musketeers."

The phone was replaced at the Major's end and Jack felt that it would have happened abruptly and noisily. He glanced toward the office and noticed a discussion between Alenti and the two officers was in progress. Suddenly Alenti leapt from his chair. With eyes and mouth wide open his shout could be heard from the main office.

Jack, Feargal and Monica all stopped and stared at the window of the office. Even Duthie the man in the black suit and hat whom Jack now knew was from the Department had turned around at the sound of Alenti's exclamation.

"What's going on Jack?" asked Monica.

"Shouldn't you go and check?" Jack was still having an internal debate as to what his responsibilities were in regard to Alenti.

"No. Not yet anyway. Let's give it a little longer and see what transpires."

By this time Alenti had resumed his seat and was wiping tears from his eyes. The Red Cross men seemed to be trying to calm him down. There was much gesticulating from them, but a seemingly stunned silence from Alenti. It looked as though he was concentrating on every word that came out of Erskine's mouth and now and then the Pole's hands would move as he asked a question, then rested back on the desk when he had an answer. At this point, the man from the Department went in to the smaller office and shut the door behind him.

Jack was wishing he had done the same but felt that he would have been asked to leave. He recalled and wondered again at the major's concerns over causing an international incident.

He and the other two stood and watched as the third man entered into the discussion which seemed to be mainly between him and Alenti. The Red Cross men were not actively involved in the discussion anymore.

After five minutes or so, Duthie stood up and left the office, lit up a cigarette and walked across the room to stand looking out onto the corridor. Jack was annoyed that he hadn't spoken to him, he felt justified in wanting to know what was going on. He walked over to him.

"What is going on there? Why all the excitement?"

Duthie looked at Jack and inhaled strongly on his cigarette so that when he gave his reply, it would emanate under a cloud of stale tobacco.

"Whatever is going on in there is none of your business. Everything's ok. Your Polish friend is safe and happy and the Red Cross say he is in good physical condition."

"But what about his mental state? Why did we hear him shout out?"

"Did he?" responded Duthie.

"Wasn't aware of that." and he resumed smoking.

"Bullshit Duthie!" exclaimed Jack. "You heard him just like the rest of us I saw you turn around." Duthie showed some surprise at learning Jack knew his name.

"How did you know my name. I didn't tell you."

"You sure didn't." said Jack. "You didn't have the common decency to introduce yourself when you came in, so I rang the Major and he didn't hesitate to tell me." Jack also recalled Sanderson telling him not to intimidate Duthie, so he stepped back a little allowing some of the tension dissipate.

"Listen to me and listen carefully."said Duthie with his index finger pointing at Jack. "You need to know nothing about this. In fact it's better you don't have knowledge that could get you into a lot of fucking trouble. If it's true that you spoke to Sanderson then you'll know that this could explode any minute and it wont just be your wee corner of the world that will be affected. The file on this job has been stamped I.C. meaning International Concern. And the only other thing I will tell you is that there is an attempt right now to stop it developing into another conflict. So back off and get back to your adventure soldiering."

By the time he had finished speaking, Duthie's cigarette was little more than a red spark on a butt. He looked at it then put it to his lips and dragged the last possible inhalation out of what was left of the tobacco. He then let the smoke out again in Jack's direction and dropped the butt on the floor and stood on it.

Jack tried not to flinch when the smoke reached him, but it was impossible not to cough. He briefly wondered how he ever was a ten Capstan a day man, but it was during the war so maybe that was an excuse. He feared no likelihood of him returning to the habit.

No response was necessary to Duthie who had walked away from him anyway, but Jack's mind was so full of questions. What was making this a potential International Incident?

What danger was there in returning to years of conflict? Was Duthie telling the truth or or exaggerating it to frighten Jack and his team off ? How connected was Alenti to a resurgence attempt by the Nazis? The other thing to wonder about is how much does Alenti know. By the look of his excitement earlier, he does know something and it is pleasing him.

Monica drew near to Jack "Watch him boss, he looks dangerous to me. Hey can I go for a pee and if so, where is the pee palace?"

Jack opened the main door and pointed to a set of stairs to the right. "Up the stairs we came down when we brought Alenti in, back near reception and I think it's second on the left. You know how to tell the Gents from the Ladies?"

Monica replied "If Gentlemen and Ladies are the criteria for entry then both you and I are leaving with full bladders."

SEVENTEEN

Craig Erskine remembered hearing while hiding in the Brake that they were taking Alenti to the Infirmary and that the Red Cross would be involved. So he decided that he would make his way there but had no idea what he would do when he arrived. He hoped it would settle his curiosity a little and make contact with his Father. He had only enough money for a one way bus fare so he would have to walk back. It was just over five miles but he didn't want to ask his Mother for a loan because she would only quiz him on where he was going and try to discourage him.

He took the number 16 bus which travelled via the Leith docks. The fine weather had brought families out and the exhausted children, faces dusted with sand, tried desperately to stay awake after a day at the beach Craig recalled that childhood resistance of drooping eyelids that threatened to wipe out that day of fun and the fear of missing out on something wonderful. At one end of the bus a few children had succumbed to the Sandman then being woken by a sudden jerk of the bus then they became intent on telling the world about their feelings in high loud voices. He was amazed how the angelic look of a sleeping child suddenly transformed into Les Enfants Terrible, it was an instant change. Memories of Portobello Beach and trips to North Berwick Rock where he was given his first pair of sunglasses. He remembered that his Father had a heated discussion with Mr. McIntyre, the chemist, who felt that Craig was too young to have sunglasses. There was some belief that the young boy's eyesight would be damaged. Craig remembered being proud of his father for persisting with his right to have them. When the chemist noticed Bill Erskine taking an interest in a camera as well he relented over the sunglasses in the belief that he would make an add on sale. He was right, Craig's father bought sunglasses, the camera and two rolls of film and presented them to the lad in the hope that it would make his holiday happier. Now, many years later, Craig mused on the fact that he thought of his father then as being a hero and courageous for standing up to the chemist. He still had the Kodak 127 and recalled the event each time he looked at it. What a contrast to now when he was having such negative thoughts about Bill.

That thought brought him back to awareness of the present. The hospital could be seen now just behind Duddington Golf Course. The next stop would be at Craigmillar Castle renowned for the Craigmillar Bond that sealed the fate of Lord Darnley, husband to Mary Queen of Scots.

Everywhere he looked, Craig saw evidence of a very rich history but history which saw political games played for high stakes and almost no matter where you looked it was borders and faiths that were the root cause of conflict. Clan and tribal borders, National Borders the cause of so many deaths in both England and Scotland. Craig mused that mankind doesn't seem to learn. It was as if each generation had to have its war to define itself for the years following as though it was a rite of passage.

The bus arrived at the hospital stop just as a late afternoon shower created a rainbow at sunset but there would be daylight for a few hours yet. Craig got off then waited for the bus to pass and he stood looking at the Royal Edinburgh Infirmary. Once it was the largest hospital in what was then the Empire and physicians of the ilk of Joseph Lister who pioneered antiseptics was Professor of Surgery. Facts like these were recalled by Craig as he looked at each historic building. The Scottish History that he undertook at the Academy had served him well and he was proud of being able to recite salient facts.

As he entered the grounds, he saw the car park just off to his right. There were few cars in it as evening visiting hours wouldn't start for another two hours. One car in particular interested him. It was a Wolseley, he had wanted one of those ever since his aunt had given him a ride when he was very young. Another reason for his interest was that he was sure it was the black car that had picked his Father up earlier. That pleased him a lot because he was looking forward to having an overdue discussion with him and it also meant he could get a ride home again.

He also thought that it could give him a way into the hospital by asking for his Father at reception. That way he would also be able to see what happened to Alenti.

"Sir, you do know that visiting hours don't start for another hour?" A cultured Midlothian accent stopped him in his tracks before he could even get to the front desk.

The owner of the accent seemed to take her job very seriously and held Craig's gaze as he approached her. Craig had noticed this trend in institutions such as the hospitals and his own university. Front line staff on welcoming desks were always a little short in injecting warmth into their greetings. It certainly put it back on the visitor to come up with strong reasons for being there.

"It's ok I'm not here to see a patient. I want to see Bill Erskine, the Red Cross Commandant. He is here with a refugee who is being checked over."

"You can't expect me to confirm that fact, young man. What is it you want with him?"

Craig noticed her name badge but looked away quickly so as not to give the impression he was ogling her bust. It was one of the biggest ID badges he had ever seen no doubt to accommodate the length of her name and he thought it unusual to contain an honorariam.

"Mrs. Farnon-Glendinning I am actually Bill's son and it's important that I see him as soon as possible."

"This is no place for parental meetings I am afraid. Commandant Erskine will be about his business and I suggest that you wait for him at home, this is a hospital you know?"

Craig could feel a little tension rising and he was mainly disappointed that this woman had taken it upon herself to interrogate him in this manner and suggest that it wasn't appropriate for him to see his Father.

As he stood there contemplating his next move, he noticed a woman coming up the stairs off to his left and looking closely at the doors on her left. He recognised Monica immediately and he headed towards her direction with the intention of following her. That haughty version of the Midlothian accent followed him.

"Excuse me my good man, you are not allowed to wander around these corridors and if you don't leave immediately I will call the janitor."

Craig smiled as he wondered what danger a janitor armed with mop and bucket would present. He felt he could take the risk so he continued to the stairs. As he proceeded down the corridor he noticed the door on his right with the design of a female in a hat and smoking a cigarette in an elegant holder, close with a loud bang. He walked slowly toward the stair and started to read notices on a board in between the male and female toilets.

Eventually, Monica came out of the toilets and headed back down the stairs, this time with Craig following. He made his steps firm and confident looking even if it meant he would overtake her in the corridor. In fact he had drawn alongside her and was about to pass when she almost bumped into him when she approached the door of the Red Cross Clinic. They exchanged a polite smile and Monica closed the door behind her. Craig walked on down the corridor and fortunately the office next door was unlocked and he went in.

EIGHTEEN

As Monica entered the room, she became aware of a different atmosphere. There were tense looks on both Jack and Feargal. Alenti was still in the other office but this time he seemed to be talking to Duthie. Bill Erskine and his colleague were out of the office talking in hushed tones.

Monica asked Jack what was going on as she felt that the dynamics had changed. "Duthie there just took a call from Sanderson in Whitehall and after that he went in and told the Red Cross guys to get out. He is now having a heavy chat with Alenti."

"Do you know what the call was about?" asked Monica.

"No, but it didn't please the fat man" said Jack. "Listen, would you and Feargal stroll over and have a casual chat with the Red Cross boys? Use your subtle persuasive ways to find out some of what they talked to the Pole about in there, but make it subtle and not like you're investigating anything. I'm going to have a chat with Sanderson. He has just got to tell me more about what's going on. I have an uneasy feeling."

Once Monica and Feargal had made it across the room and started to engage Bill Erskine and his colleague in conversation, Jack lifted the phone and asked to be connected to London. Surprisingly the Major answered quickly and sounded as though he had been expecting Jack's call.

"Now Major," said Jack in an aggressive tone, "My loyalty to you and my obedience to you is as long as the noughts on the cheque you're going to put in my bank account once I've finished this job. I'm your gun for hire and you only use me when its convenient to you. There's nothing to stop me just walking out of here and you'll never see me again. So stop your fucking around and tell me what was the burr you put in Duthie's knickers a while ago and why is he in there haranguing the Pole?"

Jack worried for a second or two that his heavy approach may backfire on him and that the cheque that the Department would put in his bank account could have a couple less noughts on it. But it seemed to have worked.

"Ah Archer" said the Major. "I was just thinking of ringing you. There has been something of a development and you probably should know about it."

Too darned right I should know about it, thought Jack, but thought better of interrupting Sanderson.

"We got a call from the OIC of the Midlothian Signals who are providing guard duty at Tynecastle. One of their sergeants seems to be suffering some ill health due to a syringe full of your magic juice, and wondering what the hell hit him. He will be nursing a sore head for a while but he managed to tell us that he found evidence that the Pole has received contact with the Morningside Group."

Jack had heard of them but couldn't quite recall their reason for existence. "Who or what is the Morningside Group?"

"It's the name of an office in Falcon Avenue Morningside which includes a solicitor, a land valuer and conveyancer and an insurance agent. We are of the belief that this group is a movement dedicated to the rebuilding of the Nazi Party."

Jack was stunned at this possibility. Perhaps the free world became too quick to assume that Nazism had died out along with Hitler and the very public demise of the party. He asked the major why this was happening in Edinburgh and why Scotland.

"Our intelligence picked up a signal back in the last year of the war, that a group of three Germans found their way over here courtesy of a boat leaving Normandy. All we had to follow it up here was the Home Guard and a platoon was waiting for them at Dover when the boat arrived. It actually crashed into the harbour wall and everyone was anxiously trying to get the crew off before it fell apart. Unfortunately those guys had the best of intent but concentrated too much on being social that they failed to notice that the three Germans had left the boat before it docked."

Jack was curious. "They swam ashore?"

"No, they had taken the dinghy life raft before the boat docked and sailed away back out to sea. They had knocked out the captain and locked the crew up."

"Did the captain expect to be bringing three enemy soldiers back with him?" asked Jack.

"He was expecting three people but was told they were operatives returning here and to say nothing."

"So how did they get to Edinburgh?"

"They had some help. They were given some intelligence including maps and directions and they headed north along the west coast of England heading for the Island of Inchgarvie in the shadow of the Forth Railway Bridge."

Jack was puzzled. "But wasn't that place occupied during the war by the Royal Artillery and an anti aircraft unit?"

"Such was their cunning." said the Major. "You've heard of the expression in plain sight, well there was only four of our chaps stationed there towards the end of the war, because the threat had diminished with Germany falling apart, so these Krauts managed to perch themselves in the ruins of the monastery."

The major went on to say that the Germans must have had enormous help from someone on the mainland because when the place was searched later, they found enormous quantities of army ration food packages.

"Hold on," interrupted Jack. "So you knew they were there?"

"No, we only found out later when the artillery were doing a final tidy up sweep of the island before heading back to the mainland. Then with what we learnt from the captain of the boat that crashed in Dover, Intelligence has deduced that they had planned this visit along with some local help. Three men were sighted in Edinburgh shortly afterwards and only attracted attention because everyone was nervous straight after the war and wary of strangers. They had passed themselves off as Dutch, looking for work on the bridge. They weren't seen after that until we became aware of this Morningside movement."

"Why do you suspect that office in Falcon Avenue?"

"One of our men happens to live near there and became a bit suspicious of the activity that was going on. He was told that it was a branch of the Dutch Royal Insurance setting up in the UK but in conversation with a couple of the staff, he detected more of a German accent than Dutch. Also he suspects that regular meetings are being held there which have little to do with insurance. We have also run a check on their telephone service and there seems to be a heavy amount of calls to and from Warsaw and Berlin."

"What has Poland got to do with Dutch Royal Insurance setting up in the UK?" asked Jack.

"Yes interesting question. One would think that the last country to want anything to do with new or old Nazism would be Poland." said the Major.

Jack agreed and suggested that it may well be another case of 'in plain sight'. He asked if the office in Falcon Avenue was under surveillance.

"It sure is, we have some of our people walking up and down the avenue regularly and a camera team in the apartment building opposite. We are just waiting for someone to slip up. We are very keen to get our hands on whomever has been helping them from these shores. Whoever it is has quite a sway in Edinburgh. Archer, I am getting a little nervous, I can't helping thinking that something is about to happen either here or in Poland. The answer will become apparent once we find who their main lead is here. By the way, we could know in an hour or so when the latest surveillance film is developed."

"OK Major, please call me here when you know anything more. I still haven't had a chance to speak with the Pole but I'm going to do that now and I'll get back to you." Jack returned the receiver to its cradle and when he looked up he saw Duthie leaving the room.

Alenti was on his own looking out of the window and Jack saw a good opportunity to talk to him on his own, so he start to walk across the room.

Bill Erskine seemed to be finishing a conversation with Taylor, the other Red Cross Officer and met Jack half way across the room "Jack I was wondering if the telephone was working ok, I need to use it to call HQ for some further instructions."

"Yes it's clear as a bell. I'll have to ring my upstairs again in a moment to find out what they want me to do with Alenti."

"Yes it seems your upstairs is as good at communicating as our upstairs. I'm supposed to be the Commandant here and I swear to you that our janitor knows more operational stuff than I do. I can tell you though that we will look after Alenti and get him back to

Tynecastle. He is in good condition now apart from the bump on the nose, which I believe you had something to do with?"

"Needs must, Commandant." said Jack. "It was the only way I could get him out of there with good reason. Why didn't you fellows do it while you were there? I have no objections because they paid me to do it and I needed the cash, but I felt like a bounty hunter."

"What do you mean, while we were there?" asked a curious Bill. "We weren't there today."

"You weren't?" asked a puzzled Jack. "I was sure that it was you that I saw disappearing out the gate when we were getting Alenti into our vehicle. I'm sure it was the back of your uniform I saw striding out of the gate."

Bill laid his hand on Jack's arm as he smiled and made his way to the phone. "Our eyes do fool us at times, Jack. One uniform can look quite like another, especially when the light is dimming. Eat some more carrots lad, see clearer!" he laughed as he walked away from Jack.

Jack paused for a moment then shrugged it all off, accepting the fact that he could have been mistaken. The other Red Cross man, Taylor who had been speaking with Duthie was sitting at the desk in the office where they had interviewed Alenti and he brought out of his bag a travelling version of draughts complete with a fairly good sized board and all the draughtsmen.

NINETEEN

Alenti turned around from looking out of the window to face Jack coming towards him. "Alenti, we haven't had a chance to talk since we arrived here. How are you feeling?"

Jack was expecting a sour reception because of the way Alenti had greeted him when he woke up from the sedative.

"Things are improving thankyou but no thanks to your government. Jack I will always be grateful for the help you gave me in Warsaw, you rescued me when I was in trouble and I have no way of thanking you other than my words. It's true also that I have met some wonderful people here who have also helped me, but the government's attitude towards me is hurtful. All I wanted was to make a new home here but no, they did nothing to help me. But things are changing, I take my own affairs into my own hands and you all won't have to worry about me for much longer."

Jack had heard the story several times before but he had to realise that this man did feel hurt and almost singled out for bad treatment. He thought that the least he could do was to listen to him, and it did seem that something had happened or had been said that had lifted Alenti's spirits. However he was becoming increasingly concerned that the Pole was perhaps unintentionally becoming involved in something sinister and perhaps life threatening.

In thinking over previous discussions Jack worried about the man's thoughts on Hitler. Even though acknowledging the horror that Germany had brought to his country, Alenti seemed to be strangely aligning his own political thoughts with the original intentions of the Third Reich

Monica approached Jack with a concerned look on her face.

"Jack, I may be imagining it all but I'm feeling there's been a definite change in this room's dynamics. Your Polish friend seems in remarkably good spirits, and the Red Cross Men have a determined look on their faces apart from the one in plain clothes, he seems a little jittery."

"You're right." answered Jack. "Something has changed."

Jack leaned in towards Monica. "Go over and get Feargal, start to pack up your gear and meet me in the corridor. Don't give any impression that there is a problem, just act casually."

"Is there a problem Jack?"

"Corridor Monica now!"

Jack picked up his backpack and opened the door of the office and placed it in the corridor. The other two were doing the same and eventually the three of them were standing in the corridor outside.

Jack closed the door and the three of them feigned a casual conversation while looking into the room containing Bill Erskine and his Red Cross colleagues and Alenti.

"Even though what I'm about to talk about is serious, try and keep a smile on your faces. I don't want them to be suspicious. Monica you are right, the dynamics have changed. Firstly I have to tell you that the chap in plain clothes is not from the Red Cross."

Feargal's eyes opened wide. "But to be sure was he not the secretary fellow that looks after all the paperwork?"

"No." said Jack. "That chap's name is Duthie and he is from Intelligence and he has been assigned to accompany the other two when it comes to dealing with the Pole."

"Do they know where he is from?" asked Monica.

"No, they believe that he is in fact the secretary and he is there to look after any welfare paperwork for Alenti."

"Now listen, you two." continued Jack "I think that our time here is done and we should exit stage left while we can. Have you got all your gear out here?"

"Yes we have" said Feargal. "Is it that we should say goodbye or something or just get going."

Jack smiled and mimicked him in return "Ah to be sure my dear emerald eyes, is it not that that would be rude? Seriously though, you both stay here and I'll go back in and ring the Major and tell him we're off."

Meanwhile in the next room Craig Erskine decided that he couldn't really wait in the darkened atmosphere any longer and that hiding in there was not achieving anything. He knew that the three that he shared a bumpy ride with while hiding under a stretcher, were congregated around the door of the bigger room next door. Looking around the room he was in he found a dusty clipboard with paper and some typewritten words on it, so he decided that if he was challenged he would pretend that he worked at the hospital.

Opening the door attracted the attention of Jack's trio and they turned towards him. Craig immediately became nervous but then he remembered that although he had become familiar with them, they had never seen him before so there was no need for them to be surprised when they saw him pass by.

As he came closer he saw into the room next door and he all but froze when he saw his Father inside. Craig wanted to avoid attracting attention so he had to quickly decide whether to throw caution to the wind and go directly in to speak to his Father, or to simply keep walking. He noticed the iron lungs stacked near the back of the room so decided to put his dummy clipboard to use and pretend to do some sort of audit. Timing would have it that Jack was re-entering the room to call the Department, so Craig followed him through, taking care not to let his Father see him as he felt that he needed a few minutes in there to gather his thoughts. Fortunately, Alenti and the Red Cross men had their backs turned to the door as Jack and Craig entered, and by the time they had slowly turned around, Craig was in the far corner wearing a white coat that he had found next door and was studiously inspecting the iron lungs, referring now and then to his blank dusty clipboard.

"Major Sanderson please" Jack was becoming a little weary of making a call to the Department. He knew that he wouldn't get through in a hurry.

"Who is calling please?" came an uninterested reply. "I would rather not say but I assure you that he will take my call."

"I am sorry but I have to have a name." said the receptionist.

"For an organisation specialising in Intelligence and privileged information, you don't seem to be very secretive." said Jack unsuccessfully keeping irritation out of his tone.

"If you don't give a name then I will discontinue this call."

"Listen madam." Jack's severe tone intensified. "What I have to discuss with the Major is high priority and of great importance to the safety of this country, so put me through immediately." He took a pause then added "Please."

Unlike Jack's the tone of the receptionist was unchanged.

"I have to advise you that if you do not identify yourself, I will discontinue this call in ten seconds."

"General Stonewall " Jack quickly quipped.

"Thank you General, I will see if Major Sanderson wishes to take your call. May I ask what is the nature of the call."

"No you may not ask because if you do, I will not answer. You are wasting valuable time." Jack's tone reached a more moderate level. He wasn't sure if the operator had really believed the name Stonewall as the monotone tone continued.

"General, with respect you must adhere to agreed protocols regarding calls to this Department. I shall read the points relating to you. When a call is received at general reception the caller must state…"

"Christ, get me the Major immediately or you will find that this is the last call you will have anything to do with in that Department." Interrupted Jack. "In fact I will make sure that you do not get a similar position within the Government ever again. What is this Protocol rubbish."

For all his international experiences, Jack had not encountered the word or the notion of Protocols before, other than in the movie Stalag 17 when William Holden spat out the word to the Otto Preminger character.

Silence at the other end indicated that the call may have been disconnected, but just as he was about to hang up the receptionist's voice returned.

"General Stonewall, the Major will accept your call, please wait while I connect."

Jack could imagine a prune like faced switchboard operator reluctantly pushing the red cord into the hole marked 'Sanderson', then reaching for the brown cord which would connect the two. She would not be a happy person, he was sure.

"Protocol! What crap" he muttered noticing that he was using that word crap more often these days. Hollywood was changing the English vernacular.

"Sanderson." the familiar voice responded. "I believe you are General Stonewall and I am sorry sir but I am not aware of you, may I ask where you are from?"

A huge smile broke out on Jack's face. "Major, it's me Archer."

"What are you playing at Archer, who is Stonewall?"

"There's still room for a sense of humour Major, tell that to Bodeacia of the switchboard."

"Archer, get on with it and stop playing stupid games." Jack was tempted to justify himself but decided to let it pass.

"I thought that I should advise you that we are assuming our mission is complete and are standing down. We would like to leave the building."

"Stay where you are man and listen to me carefully." retorted Sanderson.

"I want you to tell me exactly who is in the room and what they are doing."

Jack explained that Bill Erskine and Taylor were in the middle of the room with their backs to him and Duthie had left the room a few minutes ago. He mentioned that Monica and Feargal were outside in the corridor awaiting instruction, and also in the room was a guy from the hospital checking the iron lungs.

There was a slight pause then Sanderson's voice returned.

"Archer, someone wants me urgently on the other phone. I'll ring you back."

Jack had not heard this level of urgency in the Major's voice before and his curiosity increased. It seemed as though there was much that he didn't know and he hoped that when Sanderson rang back, he would find out.

While he waited, he walked over to where Craig was pretending to be one of the hospital staff carrying out an audit on the equipment stored at the back of the room.

Craig was aware of Jack's approach but pretended to be engrossed in checking the iron lung machines.

"I bet I know what you're doing there." said Jack.

TWENTY

Craig froze in his position crouched over a machine. What did he know? Had he actually spotted him in the Brake? What sort of response should he give? He rose to Jack's level.

"I'm sorry, I couldn't hear you properly down there."

"Those damn serial numbers." Jack replied. "Why do they put them in such unreachable places? Doesn't seem to matter what equipment it is from a bicycle to a car and I remember doing an audit at an airport once and we had to run a competition to see who could find the serial number first!"

Craig was relieved to hear the subject of Jack's enquiry.

"Yes, this should be a five minute job but it's taken me forever to find the darned things. It makes it worse that each machine seems to have their number in a different place."

"Jack Archer." Jack extended his hand towards Craig who had to quickly think what name he would give.

The first name that came to mind was that of his old neighbour, the Australian returned soldier who had fought at Gallipoli and had told Craig such wonderful stories of his time in the army.

"Mac Penfold, nice to meet you "he said as he shook Jack's hand.

Jack was studiously looking at the iron lung machines and Craig was worried that he would ask questions about them so he tried to counter that possibility. "What's going on here, what are you all doing?"

"We brought in someone from Tyneside camp for a medical check over." "Where is he from? Is there anything wrong with him?" continued Craig.

Jack could see no reason for giving out the information but didn't want to elaborate. "Poland and no nothing wrong with him really other than a bruise to his face when he had a fall."

Having seen that injury closely, Craig felt he had to tread carefully in his conversation.

"What's the Red Cross doing with him?"

"They are the ones charged with looking after the welfare needs of refugees whether they are staying here on a visa or being deported." Again Jack didn't know how much information to impart to this stranger.

"Are they doctors?" asked Craig. "I didn't think they were qualified to do anything beyond basic nursing."

"I really don't know about that." Said Jack and it was true that he hadn't questioned why a doctor wasn't here. It wasn't really his business but the thought had never crossed his mind, he just accepted that the Red Cross were in charge. Maybe this guy Penfold has a point.

Craig thought that he would press Jack further. "This Polish guy, is he staying in Scotland or heading back?"

"Well he has tried a few times to get a residency visa but keeps being refused, so if it doesn't happen in the next couple of weeks, he'll be on the next boat out of here."

"Have you talked with him? Do you know what he wants to do?" pressed Craig. "Funny you should say that, apparently he was pretty unhappy at being refused residency. He felt that he was entitled to it given that he had served with the Allies during the war, so he had a real attitude problem with the government over that. However lately, while he's still pissed at not getting a visa to stay, he seems a little happier about the prospect of going home." Jack felt that he should leave the subject right there.

Likewise, Craig felt the conversation had gone on long enough without risking some sort of blunder into revelation, so he resumed his mythical search for serial numbers on the iron lungs. It was an odd situation with both men meeting for the first time and both with something to hide and both trying to divert the conversation.

Any further possibility of that happening was averted when Jack strode across the room to answer the phone.

"Sanderson here, is Duthie back in the room yet?"

After a look around Jack replied that he wasn't. In fact Jack had to admit that he hadn't noticed that he had left the room.

The Major continued. "Well I have just been speaking to him and there's been a development with the Pole. Apparently he has had more than a medical examination, and I am piecing it together with what you told me about the angst he's holding and the political activity he's been involved in with the Polish Freedom group. The guy is ripe for the picking by those that want to push some sort of nationalistic monoculture."

Jack was piecing together a picture that didn't auger well for either Britain or Poland, should a resurgence happen.

"You talking about Nazism, Major? Because if so then its darned hard to understand how Poland would be a place of rebirth, given the horror of the last few years."

Sanderson agreed. "That saying 'in plain sight' keeps recurring Archer. Nurture it where people would least expect it, then by the time its fully nourished, it's too late to stop."

The Major concluded his call by warning him that once Duthie returned things would be escalating and it may be advantageous if he and his "two musketeers" became allies if not friends.

Duthie looked towards where Alenti and the other two seemed to be in another meeting then he exchanged looks with Jack and sidled over to where he was standing between the phone and the iron lungs being checked by Craig.

Monica looked into the room from the corridor where she and Feargal had been waiting for their boss. Then she and Feargal came back in and walked to where Jack and Duthie were talking in hushed tones.

"You know don't you that I am not with the Red Cross and the Major told you what I am doing here?"

"I know that you're not the secretary type yes but Sanderson didn't exactly tell me what you were doing here other than pretending to help in the welfare of Alenti." Jack looked again at Alenti now in the other office with the the two Red Cross men and he still had a look of satisfaction on his face. It was still a mystery to him as to what the reason was.

"To put it simply, I am here to stop another recruit joining the re-emerging Nazi Party and stymie their chances of starting up again"

"So you know who has been aiding and abetting?" asked Jack.

"Let's say that the trap is set but we don't know which mouse is going to go for the cheese. Intelligence wise we are close to busting open the organisation. I'm just waiting on a call from the Major to tell me it has been done."

"What has been done Duthie? You're losing me." pleaded Jack. "A bit of concentration would stop that Archer." snapped Duthie.

Jack's patience was draining. He wanted to get out of the hospital and the whole scene and take Feargal and Monica for a game of darts at Rutherfords on Drummond Street and enjoy another heavy.

The phone that Jack had been using rang but as Duthie was close to it, he let him answer it.

Jack watched Duthie absorb what he was being told. As he waited, he noticed that Bill Erskine and Red Cross Officer Taylor had come out of the interview office along with a very cheery and satisfied looking Alenti.

From the look on his face that things were now developing at a much quicker pace.

Duthie used the phone receiver to signal to Jack to join him.

"It's on. Major has some instructions – for you."

Jack really couldn't quite understand what that meant but was glad to be included in the conversation. "Major, what's happening?"

"I am on my way to you now with police backup. I want you to ensure that no one and that includes you and your musketeers, leaves that room."

"Sure thing, but does that include the Red Cross guys and…"

"Everyone Archer, not one person to leave."

The call was terminated. Jack wasn't sure if he should make some announcement to the effect that no one could leave, or should he just keep everyone engaged until the Major arrived. Fortunately everyone seemed to be still in discussion with each other, so he saw no reason to bring any more tension into the arena. As he looked up at the other end of the room he saw the hospital auditor that he had helped check iron lungs with.

"Shit!" he muttered. "What the hell do I do with him? He's got nothing to do with any of this."

As Jack was thinking of a strategy, The Red Cross Officer Taylor, who Alenti recognised as the one who visited him at

Waverly before he went to Tynecastle, asked him if they were able to use the phone.

"Not my phone mate, go for your life. You just got to go through the operator. Do you know the number?"

Taylor checked a scribble on the piece of paper in his hand. "Yes its local, just to Morningside."

"Well you won't have a problem." Said Jack who went back to working out what to do with Craig.

TWENTY-ONE

Craig could tell that he was the subject of Jack's thinking right now, by the way he was staring straight at him. He hadn't yet approached his Father so as far as he knew, his Father had no knowledge of his presence. Craig had to decide whether to go across the room and speak to Bill, or leave the room and the hospital and deal with the matter at home.

He decided on the latter and collected his clipboard and moved to the door. On seeing him move, Duthie crossed the floor and stood in front of the door.

"I must ask you to stay in here." Craig thought this a strange turn of events. "I have nothing to do with whatever is going on here, I have to get these figures back to reception."

He waved the clipboard as a way to confirm the fact. Duthie neither moved away from the door or spoke, but what he did do next alarmed Craig.

The man who he thought was the Red Cross secretary, undid the button on his black jacket allowing his restrained stomach to lurch forward no doubt grateful for the relief, but the action also revealed a gun resting in a leather holster.

Craig realised then that this had become a most serious situation, but he couldn't fathom why a Red Cross Officer would be carrying a firearm. He also couldn't work out what this had to do with Alenti and moreso with his Father. Then he heard a familiar voice.

"Craig, is that you?" Bill had come out of the inner office having been attracted by the commotion at the other door.

Craig turned around slowly to give himself a second or two to decide how to deal with this situation. Alenti also looked surprised as he realised that the young boy that he encountered a few years ago outside 356 Easter Road Leith was now this young man dressed in a white coat and seemingly working for the hospital.

Bill Erskine's expression was a mixture of familial recognition and strong curiosity.

Craig had not seen his Father's eyes so wide since the incident at number 356.

"Hello Dad, what a surprise to see you here." he walked towards him gauging his Fathers response. Would shaking his hand be an appropriate response?

Bill placed his hand on Craig's arms which suggested that the Commandant was also unsure.

"Are you working here?" Craig had almost forgotten that he was wearing the white coat of a hospital employee and holding a Health Department clipboard. He decided that he would continue the lie for the time being.

"Yes, in a fashion. The University was approached with a request to provide some students as volunteers to carry out audits on the equipment on hand so as a submission can be made to the Government for updating and replacing."

Craig couldn't believe how his mind could fabricate such a story free range. It was if some automatic pilot was keeping the engine alive while in reality he was trying to find somewhere safe to land.

"I had no idea you were doing this son."

"Dad, you haven't been around much lately so its been a bit hard to have any sort of discussion with you. You have had a few trips away you know."

Both men let the conversation hang there for a few moments. In that time they realised that their reunion had attracted the attention of the others in the room. A glance back at Duthie showed Craig that his jacket was still hanging open and loose, and the man's eyes were staring straight back at him. An almost tangible tension had started to elevate.

Bill, in a half whisper asked his son if he had spoken to Alenti.

"Not really, he seemed a little shocked at seeing me. I'm not sure what I should say to him."

"Son, a piece of advice. As you can probably imagine, Alenti has been through a tough time lately, he's been in prison, refused a residential visa here and for the past little while he has been out at Tynecastle camp."

Craig reminded himself that his Father did not know how well acquainted he was with Alenti's travels and travails.

"I mention it because while he seems to be physically fit, his mind is a little troubled and has some fanciful ideas."

Craig looked puzzled. "Fanciful? How so?"

"Well what I mean is that he is likely to have a different interpretation of conversations that he has had of recent times. Taylor and I have been having a discussion with him today while examining him and I'm thinking that his understanding of what is being said to him is fanciful. He has a perception that is quite distant from reality and truth."

Perception. That word conjured up memories of Craig's own feelings about his Father and how they were mistaken and misplaced. Yet Craig knew quite a bit about perception. He did wonder what fanciful ideas Alenti had and would he share them with him.

Taylor had concluded his phone call and came across to Bill. "I have to tell you Bill, I am slightly bored. What are we really waiting for here, when can we leave?"

"I agree it is tedious" said Bill "But we can't really go until the hospital clinic signs the document of examination on Alenti. That should be pretty soon though."

"Well I need something to keep me from falling asleep. Come and have a game of draughts, I think from memory you owe me the right for a re-match after last time."

"It's not what I had in mind," said Bill "But it might be good for the brain. Craig, come over later and you can play the winner or loser if you prefer Taylor" he jested.

"No thanks Dad, I might have a chat with Alenti."

"OK but don't forget what I said about his state of mind at the moment, his perception of what's going on is a little clouded."

Perception, there's that word again thought Craig as he walked over to Alenti who greeted him with a smile.

"Craig, my friend. I want to tell you what a wonderful man you have turned out to be. Your Father has been telling me about your studies and what you want to do. I am so glad that I got to see you before I went back to Poland."

Craig asked when that would be.

"Very soon. Your Father is arranging my voyage now. I can't tell you what a help he has been to me and to think that I will see my own family again, fills my heart and I owe that to him."

"What family have you still got in Poland, Alenti?" asked Craig.

Alenti fell silent and the joyous look vanished. Craig noticed the change and thought it curious.

"Alenti?" he reached out to the man who all but shirked away. "Alenti what is it?"

"I am sorry but I am not allowed to say anything."

"Why not? If you're going to see your family well that's a great thing. If it was me I would be telling everyone." said Craig.

"Has your Father not said anything to you?" asked Alenti.
"No. What about? Why should he?"

There was a prolonged silence between the two men. One anticipating revelation and another on the cusp of doubt.

"Alenti, tell me. What is it? Is it about your family? I can only guess that it's your parents or cousins or something similar, because of course I understand about your wife and son being taken just before the war."

"They found them." Alenti said in whispered tones.

"Who?" Craig was becoming more and more perplexed about where this conversation was heading.

"My wife and son." Alenti's eyes seem to be concentrating on the floor as he spoke in a low voice.

Craig's exclamation was so loud it alerted everyone else in the room who were already deep in their own conversations. Taylor and Bill looked up from their draught game.

"What! How Where When?"

"Your Father found them. He said the Polish Red Cross had rescued them from a camp and they are waiting for me. Please don't tell him that I told you, please. They made me sign a confed umm confirm..."

"You mean confidentiality agreement?" Craig helped.

"Yes."

"Who did you sign it with Alenti?"

"Bill, er your Father and the other man from Red Cross. They very serious about it."

Craig didn't think that the Red Cross went into such agreements. Where was the need?

"What did they say would happen if you told someone?"

Alenti glanced nervously towards Craig's Father at the other side of the room, but said nothing.

"Alenti, tell me what would happen if you told someone? What could they do?"

Neither of them had noticed that Bill had come across to them. He had left mid-game and Monica had volunteered to finish it for him.

"Well it's good to see you two getting on so well, much better than last time!" he laughed." Alenti come back in the office and we'll get all those forms complete."

Craig thought for a second that the arm he stretched out to Alenti was a little forceful and he shared a look of concern with Craig, as the door shut.

Jack Archer came over to him and asked Craig if everything was ok. "Can I ask you a question?"

"Sure, fire away." Said Jack.

"Would an organisation such as the Red Cross have much to do with confidentiality agreements?

"Buggered if I know! Might be if they're involved in some government stuff, why you asking?"

Craig wondered if he should say anything because it would cause him to break a confidence and it would be like a pebble in the water, ripples and bubbles would start to expand and God knows who would be dragged down to some murky depth.

Craig turned to Jack. "There is something I should tell you. That man Alenti was involved in an incident with me a few years ago which ended up with some trouble outside our home in Leith."

Jack nodded and mentioned that he had heard about it.

"But what you probably don't know is that I don't work here. I am at University and I actually came in to find out what my Father was doing, as he tells us little at home. Mum believes its because he is still in possession of sensitive intelligence from the war and has to keep his movements confidential. My name is Craig Erskine and my Father is Bill Erskine from the Red Cross."

Jack took some time to digest this news but couldn't fathom the connection and why was the son stalking his Father?

"Jack, can I see you for a minute?" Monica.

"Yup, I am sure in popular demand today." The two soldiers of fortune walked to the window which looked out onto the hospital corridor.

"I've just been watching those two Red Cross guys playing draughts, and I noticed something strange. Something wasn't right about the way they were playing but I couldn't work it out."

Jack smiled "Mon you were just eager to take over and move the pieces for them, you were impatient to be in control!"

Mon smiled slightly, he knew her so well.

"Well any other time yes but this was so hard to pick as an observer as if they were in slow motion and seemed to be putting the pieces in strange positions. So strange that I don't think either of them would have won the game. It was nonsensical. It was only when that Erskine guy left I took his place that it all became clear."

It was obvious to Monica that Jack's mind wasn't really concentrating on what she had to say

"Have you played draughts, Jack?"

"I have, but not for a while, draughts and chess bore me a bit."

"Do you know how to set the board up?" asked Monica.

"Yes I think so, black and white pieces and each move on each others territory across squares." replied Jack.

"Right, well those pieces go on the black squares and the board is positioned with a white square on the right of each player."

"For Christ's sake Mon, why you telling me all this?" yawned Jack.

"When I went over to watch them play, Taylor set the board up and something looked strange. I just thought my brain was tired after everything that's been going on so I gave up watching until Erskine left the board and walked over here. Taylor asked if I wanted to play and when I said yes, he turned the board around and then I noticed that when he had been playing with Erskine, it was the black square that was on the right, and when I sat down to play, he turned the board around the right way."

Jack thought for a few seconds. "Well its easy to get confused with all those squares, it does my head in sometimes."

"No Jack, they weren't playing, they were communicating. Didn't you notice Taylor on the phone?"

Jack did remember that.

"Well when he finished he came right over to where Erskine was talking to that young guy from the hospital and invited him to come over for a game of draughts, and he set the board up the wrong way round."

Monica was convinced that this was a coded message between the two men and explained why Erskine had left the so called game unfinished and came over to speak with Alenti.

"What message could he possibly want to pass on that he couldn't just tell Bill about it?" asked Jack.

"Something that they didn't want all of us to know about." said Monica.

"Hold on." said Jack. "I remember something. He happened to mention to me something about the number he was ringing.

I was busy trying to work out the Major's instructions but it did ring a bell, if you pardon the pun."

Monica asked him to think harder.

"Yes. When I was talking to the Major, he mentioned an area of concern that the department had with an office in Morningside, and it was the Morningside area that Taylor was making a call to."

Monica placed her hand on Jack's sleeve as she remembered something. "Did you say Morningside?"

Jack nodded.

"Do you remember that note that we found in Alenti's cabin at Tyneside? That had a Morningside phone number on it."

Their discussion was abruptly interrupted by the sound of heavy footsteps in the corridor and then as the door opened, in walked Major Sanderson with two uniformed soldiers carrying rifles. It was an incongruous look for a hospital setting, but it did give the indication that something serious was happening.

"Everyone stand where they are." shouted Sanderson.

TWENTY-TWO

"Duthie, search everyone for weapons."

It was very much to Bill Erskine's and Officer Taylor's surprise to hear Duthie referred to like that by the Major.

"What have you got to do with all this, Brian?" asked Bill as the man whom he thought was a Red Cross secretary searched him.

Duthie did not reply. He continued searching everyone in the room, although he did allow Jack and his crew to retain their weapons. He then moved back to where Bill and Alenti were standing. As this was going on, Feargal noticed that Taylor was edging his way towards the door which had been left open by the army officers.

Feargal moved quickly to block his progress but not before Taylor had drawn a pistol from inside his Red Cross uniform and aimed it at the Irishman. No one other than Taylor would ever know if he intended to shoot Feargal, but that's what the Irishman had thought had happened. Blood spurted onto his face and over his shirt, corresponding with the sound of gunfire.

Everyone in the room was instantly alarmed and looked at Feargal, expecting him to collapse to the floor.

However, it was Taylor who fell and Duthie's gun was still smoking as he lowered it Taylor's hands desperately searched for the pistol that had slipped from his grasp. Blood ran from the gaping wound in his neck and it was only moments before his hands stilled and his blood stained the floor.

Craig immediately went to his Father whose eyes were ablaze and lips in a grimace. "Dad, are you ok? What the hell just happened? Why the gun? Have you got one?

Jesus Christ!"

Craig had certainly experienced gunfire and bullets after the incident outside number 356 but he had never seen a person actually shot before nor had he seen anyone killed.

Monica, Jack and the major rushed to where Taylor was lying and Monica placed her thumb on his neck to check his pulse. She gave the others a look of sadness combined with a tinge of fear.

"He's gone."

Duthie still had his gun drawn and to Craig's horror, he pointed it at Bill's back, propelling him nearer the door, where the two soldiers took him and placed handcuffs on his wrists. It was incredulous for him to see his Father being handled in this way.

"No! What are you doing? That's my Father, he's here to help people, this is ridiculous. Dad say something."

The pleading tone was almost painful to hear and the anguish almost unbearable to watch. Countless thoughts assailed Craig's mind, and the strongest was complete and utter disbelief.

Bill Erskine said nothing and had a vacant stare in his eyes. Craig thought that he was in shock.

"Can we get a doctor to him please? You can't do this. He is a man of peace. What have you tied him up for?"

Sanderson and Jack approached the young Erskine.

"This will be hard for you to learn, but your Father did not come here on peaceful terms. He has been under our surveillance for many months now." Sanderson gestured to Duthie who had now replaced his gun to bring over Alenti.

"Mr Pawlowski can you tell us what discussion you had with this man, in that office?" Alenti seemed to be in a state of shock also and bewildered by the chain of events.

His eyes made a circuit of the room falling on Jack, Monica and Feargal then to the Major whom he felt already knew about the abduction from Tynecastle. Next he looked at Duthie whom he now realized wasn't a Red Cross Officer at all. Next he looked at Craig who looked helpless and hapless. This young man with whom he had shared an unique connection since the incident years earlier at number 356.

Alenti then took in the sight of the two soldiers flanking the manacled Bill Erskine whose eyes became locked on his for what seemed like a long time. The almost trance like atmosphere was broken with Sanderson's voice.

"Pawlowski, we need to know what was said in that room between you, Erskine and this man on the floor."

Alenti raised his hand as a gesture towards Sanderson to be patient. He then took a few steps that brought him face to face with Erskine. There was barely room for a shadow to fall between them. The two guards brought their rifles up, as a precaution, but the Major just shook his head and ordered them to rest the weapons.

Alenti's voice was shaky at the start and he had to clear his throat once or twice. "I just heard that young man over there, call this man a man of peace. This is indeed the type of man that met me when I was at my lowest . This man understood my grief, my loss. He reached out to me with hands full of support and what I took as love and understanding. This man stood beside me in Normandy when enemy bullets flew around us."

The room was quiet and no one even shuffled their feet. Alenti's voice had strengthened as he continued.

"This man showed me and people like me, gratitude for putting my life at risk for the political opportunist. This man embraces the concept of a New World Order and will work patiently but tirelessly to achieve it. This man is a traitor."

The look on Bill Erskine's face was cold and unflinching throughout Alenti's tirade.

Craig's thoughts were in an emotional maelstrom looking for somewhere to settle.

At the start of this incident his heart and his support immediately and automatically went out to his Father and his reactions had been bold. Now, enough time had passed to allow feelings to settle and in so doing, he recalled the seed of doubt that had lain dormant within him in regards to his Father. He recalled the angst over perceiving that Bill was a coward during the war, then the relief and admiration he felt when he learnt differently. Had everything that had happened since been a farce?

What was occurring now was beyond reason. It defied logic that his Father could wear the uniform of a movement whose existence was bedded in care for humanity yet he could harbour such apocalyptic ideals as espoused by Nazism.

Major Sanderson was becoming impatient with Alenti's reticence to share what had transpired in discussions with Erskine and Taylor in the inner office.

"Mr. Pawlowski, I must insist on you telling me what arrangements you had made with Erskine and Taylor. I am reluctant to do it, but such is the threat to national security that I will be obliged to have you handcuffed also and taken away for more intense interrogation.

Alenti turned a mournful gaze towards the Major.

"Major, after five years facing death as a soldier helping to defend this country against the horror of the Third Reich, having been tossed aside to fend for myself afterwards, then be denied the right to stay, there is little you can do that would be effective in making me talk, if I didn't want to. You see, Major, I just don't care anymore. In the last few hours, I have felt betrayed by someone who was helping me only to further their own ends, then I had the prospect of finding my family again waved in front of me to find now that it was a cruel trick. I was being used to encourage the regrowth of a political and philosophical scourge that I had spend years fighting against. So Major, I will tell you but only because I want to and hopefully bring an end to all of this."

He turned to look at Bill Erskine who still looked straight ahead without showing any emotion. Alenti kept looking at him as he recounted what had happened a few hours previously between himself, Erskine, Taylor, and Duthie.

TWENTY-THREE

"I cannot tell you how wonderful it is to see you again my friend." Said Bill Erskine to Alenti as they all settled inside the inner office within the hospital.

"Taylor here whom I'm sure you will remember meeting back at Waverley, will give you a medical examination while you and I talk."

Taylor stepped forward. "Alenti it's a pleasure to see you again. Bill and I have been talking a lot about you and the incredible service you have given to us here in Britain. I'm sorry that this new government has seen fit to refuse you permanent residency. Totally unfair treatment. Now would you remove your shirt please."

Bill took up the conversation by asking about the note that he had left in the Tynecastle cabin.

"I know nothing about a note, Bill" answered Alenti.

"Strange, because I had called to see you out at the stadium but you weren't in your cabin so I waited a little while then left you a note."

"What was in it?" asked Alenti.

Bill was puzzled about the note going missing.

"You remember about a month or so ago, we had a long chat after one of your Polish resettlement League meetings at the Camera Obscura?"

"Yes, I won't forget it, or maybe I will due to amount of Polish wine you had brought with you! It was a long night."

"Yes it was, I'm not usually a big drinker but I hardly remember how I got home that night, or should I say early morning. I'm sure I saw a tinge of the sun as it started to rise over Leith the next morning."

Both he and Alenti smiled at the recollection.

Meanwhile, Taylor had used the stethoscope on the man's chest and back and now asked him to open his mouth wide.

As Alenti made the usual 'aah' sound when the throat is being inspected, Taylor quipped wondering if he was making that sound in Polish or English. Given the sublety of the joke, Alenti didn't fully understand and did not respond.

Bill sat further forward opposite Alenti.

"Do you remember what we used to talk about at those meetings?"

"Yes," said Alenti "How to get me back to Poland and then when I decided to stay, how they wouldn't let me. I think we talked about the best government to live under and I remember one word you used.

"Utopian?" Bill chipped in.

"Yes, you said it was an ideal worth striving for, yet may never be achieved." said Alenti.

"That's right, but now I believe that it can be achieved, Alenti and there are many others now of similar mind."

"Is it not pointless then Bill, if it couldn't be achieved then why dream it?"

Alenti noticed what he could only describe as a fire smouldering in Erskine's eyes and an incoming tide of passion washing over his face.

"Yes, I agree." Bill responded "But given the recent worldwide conflict we have experienced, much learning has come to the surface and revealed ways in which it can be achieved. Through positive persuasion, the minds of people can be diverted from the fanciful to the factual and they can be led into a pure and positive life."

Alenti moved his arm so as Taylor could take his blood pressure, wincing as the cuff tightened.

"Bill, I can see why Utopia will never be achieved. Such thinking can never be achieved by humans. Look at what happened in that war, the overpowering of sovereign states and the devasting raids on the bodies and minds of people of the Jewish faith by a group hell bent on achieving the impossible by any means possible."

The passionate look still burned in Bill's eyes.

"Granted, but history books show that even the great reformer Martin Luther suggested a gentle persuasion be applied to bring such believers to a clearer understanding of the search for purity and perfection. The attitudes of those we fought against in the last war can now be seen as experimental and as with all experiments some fail."

"Such as Auschwitz?" ventured Alenti.

Bill's face tightened and the joy that had underlaid his passion disappeared momentarily.

"You concentrate too much on the horror and not enough on the evolutionary. The world itself is said to have begun with a huge explosion or bang, and while all that cataclysm didn't last, it was necessary to set things in motion. It was vitally needed to set the mould then watch the pieces fall back all in their right places."

Taylor interrupted the conversation, "Bill, this man is super fit! Ideal blood pressure, heart is sound and all the limbs seem agile. I would give him a nine out of ten."

Alenti asked why not ten out of ten.

"Because no one gets full marks. No one ever gets ten out of ten yet. It leaves something to be yet achieved. Ten is purity."

"I am glad to hear you are healthy Alenti" said Bill "It is people of sound mind and body that the world needs right now to reset the balance."

"I don't think that I am the soldier of change you want, Bill. I and you too have recently spent six years fighting a German monster who had ideas of creating what he saw as a perfect world, and he literally killed millions of people in his attempt. Among them I might add, my own wife and son."

Bill's passionate look was returning to his face.

"My friend, you are exactly the type of soldier or man that we need. One that can identify the need yet adjust the means by which we achieve it. What bigger incentive would you need?"

"I just told you, Bill, my wife and child."

There was a significant silence as Alenti put his shirt back on and as he turned around, he noticed the other two men exchange a strange look. Taylor gave a nod to his colleague.

Bill looked around, and even checked that the door was properly shut before sitting back down directly opposite Alenti.

"What if I gave you that incentive?"

"To do what and what incentive are you talking about?"

"Alenti, we are looking for people to become instruments of change, and where better to bring that change about than in Poland which suffered so much. I have come to realise that Poland's pain was part of the evolutionary process. A birth pang, if you like. Taylor and I have been appointed as agents of that change and are looking for like minded souls with the determination and courage to bring it about."

Alenti took some time to digest what he had heard.

"And the incentive, surely there has to be more than just idealism?"

"There is Alenti, something much more tangible."

"Like what?"

"Such as holding your wife and child in your arms?"

"Don't do that, Bill. It is most unkind, and I am surprised that a man such as you would say that." Alenti was visibly shaken.

Bill Erskine stood up. "Your wife and son will be waiting for you once you step off the boat we are preparing to take you to Warsaw."

Another silence fell upon the room. Alenti's eyes started to well with tears. "How is that possible? Where have they been. Do they know I am alive?" Erskine took a step back while Taylor continued.

"Alenti, we need men like you in Poland, on the ground ready to restart the road to restoration. We have had people researching your wife's movements since she was taken away. We have an office in Morningside where our staff have been tracing their movements since they were released from the camps. They found her and your son in a boarding house set up to give welfare to those being released from the camps in Warsaw. We are prepared to reunite you in return for your loyalty to our Restoration Movement. There is a ship docked at Leith Docks now and if you agree to our proposition then you could be on it within hours then down the east coast of England to Hull. Then a fishing trawler will take you to Amsterdam then a two day coach drive to Warsaw. Alenti you would be home in under two weeks."

Taylor spread out his hands to show that his presentation was over. Meantime Bill had kept his back to them as he looked out over the main office.

Alenti called him. "Bill is this true? How long have you been working on this? Have you actually seen Maja and Adelbert?

"Are they well? Do they ask after me?"

Erskine drew some documents out of his brief case and put them on the table. "All you have to do is sign these, and the way is clear Alenti.

"What am I signing?"

"Oh they are just travel documents and an agreement that this arrangement will remain confidential. Just routine stuff, nothing to worry about." Bill offered Alenti a fountain pen and pointed to where he was to sign.

"What happens if I don't sign, Bill? What happens if I do tell someone what we are doing in here?"

Bill hesitated and before he could reply, Taylor butted in.

"Then my friend all is lost, we can do nothing more for you. But I promise you that once you sign, we will be out of here in a matter of hours and you will be on your way to Utopia. All that you have fought for over the last few years will have led to this victorious path to restoration. And it will be achieved in your own homeland."

Taylor then slid the documents over to Alenti's side of the desk. Alenti sat down and started to read through them.

Erskine, was still standing with his back to them and Taylor walked over and spoke in hushed tones.

"I will go and ring Falcon Avenue and see where they are at with the boat they were arranging at Leith. If it is on then I will set up the draught board over there in the agreed pattern so as you will know to encourage the Pole to leave with you."

Erskine turned and looked at Alenti who was still studying the documents then nodded at Taylor, and left the office to make the call to Morningside. No one knew at that stage that the answer would be conveyed through a game of draughts.

As Alenti had finished bringing all the pieces into place, a hush fell on the room. The two soldiers had covered Taylor's body to await inspection by the police who were on their way. A rivulet of blood trickled from under the covering and it reminded everyone that this bundle on the floor was a human being. Craig stood so perfectly still that it seemed that not even his eyes blinked. Monica noticed that not even his breathing was perceptible and from her nursing experience she recognized shock in the young man. She took a blanket that she had found near the iron lungs that were stored at the back of the room and put it around his shoulders, urging him to sit down.

"Thank you, no." he finally spoke as he let the blanket fall to the floor. Craig walked slowly over to where his Father stood.

It was almost as though Bill Erskine was in shock too as he had barely moved since being handcuffed.

Father and son stood facing each other for what could be the last time. Craig had had enough of the doubt that had clouded their relationship for so many years. He now wanted to say so much and also say nothing at all.

Finally he spoke

"I can no longer call you by the name people call their male parent. Until now, I never understood how you could love someone yet despise them. You have just taught me the final lesson in that. You had my trust but you never earnt it. I gave it to you bit by bit. The trust I had in you was necessary for my survival as a child. I trusted you were there to protect me, clothe me, feed me. In a way I was forced to trust you, it was not something that I handed to you. When I was a child, it was automatically granted to you without conscious effort on my part. Then when I was old enough to understand something about life I looked to you to find somewhere to put my trust of choice. I looked hard but…" Craig checked himself before he used the word Dad.

"…I found nowhere in you that I was totally comfortable in leaving my gift of trust There was always doubt and now after this…" Craig waved his arm around the room.

"That doubt has been justified. I admit that you proved me wrong when I accused you of cowardice, it certainly wasn't in your nature. Your mind is not a safe place for true compassion or basic understanding of different points of view. They are foreign to you."

Craig ran his hand down Bill's arm to emphasise the uniform he was wearing. "The moment you put on this uniform you were putting on a pretence. You were encouraging everyone who met you to feel safe with you because you genuinely cared. But Bill Erskine, your mind was running in the other direction."

Major Sanderson, had been helping to remove Taylor's body and arranging to clean up the blood. He approached Craig's Father.

"Erskine, the Midlothian Police are waiting outside to take you to the station where you will be assessed and duly charged. Then you will be taken to Whitehall for interrogation."

To everyone's surprise, Bill Erskine spoke.

"What wrong have I done? What charges do I face? I should be the one asking questions. You had someone infiltrate my branch with one of your agents under the guise of a of a secretary and now it is your man that has killed another. I pulled no trigger, nor did I intend to."

The Major ignored the questions and asked some of his own.

"We have been aware of your movements on behalf of the Neo Nazi organization for some time. We know that several Polish and Italian former soldiers were recruited through you to travel to Warsaw to gradually build up an organizational force to present a version of the Third Reich."

Sanderson pointed to Alenti.

"Were you in the process of recruiting this man here for such a purpose?"

"You haven't the decency to even mention him by name. This man as you call him has given up much of his life in order to fight within your army against a much greater force in mind and spirit and determination than yours."

The Major put up his hand to stop him.

"I will remind you Mr Erskine who won the war."

For the first time since Taylor was shot, Erskine smiled. It was not a smile of happiness inspired by a stimulating event. It wasn't a smile brought on by any level of pleasure. It was a smile of satisfaction hearing those words from the English soldier. The notion that they had won the war, confirmed the mindset that will eventually defeat them, he thought.

"You have not won anything. I may have thought that once as well but if you had listened to people such as Alenti at their rallies and meetings in Edinburgh, as I have, you would change the hymn that you sing."

Alenti acknowledged that Erskine had been a frequent visitor to the meetings in the Camera Obscura building. He had also been a frequent contributor to the discussions that had been held post war amongst those who had returned to find that although conflict had abated, little had really changed in terms of thought, attitude and tolerance. Now, in retrospect he observed a growing political zeal within the man who had often worn his Red Cross uniform having called in on his way home from daily duty . He also recalled that their private discussions had bordered on sensitive and treacherous areas, that a war time espionage agent would have found interesting. At the time, Alenti dismissed them as wine induced utterances of post war frustration. He had had many such discussions with plenty of others which had abated in passion as if the light of day burnt off the alcohol lacing of the night before.

Sanderson seemed slightly bemused by Erskine's utterances but he felt that the man was not alone with these thoughts. It would do the Free World well to take heed of them and prevent any strengthening of such notions. Erskine was in fact suggesting that the Allied cause may have felt victorious following a a six year battle but were a long way off winning any war.

Duthie had now joined the Major at the door and made way for the two soldiers to take the handcuffed Bill Erskine away.

As he entered the corridor he turned and looked at his son. "I love you Craig. I love your Mother. I hope to see her again but if not, I ask you to tell her that she was in my mind at the last. Whatever happens to me, this is not the end of the evolution. Someone will take my place and sadly more deceit will occur within families. This was not for my personal gain, Craig. The world just has to get it right and the formula is there, but at the moment, this world just cannot see it."

Craig's eyes had turned to the floor while his Father was speaking but he raised them as Sanderson ordered a guard to remove Commandant Erskine's uniform jacket.

"Your choice of vehicle to pilot your journey was a poor one because its sentiment is so much at odds with yours. You will disgrace it no longer." Sanderson turned back as the trio left the room.

"Oh Erskine, that formula you mentioned is missing several ingredients, two of which come to mind. And they are two that will be forever foreign to you. Compassion and Freewill.

The last that Craig saw of his Father, was a jacketless and collarless shirted individual with head slightly bowed as he was escorted to a place where some appropriate justice would be apportioned.

Jack, Monica and Feargal came up to Craig, Monica gave him a hug, Feargal shook his hand and Jack patted him on the shoulder.

"I am not the hugging type lad, but I hope you feel embraced by all of our thoughts right now. You were remarkably brave speaking the way that you did to your Father."

"Is that how you saw it, bravery?" responded Craig.

"What I said came from my soul and I hope that there was some vestige of my Father's soul that I once loved that was touched in some way with my words. But it's bravery that I need now to tell Mum who would have wanted none of this."

Jack turned to his colleagues who had their packs on their backs.

"Thank you both. I am glad that it was you two that I shared this mission with.

There's no doubt that for our part it was a successful one. What I am worried about is what Erskine said about the world still needing to learn lessons."

Feargal had just hugged Monica goodbye and as he shook Jack's hands he said. "Well Jack remember if you want to do some of that world teaching, then I'd be happy to join you in the classroom."

"I'd be most grateful for that Emerald Eyes and you too Mon, Alenti and I would be proud to serve with you."

Feargal's mouth dropped open in surprise. "Did you say Alenti? Does that mean...?"

Jack placed his hand on Alenti's shoulder, "Yes once we get this Visa 356 business sorted."

Years later, when part of Edinburgh's Royal Infirmary was to be demolished then restored, builders went into one of the rooms that used to store old equipment.

"Hey Wullie, these floorboards shouldna be tossed awa' there's a muckle lot ye kin dae with them."

"Aye Bob, ye're richt. Bit wid ye look at that stain. Whatever it is has gone really deep. Ye'd think that bein a hospital it would hae bin cleaned up better."

So somewhere a well sanded piece of maranti is lying under the feet of maybe some dancers in a hall somewhere and no one whose feet touch it, know that a vestige of human blood lies in its core.

And of course at 356 Easter Road Leith, there is at least a perception of a bullet mark lodged in the tenement building.

It wasn't quite the shot that was heard around the world, but it does mark where an extraordinary group of people shared an extraordinary moment.

EPILOGUE

The flight to Adelaide from Edinburgh was delayed by an hour, so Craig Erskine had had plenty of time in the airport lounge to go over in his mind the events of that time. He had thought that all was well again following the incident when his young life could have been snuffed out by a bullet outside number 356.

However, as he and others were to find out, something much bigger was evolving. Even thinking of that word 'evolving' reminded him of his Father's theory that everything that had happened during the reign of the Third Reich was nothing more than an evolution. An experiment that had failed but not because the mixture wasn't right. He had used the euphemism of the test tube and the bunsen burner. All the right ingredients were in the tube but the heat had been applied too high and too quickly. According to Erskine Snr. nothing changed the fact that the ingredients were right and they just had to be reset and re-heated. The fact that Poland had been selected as the laboratory to conduct the next experiment had stunned many given that the Final Solution had been practiced there.

Craig recalled the shock of seeing his Father denounced as a traitor and there was a moment of regret that he never knew what his final fate was. Not even family would be privy to what happened after Bill Erskine was taken away. That would be considered OHMS... One of His or Her Majesty's Secrets.

Craig's Mother, Janet had gone to her grave a shattered woman. Never in her wildest dreams had she thought that the man she loved had harboured any good feelings towards Nazism and its perpetrators. Close to her death which ironically took place in the same hospital where Bill was arrested in front of his son, Janet asked Craig to forgive his Father.

"He was forever seeking peace and the right way for mankind, and he would accept even the most macabre political premise, if he believed it would achieve it."

Craig begged her not to ask him to do that.

"I understand the love you held for him, Mum. You gave him such admirable support and you believed in him. When I accused him of being a coward, you defended him and you defended him well. I accepted your explanation but I never fully lost that doubt."

Craig couldn't forgive his Father. He condemned him for treating Alenti in the way he did. Bill had offered the Pole support and purported friendship, but at the centre of the offer was pure Politics tainted with evil.

To lead the man to believe that his wife and child whom he thought dead were waiting for him in Poland, was despicable. Then to offer them as a glittering prize in return for aiding and abetting a return to the very political climate that had ravaged Poland and its people was, to Craig, as unscrupulous and as deviant as Hitler's defiance of non-invasion agreements and the slaughter of millions.

Craig felt that the sight of his Father being led away for the term of his natural life, or perhaps execution was akin to having his own heart torn out.

Now at the age of 73, Craig Erskine sat in the airport lounge within the city of his birth to which he had returned as a pilgrim. The late afternoon sun glinted off the giant window of the airport's lounge causing the waiting passengers to use their hands to shield their eyes.

Craig watched as an attendant walked over to the side of the window and slowly pulled the giant drape across the glass.

Gradually the sun's rays weakened as they were shadowed by the curtain, and Craig whispered a final goodbye to his town. The curtains were like a dying man's diminishing sight as he drifted into whatever lay ahead.

Ironically it was Shakespeare's Julius Caesar that came to Craig's mind as it had done so many years ago in old Mac Penfold's flat. He recalled how in awe he was of the Hollywood version but could never quite get the lines right.

He thought that Mark Anthony's or Marlon Brando's ear tugging homage to his dead leader quite fitting. And under his breath as he watched the city of his and his Father's birth fade away, he recited his own interpretation with apologies to the bard.

"I come to Bury Caesar Not to Praise him."

www.ingramcontent.com/pod-product-compliance
Lightning Source LLC
LaVergne TN
LVHW040136080526
838202LV00042B/2924